I0782080

Southern Kin

A MAX PORTER PARANORMAL MYSTERY

Stuart Jaffe

Southern Kin is a work of fiction. Names, characters, places, and incidents either are the product of the author's imagination or are used fictitiously, and any resemblance to any persons, living or dead, business establishments, events, or locales is entirely coincidental.

SOUTHERN KIN

All rights reserved.

Copyright © 2024 by Stuart Jaffe
Cover art by Mari Morgan

ISBN 13: 978-1-963517-17-0

First Hardcover Edition: July, 2024

For my wife
For my son
For my parents
For my brother
For my sisters

For all my family

Also by Stuart Jaffe

Max Porter Paranormal Mysteries
Southern Bound
Southern Charm
Southern Belle
Southern Gothic
Southern Haunts
Southern Curses
Southern Rites
Southern Craft
Southern Spirit
Southern Flames
Southern Fury
Southern Souls
Southern Blood
Southern Graves
Southern Dead
Southern Hexes
Southern Hart
Southern Kin

Nathan K Thrillers
Immortal Killers
Killing Machine
The Cardinal
Yukon Massacre
The First Battle
Immortal Darkness
A Spy for Eternity
Prisoner
Desert Takedown
Lone Star Standoff
The Puppeteer
Blowback
Prime

The Ridnight Mysteries
> The Water Blade
> The Waters of Taladoro
> Waterfire

The Parallel Society
> The Infinity Caverns
> Book on the Isle
> Rift Angel
> Lost Time
> Pages of Glass
> The Bold Warrior
> City of Infinity

The Malja Chronicles
> The Way of the Black Beast
> The Way of the Sword and Gun
> The Way of the Brother Gods
> The Way of the Blade
> The Way of the Power
> The Way of the Soul

Gillian Boone novels
> A Glimpse of Her Soul
> Pathway to Spirit

Stand Alone Novels
> After The Crash
> Real Magic
> Founders

Short Story Collection
> 10 Bits of My Brain
> 10 More Bits of My Brain
> The Bluesman
> The Marshall Drummond Case Files: Cabinet 1
> The Marshall Drummond Case Files: Cabinet 2
> The Marshall Drummond Case Files: Cabinet 3

Non-Fiction
How to Write Magical Words: A Writer's Companion

For more information, please visit ***www.stuartjaffe.com***

Southern Kin

Chapter 1

STANDING BEFORE THE DOOR with an etched plate reading 202, Max Porter paused to take a breath. For several years now, a whispering part of him had doubted they would ever reach this door, yet here they stood. His wife, Sandra, squeezed his arm. She must have shared his doubts on some level because she acted every bit as excited as he felt. Behind them, their business partner and the ghost of a 1940s detective, Marshall Drummond chilled the air against Max's back.

"Why are we waiting?" the ghost said. "Did you lose the key already?"

Flashing a perturbed eye over his shoulder, Max said, "Can't we savor the moment? This is a big deal."

"Don't see why. You signed a lease, wrote a check, and now you have an office. You've had one before."

Sandra said, "Stop teasing. It's big to us because we can afford it now, and you know it."

"Then let's stop gabbing about it and go enjoy our new digs."

Max pulled the key from his jeans but hesitated. "Should we wait for J?"

Swiping his fedora from his head, Drummond said, "You really want to wait until school's out? That's another four hours, at least. Plus, doesn't he have some clubs or something?"

"He's part of The Porter Agency, so yeah, we should definitely wait."

Sandra said, "Now it's your turn to stop teasing."

Grinning, Max kissed the side of her head. "And it's your turn to do the honors." He handed her the key. "I did it the first time we moved down here with the place on Spruce. That one got demolished by witchcraft. I also opened the door to our second office, and that one burned to the ground. This place isn't as nice as those, but it's a start, and I want us to have better luck. So, it's up to you, this time. Go for it."

With a brave face, she set the key in, turned the knob, and pushed. And pushed again. And pressed her shoulder against the door, giving it a firm shove. With a sharp whine like a frightened terrier, the door peeled open. Sandra stumbled into their new office. Both Max and Drummond had the good sense not to giggle.

Situated on the edge of the revitalized northern section of Winston-Salem, the old brick building had once been a warehouse back during the heyday of Reynolds Tobacco. For the last decade, it sat fallow, decaying like a carcass in the woods. But where most saw a blight, somebody saw possibilities. A business group — the Palasco Brothers — bought the building, divided it into two floors of offices, and started selling space.

"I want this corner," Sandra said, crossing the large, empty room and stopping at the only corner with a window next to it. She pointed to the area in front of her. "Or you could put your desk next to mine and we can share the view."

Max joined her and glanced out the window — an alleyway festooned with weeds, garbage, and a few rats. "Lovely."

The floor needed covering — concrete at the moment — and the walls had the faded brown of dying brick. Odd splotches of white paint from some Jackson Pollack wannabe marred one section, and a long water stain stretching down like the trail of an ambling snail finished the décor. The place smelled of oil and trash, and a single length of fluorescent lighting buzzed from the ceiling.

"Any objections to making this wall my home?" Drummond said pointing to the side area next to the door.

Max said, "Looks good."

It did. About as much as the rest of the office. But with some work, he thought they could either clean the walls or paint over them, lay down some carpeting, and build a bookshelf for Drummond. The air would freshen with time and some open windows, and if he cleaned up the alleyway, the air might stay fresh. They could find a few couches and a coffee table to make a comfortable sitting area, too. He needed a priority list — they couldn't afford to deck the place out all at once.

"Look here," Sandra said with an excited coo.

A narrow door led to a narrow hall. On the left, Max found a breakroom; on the right, a space that could be a conference room. And in the back, a bathroom.

Though he felt the thrill of watching a loved one opening a birthday present, he had to bite back the frustration of having to sign a lease on the office without ever stepping foot in the place. He could thank the late Cecily Hull for that one. Even dead that woman continued to cause him problems. She had threatened to use her political reach against the Porters, to make sure nobody would rent them an office, and apparently, word of the threat had been enough. No way to be sure how that word got out, but Max suspected Madame Ti — the former Hull witch who spearheaded the current witch war. Also possible, Mr. Van Horn who had worked for Hull as her assistant but truly worked for Madame Ti as her spy.

The Palasco Brothers were new to the area when they bought the dilapidated building. Transplants from Connecticut, they didn't know anything about Winston-Salem, the South, or the Hulls. They had been thrilled to receive the Porters' business, and all the preliminary phone calls went smoothly. But the day Max had scheduled to view the space, they changed their enthusiastic tone. Suddenly, they would only do the deal if he would sign right away and agree to backdate the lease. Max figured they would tell Madame Ti, or whoever threatened them, that the lease had already been signed before the threats and it was too late.

Max had to give them a little credit. They didn't back down from the witches. Only rearranged the situation. Then again, the Palasco Brothers probably didn't know about witches or simply didn't believe in them. If they heard anything, they discounted it as Southern superstition.

Pointing toward the last unclaimed spot in the office, Sandra said, "What about here for my casting circle?"

"Looks good to me," Drummond said. "You might want to

start putting some wards on this place. It's been quiet lately, but that only makes me think these witches are working on something we don't want to know about."

"I was already planning on it. Until the witch community sorts out its disagreement —"

"Is that what you're going to call an all-out war for power?"

"Okay. How about this? Until the witch community stops attacking each other and one of them comes out on top, we should all be extra cautious. Not just wards for the office, but Max and I should be wearing some, too. Once we have the casting circle put in, I'll get on all of it. Brenda can help me. She's getting quite good at the basics."

Brenda Byrd had been more than a help, more than a woman they had saved from a haunting and curse, more than an ally in this dangerous war. She had become an integral part of The Porter Agency team. Part of the family.

For Max, that was an important distinction. It had taken him a long time to admit that he could not control everything. Life was in constant flux, and the second he succumbed to the delusion that he could shift the flow of life, it would smack him down, remind him he had scant influence, and possibly screw with any success on the horizon out of spite. But he could control one small bit of his world — protecting his family — and let the rest fly to wherever it went.

Gazing around the empty office, seeing how Sandra and Drummond appraised the space with hope, Max trusted the future could be manageable. They had endured a lot over the years. It came with the job. Too often, though, Max had the deep-bone sensation that they teetered on the edge of failure — which meant death in their business. But at that moment, despite Madame Ti and her witch war, Max agreed with the satisfied smile on his wife's lips. They had turned a corner, looked up and saw dark clouds parting, felt the shining warmth of a brighter future, and —

His phone rang. Detective Jorge Osorio, Winston-Salem PD and part-timer with The Porter Agency.

When Max answered, Osorio cut right into it. "You need to

drive out to Yadkinville immediately. And bring five hundred dollars."

If not for the harshness in the man's voice, Max would have assumed he joked. Instead, Max said, "What's wrong? You need help?"

"Not me, no. But you may need some. Police picked up a woman on a B&E charge."

"And?"

"And it's your mother."

Chapter 2

THE SMALL TOWN OF YADKINVILLE could have been used in a John Mellencamp video to symbolize the heart of America decaying away. Once a beautiful place, it clung to a yesterday long expired while struggling against too many modern pressures. The biggest among them being money. Yadkinville didn't have much of it.

While only on the western edge of Winston-Salem, it took Max forty-five minutes to reach the town. The entire drive he had two emotions battling in his head — concern for his mother's safety and anger at whatever she had done. And why all the way out here? Watching the city drift away into this tiny town, he added a new thought — how the heck did she even get out here?

Both Sandra and Drummond wanted to come along, but Max insisted on going alone. Assuming Osorio had not been mistaken, Max's mother would be embarrassed, angry, maybe ashamed, and certainly not in a good mood. Sandra's presence would only upset her further. As for Drummond — Max didn't need the added pressure of navigating two conversations at once while making sure the living failed to notice that he spoke with the dead.

He turned onto E. Hemlock Street and spotted the police station on his right. A squat, red brick building with an odd roof that looked more like a hobbit hole raised out of the ground and bricked over than a hub for local law enforcement. An American flag flapped in the wind, centered in a circular landing that led to the entranceway.

Osorio had instructed him to park on the street several blocks down near an elementary school. Max did as he had been told. He sat in the car, letting the air conditioning keep him comfortable, and waited. A few minutes later, when he caught Osorio in the rearview mirror, he stepped out and offered a grateful wave.

Overcast skies threatened to darken with rain, but Max didn't hold out hope. Mid-April and temps had already hit the 80s. North Carolina often went over 100 in July, but this early heat in Spring suggested worse would be coming. Rain would cool things down for a short time, but the overcast had been around for days now and all they had was thicker humidity and rising temperatures. Beyond that, nothing.

Except sweat. Max could feel the trickles running down his spine, and he watched Osorio patting his forehead as he lumbered closer. The man had a leather satchel slung across to his side and his one hand gloved. The satchel went everywhere Osorio went, and the glove never came off. Max had no idea why Osorio loved the satchel, but he knew all about the glove. He was there the day Osorio's hand suffered a curse. Anything the man touched directly would wither away. Without the glove, Osorio would become King Midas — only with death instead of gold.

"Did you bring the money?" he asked as way of a greeting.

Max patted his pocket. "You going to tell me what happened? Where's my mother? Why can't I go into the police station? And what's the money for? Is it a bribe? Are you having me a bribe a police officer?"

"Take a breath there, boss. Trust me. I've got it all sorted out. Everything's going to be fine."

Holding back another panicked blurt, Max said, "Then please tell me something."

From his satchel, Osorio brought out a small bottle of Gatorade — traditional lemon-lime flavor — and guzzled half of it before resting his back against the car. "Yadkinville police got a call of suspicious activity in Olin."

"Where's that?"

"Further west. A bit north of Statesville. Very rural small town. Makes this place look like a buzzing metropolis. They don't have their own police, so the neighboring stations take turns helping out. Anyway, a Yadkinville cruiser was sent to check into it, and they found your mother had broken into a home."

"That's crazy. She wouldn't do that."

"She did."

"But how the heck would she even get out here?"

"Uber, I'm guessing. Police searched the area and didn't find any accomplices, so she didn't have a getaway driver. Doesn't look like she stole anything or damaged anything other than the front door lock — she bashed that with a hammer. The house was empty until a few weeks ago, and the new couple that bought it only just moved in. They hadn't gotten around to putting in a good door lock, yet. I'm guessing they'll change that attitude now."

"So, they arrested her and —"

"No, no. Nobody's been arrested, and no charges are filed against her. Your mother is smart. The moment the police arrived, she started acting lost and confused."

"What makes you think she's acting? None of this sounds like her."

"I've met your mother. This was an act. Plus, she had the sense to attempt calling her grandson for help. The younger one — J. But she couldn't get through. She then told the officers that she was your mother. A few of the guys knew you from the television spots you've done, and they didn't believe she was related to some TV guy. They started treating her as a dementia patient, and she played along. They put out a silver alert which is how I found out. All amber and silver alerts ping my phone, and when I saw the details, I knew it was her. I called the Yadkinville station — I'm friends with two of the officers here — and told them I was familiar with the woman. After I sorted things out with them, I called you, and here we are."

Wiping his soaked forehead, Max said, "I don't know what that means. Is she going to jail?"

"I already said no charges were being filed. The homeowners bought the story of a woman lost with dementia. If anything, they felt sorry for her. So, stop freaking out, give me the money, and I'll be right back with her."

"You said you had it all sorted out *before* you called me. What's the money for? Bail? You said she's not being arrested."

"You are making a gracious contribution to the police fund drive. That's all. In return, all record of this incident will disappear. Simple as that."

"Sounds like a bribe."

"Can't be. Not a single person is getting the money. It's going in the police fund."

"Isn't that semantics?"

Pushing off the car, Osorio said, "It's semantics that makes everybody happy and nobody gets arrested. Or would you rather your mother spent a few nights in jail until she can be arraigned?"

Max handed over the money. He had no intention of making her undergo further disgrace, but his mind had taken the roundabout path to putting everything in order. As Osorio headed back to the police station, Max went over it all once more. None of what his detective friend said made any sense, but he couldn't deny any of it, either. After all, he stood by his car in Yadkinville waiting for his mother to be released.

Rubbing his sweaty face, Max let out a long breath. He wanted to believe things had grown complicated, hectic, overwhelming, and he only needed to make it through the week for life to return to normal. But he had been telling himself that much for years. He could not evade the simple fact of adulthood — it always would be complicated, hectic, and overwhelming. When any single pressure relieved, another took its place. One had to snatch the peaceful moments when they dared to peek above the daily tumultuous waters. Max had his moment earlier that day — enjoying the new office with his witch wife and his ghost friend. Now, no matter what he wanted, his mother had made things difficult.

His mind churned around the idea that his mother could do something like this, that she thought to do it, prepared for it, and called a driving service to take her here. Breaking and entering? Maybe she did have a little dementia. Maybe that went hand-in-hand with her MS.

Before her diagnosis, he knew nothing about multiple sclerosis other than it was bad. Since then, however, he had learned to be comfortable with a steady stream of new ailments that accompanied the dread disease. Perhaps he would have to adjust to her having dementia now. While certainly not something he wished on her, it would, at least, explain why she ended up all the way out in Olin.

His eyes roved around the little street. Not much activity. Most people worked inside, in school, or out in a field somewhere. Though maybe the latter had taken the afternoon off. It was far too hot to be plowing.

He should have brought Drummond along. The ghost's non-stop wisecracks would have been annoying, but his cold, ghostly chill would have been welcome right then. Plus, he could have sent Drummond into the police station to scout information, instead of standing in the sticky heat letting his mind drive him crazy.

Glancing up the street, he waited. No sign of them yet.

Hold on. His mind replayed Osorio's words — something about J. *She had the sense to attempt calling her grandson for help. The younger one — J.* Why did his mother call J?

Sure, the two of them had a close relationship, and she probably wanted to avoid dealing with Max, but the idea gnawed at him. Not jealousy. Not much, anyway. Something else.

When as a kid, he got into a troubling situation, the kind where he saw no safe way out — stuck at a party where everybody was too drunk to drive, for example — Max knew he could always call his mother. He'd suffer the consequences, no free pass with her, but he would call her nonetheless. He knew that she would rescue him. She had to know it went both ways.

Of course, she did. She had called Max for help many times over the years since moving to North Carolina. And with her MS, she reached out even more. So, why J? Unless J offered a way out.

Back in the old days, at those old parties, if he did have a way out, a way to get home without having to call his mother, without her learning where he had been and what trouble he had found, then he would take it. Had done so many times. Far better than admitting the truth to her. And far, far better than letting his peers know he had called Mommy to come get him from the party. Never mind the facts that nobody at the party cared about him, that any party filled with drunken kids had not invited him, that he had never enjoyed any popularity to be in a situation like that.

Max fished out his phone and called J. With school still in session, he got voicemail. "Your grandmother got arrested on a B&E. Seems like you know something about it. I'm picking her up now and taking her back to her apartment. I want you to meet us there after school. Be ready to tell me the truth."

After he ended the call, he thought it had sounded too harsh. His bouncing mind had riled him up, and he let it out in that terse message. Then again, the kid had some answers to give.

Ten minutes later — ten excruciating minutes — Osorio ambled down the sidewalk with Mrs. Porter in tow. She kept her eyes down and her shoulders hunched as if dragging a heavy bundle. And she was. On a bad day, every step could cause her great pain. The guilt or embarrassment at what she had done, at getting caught — those things paled against the anguish of her body's brutal war with itself. Cancer got all the attention. But MS — fuck MS, too.

All his sympathy, however, did not overcome his frustration with her. Being old, being in pain, being challenged with every stride — none of that excused her for committing crimes. When Osorio reached the car, he opened the passenger door and ushered her into the seat. She never met Max's eyes. Osorio put his back to Max, jutted his chin toward the driver's side, and said nothing.

Max got the message. Not only to get in the car, but to keep any scene from developing on a public street. Whatever the Porters needed to work out, Osorio wanted them to work it out elsewhere. Far away from the police station, preferably.

Once Max settled into the car, Osorio made sure Mrs. Porter had buckled in. Then the detective walked around the front of the vehicle and motioned for Max to lower the window. He leaned on the rim of the door.

He handed Max some papers, and in a low voice, he said, "Those are the originals. No other copies around. It's got all the information from the officers called to the scene. As far as the paperwork goes, and that's the same as the department itself, this never happened."

"Thank you." Max folded the papers and stashed them in his pocket. "I owe you one."

"Don't worry about it. The work you do is important. I'm happy to help when I can." Osorio checked up and down the street. "But I can't be a part of it. Not this time."

"There's no *it* to be part of."

"I hope not."

Max's hand dropped to the pocket with the papers. "Did something else happen with her? Something not in the report?"

"No, nothing like that. It's just weird that she's out here breaking into a home. And when weird things happen around you —"

"I get it. But this isn't part of an investigation."

"Good. I'm trying to get a pay raise, so I can't be seen involved in a typical Porter Agency matter. You understand?"

"Absolutely." Max put out his hand. "Good luck."

Osorio shook the hand, then patted the roof of the car. "Get out of here."

Max pulled onto the road. As he worked his way through the town and towards the highway, he peeked over at his mother. She bent forward a bit and held her mouth in a tight pout, staring ahead and looking ...

Haunted.

The word popped in Max's head, and it fit. Too well. Frighteningly well.

Chapter 3

THE DRIVE BACK TO WINSTON-SALEM continued in silence. Max tried to engage a conversation, but Mrs. Porter remained uncommunicative. Like a sullen teenager, she rested her head against the window and watched the landscape roll by. Every utterance from Max received a huff or a grunt or an exhausted sigh. At most, he would hear a monosyllabic response. Dealing with the Sandwich Boys through the worst of their teen years had never been this frustrating.

With each grumbling mile, Max's worry grew. The unusual way his mother behaved coupled with the cautious way Osorio had phrased things launched his imagination into dark realms. He feared she might be possessed or cursed. Madame Ti or Sister Sadie or one of countless other witches could have performed a spell against his mother in an effort to control The Porter Agency. Max's ego didn't once think it would be for him. No. Those witches wanted control of Sandra, control over one of the few women trying to be a good witch, control over the one good witch that showed untapped strength and talent for the craft. He had no trouble believing they would attempt any path toward that end — even abusing an elderly woman with a fatal disease.

With twenty minutes left to drive, Max called Sandra, gave her a quick rundown, and asked her to meet them at his mother's apartment. "Bring our friend, too."

She paused, digesting the request. "Sure. How bad is this?"

Max snatched a look at his mother. "I have no idea."

When they entered Mrs. Porter's apartment, Sandra, Drummond, and J settled in the narrow living room. J had a key to the building and played host, providing Sandra with a cup of coffee while they waited. A couch ran the length of one wall while heavy furniture dominated the rest of the cramped space — two high-backed reading chairs, a thick end table, and a coffee table with carved corners. Above the couch hung a painting of the sea crashing against rocks near a lighthouse.

On the opposite wall hung a painting of colored circles with swirling lines wisping off into the void of the canvas. Both struck Max as generic and innocuous, the kind of thing decorating a hotel room, and he often had wondered why these paintings spoke to his mother — enough for her to purchase them and hang them on her walls. What could they possibly say to her?

Well, the paintings might not have much to say, but he expected more from her. As he sat in one of the reading chairs, feeling like an imposing judge, he rushed straight into the matter. "Don't make me have to pull teeth in order to get this out of you. What is going on?"

Mrs. Porter turned her head toward J as she perched on the far edge of the couch. She looked smaller than usual, rubbing her hands and rocking slightly, a fragile figurine precariously balanced on a ledge. "You have to understand," she said, and her voice creaked each word with pain and uncertainty. "You need to believe me. I didn't believe it, not like — well, not for real. But the pain had become so bad. Just awful. This MS hurts all the time. I was looking for anything to make me feel better."

"Breaking into a stranger's house alleviated your pain?"

Sandra set her coffee mug on the table with a clear clink. "Let your mother talk."

Swishing into the ceiling corner, Drummond snickered. "Listen to your wife. She's far better at dealing with people."

Max wanted to snap back a witty reply, but his mother would have turned the discussion to why he was talking to the ceiling, and he would never get her back to the real topic. Instead, he used one of the interrogation techniques he had learned from Drummond. He stayed quiet. Most people felt the need to fill such silences and they simply started talking.

Mrs. Porter obliged. "You know I've tried. I tried acupuncture. I still go to physical therapy, but that's more about keeping me mobile, not pain free. I've had massages, and I've talked with therapists, and I've even tried marijuana."

Max raised an eyebrow.

"Don't give me that look. When you were a boy, smoking that stuff was illegal. Still is in a lot of states. I don't really know about here, but you can't imagine how a bad day feels for me."

"Did smoking pot help?"

She shook her head. "Only made me nervous. And hungry."

Max caught his wife hiding a grin behind her hand. He even heard the ghost above chuckle for a second. But he found none of this amusing.

Mrs. Porter shriveled back in the couch as her wrinkled skin quivered. "You simply can't understand how awful I feel. Not that a mother ever expects understanding from her children, but we do hold onto the hope — the expectation — that, in our old age, our children will take care of us, ease our suffering, make our final years bearable." She lowered her voice toward Sandra. "It's okay, dear. I don't blame you. You've never had children of your own. You wouldn't understand."

Sandra's fingers rolled into tight fists. Interjecting before a brawl could begin, Max said, "We've done everything we can to help you, make you feel comfortable, and still give you plenty of freedom."

"But that won't last. There will come a time when you've had too much, and that's when you'll send me to a home."

"We won't do that."

"You will. That little house of yours doesn't have enough room for you three. Even if it did, I'm no fool. I know Sandra doesn't like me."

Sandra said, "I'm right here."

"I have to get better. I won't go to a home. That's why I had to try."

Her words disturbed enough, but then Max spotted J's inability to maintain eye contact. "Try what?" he said. "What did you do?"

Mrs. Porter reached over and clutched J's hand. "It's not his fault."

"J? What happened?"

"Over the summer, when PB and J took me to the Appalachian Mountains, it wasn't just a vacation. I … well, I asked them to take me to see a granny witch."

As Max and Sandra's eyes widened, as Drummond choked on the idea, J put out his free hand as if to stop an oncoming stampede. "It's not what you think," he said, waving his hand as if to erase Mrs. Porter's words. "I swear. I looked into it. They call her a granny witch but it's a misnomer. They're also called granny healers. That's what they are. It's mountain medicine, herbs and roots and strong drinks and stuff like that. That's all."

Drummond said, "What the kid's saying is sort of true. The granny witches are mostly local folk healers. A lot of mountain people don't have much money, and while there are doctors up that way, many people prefer the old methods. But I've also heard a lot of weird stories. Enough to say that I wouldn't be trusting anybody who willingly uses the name *witch*."

"Don't go getting mad at J," Mrs. Porter said. "I would've gone no matter what. I know you think I'm computer illiterate, but I know how to use my phone to call a car service. Got myself out to Olin, didn't I? If those boys hadn't joined me, I would've found my way to the Appalachians on my own."

"She told me that, too," J said. The mixture of guilt and pleading that painted his voice struck Max's heart — both in its authenticity and its concern.

"You went there to protect her?" Max said.

"Of course."

Mrs. Porter smacked her hand on her thigh. "Stop interrogating him like he did something wrong. He and PB gave me a wonderful vacation. A final chance to spend some time with them that I loved and will cherish with what little time I have left. The fact that we went to a granny witch or two —"

"Or two?" Sandra said.

"The first one gave me a concoction to drink — tasted like rotten fruit mixed with coffee grounds and peppermint. Just awful. We stuck around for a day or two, but I didn't feel any better. Actually felt worse because that stuff did a number on my digestion. But then we went to see Granny Witch Westra. There's another lady at my infusion treatment sessions, the ones I had before we did it privately, and she told me about this Granny Witch Westra. Said this woman in the Appalachians saved her from losing three toes. Scared me to death back then. I'm still scared. If this MS starts taking my toes — I don't want to even think about it."

J said, "I thought after the first one she would've stopped, but she insisted we take her to this other granny witch deeper into the mountains."

"We were already up there. I might as well try all that I could. I didn't want to have to go up there again."

Max had a hard time swallowing his words. One objection after another rose in his throat, and he had to remind himself that there was no arguing to be done. His mother had already acted. He wanted to be angry at J for allowing this to happen — whatever this was — but would he have done any different in the same situation? He would not have physically restrained his mother, so the best he could hope for would be to tag along and make sure things didn't get worse. If anything, Max thought he would have to thank J for putting in the effort. Yet that didn't make any of this sit better in his tumbling stomach.

"When we finally reached the granny witch," Mrs. Porter continued, "I had a sense that things would be different. She was an old lady — even to me — nothing but a tiny ball of wrinkled skin. She wore a simple outfit of handmade clothes — looked like she stepped out of the 1930s or something. The other granny witch, she looked modern. Even had a cell phone. But not this lady. That gave me hope."

Bursting to his feet, J said, "But this lady turned out like the other one, didn't she? She just gave you some herbs and told you to make a tea with it and that was it. That's what I remember. You were disappointed and said that the whole healing part of the trip was a bust. Nothing to worry about because nothing came of it all."

Mrs. Porter rubbed at the back of her hands. "That's not quite true."

Chapter 4

TRYING TO RECAPTURE HER STERN-MOTHER FACE, Mrs. Porter said, "I don't want any of you being mad at J. Or PB, for that matter. Those boys did nothing wrong. They were trying to help their grandma out."

"Why should I be mad?" Max asked, a simmer under his voice.

"Because," Drummond said, "it doesn't end there. This Granny Witch Westra said something."

"Well?" Max ground his teeth. "What did the Granny Witch say to you?"

Straightening her back, Mrs. Porter said, "She waited until the boys were outside. I told them to get the car started, get the air conditioning going, and I'd be right out. As I paid for the herbs, she put her hand on my wrist and pushed it back. Said she didn't want my money. Said that if I really wanted to stop the pain, I should come back later that night. Alone."

J's shock turned into dark understanding. "That's why you insisted on staying in that crappy motel. You wanted to be within walking distance of her house."

She patted his arm. "I'm sorry. But if I had told you what I planned, you would have thought I was crazy. You would've assumed that I was being set up, that they were going to rob me or something like that. And you would have insisted on coming along."

"I should have been there with you."

"I couldn't have that. Granny Witch Westra wanted me alone, and I wasn't going to mess that up. Not if she could really help me. You've spent plenty of time with me. You know how I hurt. Please, tell me you understand."

Max watched the dilemma play out for J. The young man

wanted to be mad at his grandma. He must have felt betrayed, but also, he probably felt guilty — that he had somehow failed by letting her manipulate him. In the end, much as Max expected, J took the burden on his own shoulders and absolved his grandma. With a nod to her, he simply said, "It's okay."

She scooped up his hand and gave it a kiss. "Thank you."

"Can we back to why you're now a criminal?" Max said.

"Watch your tone. I'm still your mother."

For a flash, a soft comfort covered Max by his mother's sharp snap. But she quickly shrank back, as if shocked at her own outburst, and his anxiety spiked. Lowering J's hand, Mrs. Porter picked at some lint on the couch.

"That evening," she said with a sigh, "after dinner with the boys, I waited until they thought I had gone to sleep. Then I snuck out and walked up to Granny Witch's house."

Max couldn't take anymore. He thrust out of the chair and paced by the opening to the tiny kitchen. A memory flashed in his head — watching the Sandwich Boys trying to cook eggs and toast one morning while his mother clucked around them. How could that doting grandmother be the same woman?

"She was sitting in a rocking chair on her porch. Said she was waiting for me. We went inside, and I swear the entire place looked different. It wasn't that the sunlight was gone or that I was nervous — and I was — but something truly had changed. I couldn't see it, but I felt it. That's when I thought that this granny might actually be able to help me."

"You didn't think it might be dangerous?" Max huffed. "You didn't think any of those nerves should be listened to?"

Mrs. Porter snapped her head towards Max. Her eyes blazed, and part of him shriveled as if he had broken her favorite lamp playing ball in the house. She let her attention rove toward Sandra, then J, then to her hands in her lap. Firm but with less fire, she said, "Do you have any idea what it's like to wake up in the morning in such pain, every muscle, every bone throbbing, and you need to go to the bathroom, but you can't move that much? Just trying to get out of bed would require more strength than a hundred of you would have. Do you think you can understand what I feel knowing the dark end I have awaiting me? I don't mean death. I mean the journey to death. It won't be a pleasant, peaceful end. I won't get to drift away slowly, crossing the finish line by going to sleep one night and never waking. I have pain, nausea, injections, maybe amputations, and plenty of other indignities ahead of me. The fact that an old lady in the mountains made me nervous meant nothing compared to what she offered. And she didn't even want to charge me."

"No," Sandra said, quiet and full of dread.

"Oh, Mom. You didn't — tell me you didn't strike a deal with her, did you?"

Mrs. Porter's head lowered further. "I wanted the pain to end. It wasn't anything crazy. At least, at the time it didn't seem crazy."

"What did she ask for? What did you agree to?"

"She said that sometime in the future, maybe never, she might ask me to do a favor. She promised it wouldn't be anything dangerous, but I didn't care. How many more years do I have left? Besides, the whole thing sounded like the movie, *The Godfather,* so I figured, at worst, hiding a body or something."

"Mom!"

"That's where my mind went. What did it matter? She knew nothing about me. She didn't know where I lived, didn't ask — she couldn't possibly find me. So, I made the deal."

"Except she never delivered. You've had plenty of bad days since you got back from that trip."

Another guilty look. "Not really. I pretended so you wouldn't be suspicious. Truth is — I have felt fantastic ever since. Better than even before the MS started up."

Sandra said, "But then she showed up."

"A week ago. She arrived with two young men, big fellows, scary looking. She came here to the apartment and said that she had a job for me. She wanted me to break into that home and leave this weird looking hairball in the house where nobody would find it — in the walls. I tried to ignore her. But every day she and her men would be standing across the street, staring at my apartment. I'd watch them from behind my curtains, and I could feel them looking right at me. Then the pain came back. Bad. So, I did it. But I failed. The police caught me before I could finish the job." She lifted her head, and her face glistened with tears. "I didn't do my part of the deal, and the pain is getting worse. I don't know what that crazy lady will do to me when she finds out I screwed up."

All of Max's anger flowed away along the water shedding from his mother's eyes. He rushed to her side and held her firm. "It's okay. Don't worry about any of it. I promise you we'll take care of everything."

Sniffling, she said, "How? What can you possibly do?"

"You'd be surprised."

Chapter 5

FOCUSING ON THE ROAD, Max headed back across the city. When he left, he told J to stay at his mother's apartment and keep watch. If they were going to fix this, he had to trust that she would remain in her home. But he didn't trust her. He knew her too well for that. Mrs. Porter did not like to stay still. So, J would have to play prison guard.

Sandra said she would dig into Appalachian witch deals. If they were anything like the North Carolina variety, they would be difficult to break. But they needed to understand what they were dealing with, and that was a logical first step.

The other first step — smoothing things over with Wyatt and Callie Vellmer. According to the police report Osorio had provided, Mrs. Porter broke into the Vellmer's home while they were out at work. The report also gave an address on Tatum Road in Olin. Max wanted to make sure they wouldn't change their minds and suddenly press charges.

Drummond floated over the passenger seat. Max caught the ghost snatching glances his way. After the third time, he said, "Just let me fume for a bit longer."

"I didn't say a word."

"I can feel you not saying a word."

"You want me to leave, I can. You can call for me before you go in that house."

"No offense, but I don't really need you for this."

"You certainly do. Partner, you are red faced, white knuckled, and muttering to yourself. I know the way you think, and you are not in a thinking frame of mind. You need me to make sure you don't blow it because you're still pissed off at your mother."

Max slapped the steering wheel. "Don't I have a right to be mad?"

"Absolutely. It's understandable how this desperate lady got herself in this position, but if she only believed you even half-the-time, she would have known to come to you first."

"Exactly. She has spent so much energy denying things, yet suddenly she's an expert on witchcraft. For crying out loud, she's lucky the only problem is a witch deal. She could've gotten herself cursed beyond the grave."

"Yeah. I have a few words for J, too. I love that kid, but he should never have let —"

"You're right about that. I mean I know his heart was in the right place, but —"

"This isn't the kind of thing to take chances with."

"Exactly."

Drummond pushed his hat back. "I don't know which is scarier — when we argue or when we agree."

That got a chuckle, and that small release eased Max back into the seat. He sighed. Part of him instantly wanted to thank the ghost. But another part, a wiser part, knew that Drummond would be happier without direct acknowledgement. Oddly enough, it felt better that way.

Twenty minutes later, Max parked in front of an old beige farmhouse backed by acres of field and forest. Farms dominated Olin, and as such, the nearest neighbor's mailbox looked about four acres down the road. Tatum Road connected to the center of town, yet it felt isolated. And quiet.

Two cars sat in the driveway — a maroon Ford sedan and a white work van with Johnson Electrics painted on the side. Mr. Johnson's rotund caricature smiled from beneath a bushy beard as he presented an oversized thumbs up for all passing cars.

"You ready for this?" Drummond said.

"I'm not going to start yelling, if that's what you mean."

"Okay. Let's get it over with."

Max and Drummond walked up the driveway and along a concrete path to the front door. It should have been a bland bit of traveling by foot, but the hair on Max's arms stood up. He didn't feel nervous or afraid, and he didn't notice anything that would suggest an electrical field of some sort. Yet his skin reacted, his heart reacted, and he knew not to ignore those reactions.

"Do you feel that?" he asked.

Drummond nodded. "Something's off."

"A ghost?"

"There's an old farmer in the field across the street. From his clothes, I'm guessing he died in the early-1800s or so. But he's just wandering up and down the rows, and he's too far away to be causing what we're feeling."

Max rang the doorbell. "Keep alert."

While waiting, Max noticed the doorknob had been replaced already. Shining brass. Probably the first thing they fixed once they learned that his mother had bashed the knob to pieces.

A young woman opened the door. She looked about twenty, but the older Max got, the harder he found it to judge age accurately. The young all looked like kids. It didn't help that she was all of five feet tall.

"Small and pretty," Drummond said. "Put her in a waitressing outfit, and I might —"

Max thrust out his hand. "Hi, there. I'm Max Porter. I'm here because my mother was the woman who broke into your home earlier today. I wanted to apologize for her."

She wore overalls and had her straw hair tied back. Spatters of tan paint sprinkled her outfit. "Oh. Um, come on in." Stepping aside, she called out, "Wyatt, we got company." She spoke with a thick accent Max could not place — not North Carolina but definitely from the South.

As he entered, she added, "I'm Callie. Excuse the mess. We've only moved in."

Stacked boxes lined the walls of a mostly-empty living room. One beaten couch and two folding chairs made up the only furniture. Wherever Max could see the walls instead of towering boxes, he found peeling wallpaper — white and brown stripes — and the outlines of paintings hung long ago.

Wyatt walked in from a hallway near the far corner. Dressed much like his wife and cleaning paint from his hands with a stained cloth, he stood over six feet. Had an athletic frame.

"Hey, there," he said, extending a hand as he approached. "You one of our neighbors?"

Callie appeared even shorter next to her giant husband. She rested her head against him. "No, love, his momma was the old lady that broke in here."

"Oh." He frowned. "What you want?"

"To apologize," Max said. "And to figure out a few things."

Callie smiled brightly. "You sit on down. I was fixing to bring Wyatt some sweet tea — we been working up quite a sweat painting the bedroom — so it ain't no trouble to bring out another glass."

The kitchen was visible through a double-wide archway, and as Callie poured some glasses of the over-sweet drink, Max sat on the couch. Wyatt eased his large body onto one of the folding chairs, and Max marveled the thing didn't collapse in protest. When Callie returned, she handed Max a glass first, then Wyatt, then rushed back for a third before taking the other folding chair.

She raised her glass. "Let's make it official. Your apology is accepted."

As she and Wyatt drank, Max brought the glass to his lips. He had never grown a taste for this stuff. It barely tasted of tea. More like a drink designed by a corporation to addict kids with sugar, sugar, and more sugar.

"Don't be rude," Drummond said, hovering behind the couch.

Max startled. He had forgotten about his partner. Only for a moment, but enough to be surprised.

"You okay?" Wyatt asked.

Nodding, Max took a healthy gulp and forced it down with a smile. "Thank you for the tea." He set the glass on the floor. "If you don't mind, I'd like to ask a few questions. I'm trying to understand why my mother did what she did. It's not like her. She's never broken the law before. I can't recall her so much as jaywalking. And your house is far from where she lives in Winston, so why here?"

Callie said, "I don't see as to how we can help. We just moved in. Don't know much about the area, and don't know your momma. But we'll help, if we can. Right, love?"

"Sure. Anything to help."

Max had faced enough witchcraft, enough evil, that he could find it like a seasoned fisherman finds the best spot on a lake simply by observing the water surface. The surface of this house and this couple did not match the unsettling ripple he and Drummond had felt on their arrival. Nothing about them hinted at magic. Nothing suggested ill intent.

Wyatt finished off his sweet tea and jangled the ice cubes as a request for more. Callie swiped the glass with an amused look between them. As she headed toward the kitchen, she said over her shoulder, "You got a northern accent. Where you from?"

"Michigan. But my wife and I moved down here over a decade ago."

Wyatt said, "Another ten years and you can consider yourself a native of the state."

Returning with a full glass for her husband, Callie said, "You never mind him. He says that like he's a native."

"I'm more native than you."

Max grabbed at the opportunity. "Then where are the two of you from? How did you meet? How did you end up here?"

"Good thinking, partner." Drummond flew across the ceiling toward the far wall. "It won't take me long to check out the whole house, but if you run out of things to say, focus them back on your mother. There's got to be a reason that old granny witch wanted her dealing with this place."

Sitting straighter, as if called upon in school, Callie's genuine happy demeanor brightened even more. "I'm a branch manager over at First Community, but when we met, I was a bank teller working at Bank of America in Richmond, Virginia. Wyatt's an electrician, and he's worked with different companies over the years."

"I saw your truck outside."

"Yeah," Wyatt said. "Mr. Johnson's been a good boss so far. I mean we've only been here about a week, but I've been an electrician long enough, worked for enough people, that I got a good feel for these things. I can tell he's a straight up kind of man."

"Back in Virginia," Callie went on, bouncing in her seat, "my bank had some electrical issues, and Wyatt came to fix them along with some other man. Me and the other bank tellers had to spend hours just watching these men work. I didn't know if he even noticed me, but I sure noticed him."

"Oh, I noticed. Prettiest woman in that whole building. Prettiest woman I've ever seen."

She blushed. "When it came time for my lunch, I went to the break room and sat down like always. About halfway through my tuna sandwich, in walks this handsome man. He asked me out on a date right then and there. Normally, I would've said *No*. A complete stranger asking me out? I know better than to accept such an offer. But he had this strength and this confidence that somehow made me feel at ease. Made me let my guard down. Didn't hurt that I had been watching him for hours."

"I also used a really good line."

"That's true."

Max laughed. "What did you say?"

Wyatt hunched forward on his elbows. As if bestowing great wisdom, he said, "It's not so much a line, because it was true, but I walked up to her and asked her out, and she asked me why she should say *Yes*. So I said, *Because I want to know if the woman on the inside is as beautiful as the woman on the outside*."

Callie beamed as she put her arm around Wyatt and squeezed him. "I ask you, how is any sane woman going to turn that down? Well, I clearly didn't. Wasn't but six months later that we were married."

Drummond rose through the floor a few feet behind the Vellmers. "Tell them you've got to use the bathroom. I'll meet you there to explain."

Holding back the slightest flinch, Max said, "I hate to bother you, but may I use your restroom?"

"Of course," Callie said without hesitation. She pointed down the hall. "On your left."

Even from the hall, Max could tell the room had been themed — tiled in blue, with a blue toilet, and a blue trashcan. The towels, the washcloths, even the toilet paper had a blue tinge. The hand towels had monogramed initials — WPV and CDV — his and hers in light blue. Max never understood monogramming anything. He knew his own name, and if Sandra had her initials on a towel, he'd still use it.

Worse than the overwhelming blueness of the monogramed room, the bathroom was a tight fit for one person. Add an old ghost and Max grew concerned he might accidentally freeze off something important. Before he could make a wisecrack, though, Drummond poked his head through the door to make sure nobody listened.

"Most of this house is fine." Drummond's scowl looked anything but fine. "There's a door at the end of this hall, though — blocked off from all sides. I'm not just talking the door. I tried to get in that room through every wall, through the ceiling, through the floor, and through the outside — nothing. Sound familiar?"

Whispering, Max said, "They've got a ghost ward on that room?"

"Not a ghost ward. Think."

Max wanted to snap back a witty reply, but then he saw what Drummond saw. "Like Madame Ti's special safe?" During a recent case — the one that started the current witch war — they had found a safe locked by witchcraft. Took Sandra hours to break into it.

"The idiot has a brain again."

"You think it has a spell lock on it. Strange. I haven't seen anything that even hints at witchcraft."

"Feels different than Madame Ti's spell lock, but then I'd never come across one before that. I don't know what it is, but it ain't right. We'll need Sandra to take a look."

Max flushed the toilet, washed his hands, and stepped into the hall. He peeked down at the door on the end. The dark-stained wood bore hardware that looked old and rusted, and it had a carved wolf's head near the top glowering at all who approached. Even without the spell lock, the door denied entrance to anybody. It carried a warning, a threat, and a nasty promise all in one growling visage. Max shuddered.

"I'm sorry, again, for all this trouble," he said as he returned to the living room. "My mother has never done anything like that before, and I hope she never does again."

"Think nothing of it," Callie said. "Wyatt's father suffered from Alzheimer's for a long time before he passed. We understand."

"I appreciate that." He walked towards the front door and attempted a nonchalant pause. "I noticed that beautiful door at the end of the hall. Looks like an antique."

Wyatt frowned. "I thought so, too. I'm thinking of taking it out and trying to sell it, maybe on eBay or something. I'll replace it with a regular door. Only thing is, I can't get it open. Can't even get it to budge."

"Oh?"

"I've tried everything except kicking the door down. I mean I want access to the room — we paid for the whole house — but I don't want to ruin that nice piece."

Callie laughed. "It's just another project for him. We'll figure it out." She leaned closer. "Frankly, I don't care about the door as much as I do about seeing what's on the other side. If it's big enough, I think we should make it into our guest room."

Amused at their differing opinions, the couple escorted Max out. Drummond followed nearby, frowning at the house as if it might frown back. A few steps off the porch, Max turned around.

"It's a funny thing, my mother picking this house. Usually, people who are suffering in their minds — sorry, it's hard for me to say the word *dementia,* but there, I said it — anyway, don't they usually try to go back to places they know? But you all just got here. You've never met my mother."

"I assure you we haven't," Wyatt said.

"Would you mind telling me who you bought the house from? Maybe that person knew her."

Wyatt glanced down at his wife, and she shrugged. "We don't know."

"You don't know who you bought a house from?"

Callie said, "We bought the house from the bank. It's a foreclosure. You really think the two of us could've owned all this land and this beautiful old house? We make okay money, but not like that."

Max thanked them one last time and returned to the car. Drummond joined him as he drove off. "You're getting pretty good at this," the ghost said. "I like that I don't have to feed you every question that needs asking anymore."

"I'd say *thanks*, but I'm not sure if that was meant as praise or an insult."

"Then neither am I."

"Unless you spotted something different with your great detective brain, seems to me that the Vellmers are innocent in all of this. Other than the door, I didn't see a speck of a sign of witchcraft or magic. And did you notice the wife had no problem letting me go down the hall to the bathroom? Not a single worry that I would encounter that warded door."

"Still not sure if it's warded."

"I don't think they know what they bought with this house."

"I agree with that. You need to figure out who owned that house before the bank took it over."

Max raised an eyebrow. "Are you actually suggesting that I go do research?"

"Well, I'm not going to do it."

Max smiled the entire drive back to Winston-Salem.

Chapter 6

WHEN THEY REACHED WINSTON-SALEM AGAIN, Max decided to use his favorite library — the Z Smith Reynolds Library at Wake Forest University. No other facility felt as inviting. Plus, he had spent so much time there that he knew where to find most things he needed. Or at least, where to start searching.

"While you go have fun doing boring stuff," Drummond said with a glint, "I'm going to our new office to get a better feel for it."

"Is that a euphemism for something I don't want to know about?"

"No, it's exactly what I said. Until that bookcase is built, I'm going to have no homebase and I benefit from a consistent … oh, forget it. You wouldn't understand."

"What? Tell me."

"It's a ghost thing. Just accept it." Drummond winked, too proud of himself for making an aged reference, and disappeared.

Not long after, Max entered Wake Forest University and found a place to park — his third attempt on the crowded campus. When he entered the library, all the mounting tensions of the day drifted away like steam rising off hot asphalt after a summer rain. The old paper smell blended with the studious quiet to create a solemn, reverential mixture unique to the environment. No other place on Earth created the same aura as a library.

He climbed a narrow staircase to the third floor but thought it a bit too congested with four students hunched over books and laptops. On the fourth floor, he found only a young man with headphones on, bopping his head as he tried to type out a paper for some class — philosophy, Max guessed from the books on Kant and Socrates occupying the workspace. Picking a desk nestled behind a few rows of stacks, Max soaked in the atmosphere as he opened his laptop and readied to work.

He began by looking into the Vellmers. Though he and Drummond both categorized them as innocent bystanders in this, it didn't hurt to be sure. A few easy searches produced clear results. Their stories checked out. Wyatt Vellmer worked as an electrician for Johnson Electric, and Callie Vellmer ran the Yadkinville branch of First Community Bank. They had recently moved in from Virginia, and a scan through their social media showed nothing suspicious or witchy.

Max then turned to the County Recorder's Office website. Callie said they had purchased the home through the bank off a foreclosure. All foreclosures in North Carolina were public record, and with a few clicks of the keyboard, Max scanned the listings for Notices of Default. But nothing turned up.

He checked the address twice. Then he went to the *lis pendens* listing — the official notice that a lawsuit had been filed and that a property had a claim against it. Again, nothing.

After a few other attempts, he decided to come at the property from a different angle — Olin itself. The town was part of Iredell County, and it never had a large population. More a village than a town.

"A small place like that," Max said to his computer screen, "every event, every story, everybody's business gets known."

A handful of odd tales turned up, but most fell into the category of urban legends. Of course, Max knew firsthand that some urban legends came from truth; however, nothing he discovered rose to the level of sparking his research instincts. Old Cherokee stories of the Moon Eye People entertained as well as brought a touch of another's culture, but none of that linked to the Vellmer's home or the spell locked room in their house.

The only story that stood out held no occult or witchcraft aspects to it. Maybe it was the name, but Max dove down a rabbit hole of links and information as he took careful notes about the Enigma Tornado Outbreak.

From the night of February 19, 1884 into the morning hours

of the 20th, an enormous series of tornadoes ripped through a wide swath of the country. Hitting Alabama, Georgia, Illinois, Indiana, Kentucky, Mississippi, North Carolina, South Carolina, Tennessee, and Virginia, it was one of the largest and most widespread outbreaks of tornadoes in American history. While no firm numbers could ever be gathered in 1884 — in fact, the outbreak derived its name because of the uncertainty regarding the total number of tornadoes as well as the dead — estimates suggested somewhere between fifty-one and sixty plus tornadoes touched ground. As for the dead — hundreds, maybe thousands.

North Carolina suffered its deadliest single tornado ever when an F4 trampled through Rockingham killing twenty-three people. At least eight other tornadoes hit the state that evening, including one that smashed through Olin.

"There you are," Max said.

But he couldn't get much more from the story. Maps showing the various paths of destruction marked areas in such wide bands that he had no way to be sure if the house on Tatum Road had been hit. Even if he could prove that much, he had to admit that knowing a tornado hit the Vellmer house did little to help him understand the current situation.

And if the tornado destroyed the house nearly a century-and-a-half ago, did that change anything? If anybody died in the house that night, they certainly had moved on. Drummond would have seen them, otherwise. And a haunting didn't produce the kind of spell-locked room they dealt with. That was a deliberate act cast by a witch.

And yet — Max's brain itched at this incident. Something about the Enigma tornadoes connected with the house, and something about that connection shined like a beacon. His gut told him so, and he had learned to trust those feelings.

He placed numerous question marks in his notes and rocked back on his chair. As his mind pondered the possibilities, his eyes fell about the stacks not truly seeing much beyond his own thoughts. Until he saw the large man standing at the stairwell entrance. The man didn't walk in. Just stood there and scanned the room — seeing everything. Searching.

Another gut instinct, one Drummond had been working over the years to hone within Max, came to life. It said that this man searched for him. It screamed that Max didn't want to be found.

Slipping out from his workstation and ducking behind the nearest stacks, Max pulled one book free in order to keep an eye on the man. He wanted to run further into the maze of aisles and tables and books, but he feared that making too much movement — heck, making any movement — would draw the attention of this imposing figure at the stairs. He held still, listened to his own trembling breaths, and peeked through the stacks.

The man had a hefty build and was bald. He could have been a bouncer or muscle for an organized crime boss or — but Max shivered off those thoughts. Imagining such things did no good. For that matter, if allowed a moment to think clearly, he had no reason to suspect this enormous man threatened him at all. Drummond's training could be helpful, but it also could make Max paranoid. After all, the guy probably looked for his girlfriend or boyfriend or maybe he was a returning student desperate to find a place to study or a fellow student willing to befriend an older person. He wasn't that old, though. Maybe in his thirties. Or forties. Or twenties. Sheesh, Max really couldn't guess ages at all.

Okay, that's it. I shouldn't be hiding like a fool.

He took one last peek. The man stared directly back.

Max dropped to the floor, bringing several books down with him. Wincing at his clumsiness, not to mention his stupidity — hadn't he just told himself not to make sudden movements? — he sucked up his wounded pride and clambered back to his feet. No point in pretending to hide.

But when he stepped away from the stacks, the bald man had gone. Max's eyes darted to his work area. Nothing stolen.

"What the heck was that about?" he muttered as he returned to his laptop.

Taking several deep breaths to lower his pulse, he sat still for a few minutes, then double-checked that nothing had gone missing. He would have to tell Sandra and Drummond about the bald man. If somebody had taken notice of their inquiries, then they might have stumbled into something important.

"Or," Max reminded himself, "none of that had anything to do with me."

Maybe Max's clunky clattering about in the stacks scared the man, had him thinking some kids were messing around back here and he didn't want anything to do with it. He could have simply been looking for a friend, didn't see the friend, and went to check on a different floor. There could be hundreds of plausible reasons for the bald man to have behaved as he did, and none of them pointed to Max Porter being involved.

"Focus on the research."

That sounded better. Much better. He returned to the Enigma tornadoes.

As expected, he had no trouble pulling up newspaper articles about the storm. Something like that would be big news in any era, and numerous reports had been filed across the states. Being 1884, those articles played out for weeks. No twenty-four hours news cycles to worry about back then.

While he sifted through endless interviews with survivors and somber memories in the obituaries, he had difficulty finding anybody from Olin. Survivor or victim. With one exception. It took over an hour to locate, but he managed to uncover an eyewitness account written up almost two weeks after the storm.

Mrs. Lydia Mary Elcott, 32, who lost her husband, Hank Peter Elcott, 37, and their two children to the tornadoes, agreed to be interviewed after speaking with her preacher. On his advice, she met with me at the local firehall, the only place she felt safe because her husband had been a volunteer there. These are her words:

The noise of the thing woke us up. I never been in no earthquake but that's where my mind went. The walls rattled and things in the house shook vicious. I might have even thought it might've been a hurricane, but a hurricane howls, right. The wind blows so hard, it whips around a house and howls like a mournful wolf. Not this, though. I heard it like thunder that kept rollin' harder and harder, louder and louder, until it barreled straight down the road. The winds spun round and I couldn't hear nothing but that storm. My children cryin' and my husband yellin' but I heard nothing. Next thing I know, Hank's got both the children under his arms and is racing for the horse and buggy. I should've been with them, but I stood frozen on our porch. I can't explain why other than to say that I saw this column of black twisting and turning its way toward us, and all I could do was drop to my knees and pray. I know some people don't believe in the Lord, but let me tell you this. You look at a force of Mother Nature coming down on you like that, and you'll believe to your truest heart. And as I prayed, Hank brought the buggy onto the road, yelling at me to get in. The storm took them from me right then. I watched it pick that buggy up like a leaf and toss it away. I did the only thing I could do. I bowed my head and prayed harder.

Max searched for more interviews, but if anybody else from Olin spoke up, the records of those talks had not survived. Then again, those interviews simply might not have made it into the newspapers. They still might exist somewhere.

"Because there's always more than one way to find information."

Hearing his own words bounce back off the laptop screen, Max's mouth dropped open. He had been an idiot — not the friendly-sarcastic idiot Drummond needled him with but a true idiot that knew something and ignored it. Putting away his work on the tornado, he brought back his research into the Vellmer house. Just because he couldn't find any foreclosure information didn't mean such information was non-existent. Of course, the foreclosure story could have been a lie, but Max thought otherwise.

Callie Vellmer worked at the bank. Not only worked there,

but managed the whole place. She would have access to all records regarding foreclosures in the area — particularly, those involving her bank. It would be easy for a bank manager looking to score a cheap property to search those records before they made it into the public spheres. That would allow her to snatch up the place without getting into an expensive bidding war. With housing costs rising to ridiculous heights, he couldn't fault Callie for bending the rules a little in her favor.

If that hypothesis proved true, then the best way to cover up her actions would be to make the foreclosure aspect disappear. After all, if the property went through the normal buying and selling process, it would still register for the bank's interests while avoiding the public scrutiny of the foreclosure. At least, Max guessed as much. He had to admit he knew little of how banks operated with mortgages and such beyond purchasing a house or two during his life.

Regardless of the bank's inner-workings, however, Max did know how to research the history of a property. Sandra could do it better — she had learned it all during her time as a realtor — and she had been the one to teach him, but he thought he could handle the task now. With several clicks and some energetic typing, Max discovered he could, in fact, prevail.

In satisfied triumph, he copied down the name of the former owner — *Montgomery Dun*. Less than a minute with that name brought Max an address on Sawmill Road in Wallburg. That town was to the southeast of Winston-Salem.

Of course, Max thought. It couldn't have been a town five minutes outside of Wake Forest University. Nope. He had to deal with one property in Olin, far west of the city, and now one in Wallburg, not as far on the opposite side, but far enough to be a pain.

However, as he gathered his things to go, his phone vibrated — J. Before he could say *Hello*, J said, "It's Grandma. You need to get here now."

Chapter 7

EVER SINCE OSORIO CALLED about his mother's arrest, Max had been ping-ponging from one end of Winston-Salem to the other. Each time he drove across the city, his nerves ratcheted up another notch. With all the possibilities of his mother's involvement with witches, how could he expect anything less? Weirdly, getting that call from J eased him slightly.

Not that the call had been a good one.

J had said that one of the granny witch's two bodyguards showed up at the apartment. "A real big guy. Practically blocked out the sun." This giant pushed his way into the main room. Mrs. Porter paled under the threat of the bruiser, and the man made no allowances for his victim's age.

According to J, the man said, "You made a deal with my granny, and you're going to honor that. Nobody gets out of a deal with Granny Witch."

Mrs. Porter pleaded with the man. She swore she had tried, but what could they expect? She was an old lady and had no business trying to break into a house.

"That's not my problem," the man said.

"But surely," Mrs. Porter said, "surely there must be some other way I can fulfill this deal that would satisfy your grandmother."

J made it clear that while Mrs. Porter's words were poised and proper, she exhibited none of those traits. Tears poured down her face. When she spoke, the constant shivers made it difficult to understand her.

"Only one way I know my granny will let you out of this."

"Yes, yes, please, anything."

"You can die." The man gave his words a thought. Then: "Sometimes, even that's not going to help you out."

Mrs. Porter collapsed to the floor, bawling in such a pitiful way that J teared up as he recounted the incident over the phone. The man stomped out of the apartment, and minutes later, Mrs. Porter's MS flared hard. J used all his strength to wrangle her into bed, and though she tried to assist, her wailing and spasming only complicated the difficult process. After that, he called Max.

Of course, J sounded shaken on the phone. Max wondered if the encounter had brought up long forgotten memories of the bullies J had once dealt with daily while living on the street. Then again, watching his grandma fall apart under the threats of a man who could probably break all her bones with little more than a toothpick would have been more than enough to unnerve anybody.

When Max arrived, he gave J a reassuring hug before hastening into his mother's bedroom. She writhed and groaned as pain shot through her system. Her face flushed red, and even when the twisting knots in her muscles had subsided, her brow wrinkled and her eyes clenched shut as she waited, waited, waited for the next bout to begin. Max pulled a chair next to the bed and clasped her hand. She clutched it with her weakening grip.

Letting out a shivering breath, she whimpered. "It's too much. I can't take it."

"Shhh." He picked up a dry washcloth from the bedside table and patted away the sweat on her forehead.

"No, no, listen to me." Her eyes locked open as her fingers clawed around his hand. "That deal I made, I know I made it with the Devil, but I swear I felt normal for the last several months. I felt good. Free of all this pain. And now — I can't do it again. I just can't."

"Sandra and I are doing our best to find a loophole for you. There's some way out of this Granny Witch's deal. We'll find it."

"I don't care about the granny or the deal or any of it. She took away the MS and now she's mad at me and she's brought it back. What good is a deal if she can make it come and go whenever she wants?"

"Witch deals don't work like that."

"It doesn't matter. I can't live in pain like this anymore."

"I'll call your doctor. Maybe we can get some meds tonight. Have you taken anything yet? What have you got here?"

"You're not listening. Stop and listen. I don't want to live in pain. I am done. This life is over."

The bedroom disappeared. All sound drained away as if an old volume knob slowly turned to zero. Max stared at his mother, a tremor in the corner of his mouth. He saw her isolated from all reality and tried to comprehend what her words meant — though, of course, deep within, at his core, he knew exactly what she had said. That visceral reaction lasted only seconds, yet he would have sworn it had been far longer. In the next breath, reality returned, and though nothing had changed, everything moved different, sounded different.

His body numbed as he stood and closed the bedroom door. When he returned, his mind had yet to clear from the fog of her words. All he could manage: "I can't do that."

"Oh, no, Max, no, no. I would never ask you to. A mother should never put too much of a burden on her children's shoulders. I will take care of it myself."

Involuntarily, gently, his head shook. "You shouldn't."

She winced at a short, sharp jab in her side. Then she forced a smile. "It'll be okay. I'm not telling you this to get sympathy or take the spotlight. I only want to make sure it's not a shock when you find me gone. I want to give us time to say goodbye."

"Stop it. Stop talking like that." Max pushed down the frustrated anger and tried to speak — to think — in a reasonable, logical manner. "We are not out of options yet."

With a genuine chuckle, she said, "I made a deal with a granny witch. I think I've gone to the end of my options."

"This is nuts. You're talking about — *suicide*." He whispered the last word.

"I'm talking about dying with what little dignity I have left. I want to end my suffering. I want peace."

"But you've said it was wrong. You said it was sin."

"I've said lots of things I don't believe. A mother has to do that to raise her son right. Sometimes, it was to make you a better person than myself. Sometimes, it was to protect you. The truth can be a horrible thing. But a well-placed fib — we all benefit from hearing things we don't believe now and then."

Max's face dropped open. This had to be a joke. A sick joke, but still a joke. Except nobody jumped out of the closet laughing. Nobody leapt in front of his face with a camera to capture his confused shock. Instead of sitting up in bed and pointing with mirth at his dumbfounded expression, his mother closed her eyes as her muscles spasmed.

After a moment, she said, "I'm sorry. I shouldn't have said anything. It's the problem I created by being too good a mother. It's hard for you to handle the realities of the world. It's why I never told you about your father."

"What?" The word barked out of him.

She flinched, her eyes darting around. He thought she might be faking confusion, but she seemed unaware of what she had said.

Scooting closer on his chair, Max forced a calm tone. "What did you want to tell me about my father?"

"Why would I want to talk about him?"

"You said that —"

"I know what I said scared you. It's not easy saying goodbye to the ones we love. Don't worry. I won't do anything drastic yet. I just … I guess I wanted you to know that I consider it, that it's an option for me."

"But —"

"Enough talking. I'm tired. If my body will stop hurting, I'd like to try to sleep." She rolled away from him. "Please turn out the light when you leave."

"Um … sure."

Hiking a blanket over her shoulder, she added, "If you don't want me to go, then find me a better choice. You promised to fix this, so fix it. I'd think that'd be the least you could do for your mother."

Max stood by her bed, wondering if the next hit would come, if it would a venomous strike or a somber plea. But she had finished. She always knew when the knife had gone in far enough, and so she had to do no more.

Like a marathon runner stumbling off the track, Max veered into the kitchen. He felt more than saw J watching him, but Max could not find the strength to speak. He opened the refrigerator and stared at the sad emptiness within.

Clearing his throat, J said, "We haven't had a chance to go to the supermarket. There's usually more food in there."

"You shouldn't have to be the one doing this. I'm supposed to be taking care of her."

"We all have to help out. You can't do it alone and still run the agency. If you don't do that, then there's no money for things like food."

Did any of this even matter? After all, if Max failed to find a solution, his mother had made it clear what she intended to do. He had full faith in Sandra's abilities — Drummond's, too — but he also had been through enough situations to know that when it came to witches and witchcraft, even the best solutions often ended up as compromises. Nothing ever turned out as expected.

But would his mother accept that kind of outcome? She had tasted the pain-free life she once enjoyed. He couldn't blame her for not wanting to slog out her final years stuck in a loop of drugs and misery and the terrifying prospect of even worse. Those with MS that lived a full life, that never let it slow them down, they were heroes. They were valiant and rich in spirit. Giving up always tempted the infirm. But whether through pride or willpower, stubbornness or defiance, so many people with this horrid disease fought to reclaim each breath, each moment, each heartbeat, each day of living that they could capture. If he wasn't so distraught at his mother's suggestion, Max would have been inspired by these others.

"I'm sorry." J still watched Max from the edge of the kitchen. He looked smaller. It reminded Max of when they first met.

J had been PB's friend on the streets, and it was through PB that J came into Max's life. Back then, Max thought he was helping some homeless boys by paying them for a little work. He never once thought those boys would grow up to be his sons.

"You have nothing to be sorry for."

Pointing down the hall, J said, "She wouldn't be in this mess if it weren't for me. I should never have let her go to the Appalachians. I should have told you what she was up to."

"I agree about that last part. But you tried to do the right thing for her. I understand that." The words came out of Max, but they sounded rote to him. Probably did to J, too. They were hollow because he felt hollow — his mother had gutted him.

"Look," J said, "tell me what I've got to do and I will. I want to help. I want to make this right."

Max closed the refrigerator door and faced J. He stepped closer. "The best thing you can do is stay here. Keep watching over her. Take care of her. Because it's like you said — Sandra and Drummond and I can't do our job if we're being pulled in this direction, too. Having you here makes me feel better so I can go out and work. She wants me to fix this, and that's what I want to do. Can I count on you?"

"You know you can, but I couldn't even stop her from reacting to that big guy."

"Sandra's taught you some spells over the years." Simply saying those words helped Max's brain start to reconnect. "Yeah. You're never going to be a great witch like she will, but you can pull off a thing or two to protect your grandmother. Can't you?"

"I — I don't know. I can try."

"Okay, then. Try." Though J's eyes glistened, he held firm and gave Max a soldierly nod. The heck with that Max thought. He stepped forward and wrapped his arms around the young man. Clenching his son tight, he kissed the side of J's head. "We do what we do for those we love."

Without another word, Max left the apartment.

Chapter 8

MAX DID NOT RETURN HOME UNTIL LATE. He spent dazed hours driving through the city with no destination. That had never really been his way — to aimlessly wander as a way of clearing his mind — but once he got behind the wheel and started moving, he simply didn't stop.

When he arrived at the house, he still felt numb, but some part of him, the part that keeps people pushing through their lives even after losing a loved one, that part seemed to have found its footing. He could move. He could think a little. Not about his mother, though. Each time he tried to recall what she had said, how seriously she had said it, his brain threatened to shut down again.

Instead, he entered the kitchen and breathed in the life of his home, of his wife. Sandra sat at the kitchen table with her research spread across like some obsessed FBI agent in a thriller. She had her laptop opened at an angle on her left, a few books both old and new scattered about, and several casting circle sketches filling up the rest.

With a long hiss like air releasing from a tire, he dropped into a chair and rubbed his face.

"What's wrong?" she said.

"I'll tell you later. I'm tired of thinking about it."

She lifted her head from a book and inspected him with care. "You want me to distract you?"

"I don't think I have the energy for that. Really not the mood, either."

"I was talking about sharing my research."

Glancing across the table, he winked. "I knew that."

"Would you rather have a backrub? Or a glass of wine?"

He picked up a small paperback. *The Long-Lost Friend* by John

George Hohman. "What's this? Appalachian granny witch fiction?"

Stretching her arms, Sandra said, "That book is something you will love to hear about. *The Long-Lost Friend* is considered to be the first grimoire written and published in America."

Max perked up. "Really? I'm all ears."

"It was written in 1820 by a German immigrant. Was originally in German and published in Reading, Pennsylvania. The actual title is stupid long and translates roughly into *The Long Hidden Friend, or True and Christian Instructions for Everyone.* Doesn't really roll off the tongue."

"The first grimoire was actually a Christian book?"

Sandra smirked. "Witchcraft doesn't come out of nowhere. The book was translated into English and has been republished as *The Long-Lost Friend* ever since then. Obviously, what you're holding is not the actual original grimoire but merely a reprinting of the book. I got that one online yesterday."

Max flipped through the pages and saw spells with titles like *A Good Remedy for Worms in Horses.* According to that page, a farmer should speak the name of his horse and say, "If you have any worms, I will catch you by the forehead. If they be white, brown, or red, they shall and must now all be dead." The farmer then needed to shake the head of the horse three times and pass his hands over its back three times.

"The fact that you're looking at this," Max said, "tells me there's more to this book than spells for good animal husbandry."

"Remember that the word *grimoire* only refers to a book that contains the rules that a group agrees to live by as well as useful day-to-day information that they need. Back then, things like this were considered folk magic or practical spells. Some of them are ridiculous, but not all. Some are very real. We witches kept the real ones and made grimoires of our own. Those are the books that have the rules of a coven and all their spells. The author, John George Hohman, came from Hamburg in 1802, and though he ended up in Pennsylvania, a lot of other German settlers at that time ended up in North Carolina."

"Plus, a lot of the Pennsylvania Dutch migrated down here. That's how the Moravians got here. Though that would have pre-dated Hohman."

"True. But not all Germans moving south from Pennsylvania chose to end up in the Winston area or anywhere in the Piedmont. Some of them stopped in the mountains. The Appalachians. Many of them brought *The Long-Lost Friend* along for the ride. In fact, most homes at the time could be counted on having only two books in the house — the Bible and *The Long-Lost Friend*. It wasn't until 1928 that people started rejecting the book."

"That's very specific. What happened in 1928?"

Sandra walked over to the refrigerator and pulled out a recently opened bottle of wine. She moved with a triumphant swagger that Max found appealing. "This is usually your area of research, but I did the best I could. You'll love it. It involves murder."

"You keep talking like this, and I may find the energy to take you back to bed after all."

He didn't truly feel that way, and she must have known it. She handed him a full glass instead. Pouring a second glass, she eased back into her chair. Sifting through a few papers, she pulled out something she had printed off a website.

"Okay, here — in 1928, there was this guy named Nelson Rehmeyer. Nelson's family moved to Pennsylvania in the mid-1800s. Now, Nelson knew this other guy — John Blymire. On November 27, 1928 — notice there that I got the specific date; that's for you, hon — anyway, on that night, Blymire and some friends broke into Nelson's house, murdered the guy, and then set fire to the house. Some reports are that they were attempting to destroy the evidence of what they had done. But like lots of criminals, they were not too bright. They didn't burn down the house properly, and Nelson's charred body was found a few days later. Blymire and his two pals ended up in jail."

"I'm jealous," Max said. "This is exactly my sort of research."

"You can share the fun."

"Well, don't stop. I know this kind of stuff doesn't end

there."

"No, it doesn't. At their trial, things started off rather mundane and boring. The prosecution said it was a robbery gone bad, and the defense denied everything. But a different story started circulating the rumor mill, and it got picked up by the press in what must've been a slow news week because it ended up going national. Basically, the story was that a woman named Emma Knopp convinced John Blymire that he had been cursed by Nelson Rehmeyer. I couldn't find any reasons given why she would do this or why Blymire swallowed the tale, but he blindly believed it. It's thought that he broke into Nelson's house to search for the spell so that he could break the curse."

Max gestured to the copy of *The Long-Lost Friend*. "It is a grimoire, after all."

"And like most people at that time in that area, Nelson had a copy. Now, in a normal situation, this wouldn't have been enough to push somebody over the edge to murder."

"I'm guessing this is not a normal situation."

"I'm sure you've come across this in your own research of that time period, but you probably never had to put it within this context. You see, in the late-1920s, there was this movement trying to curb certain behaviors."

"You mean like Prohibition?"

"Right. What gets less publicized is the fact that those same people trying to create a moral high ground for themselves over alcohol also got their knickers in a twist over magic books and spiritual practices and anything that was not the Bible. If it wasn't Christian, it was evil. They went after African-Americans who practiced hoodoo, and they also had a growing fascination with the idea of hillbillies. A lot of the stereotypical views of Appalachian people as backwards, slow, violent, and superstitious — it all stemmed out of this period. It was basically a group of Christians who thought they were better than everybody else trying to turn the world against things they either didn't approve of or didn't understand."

"Thus, Prohibition."

"You understand it perfectly."

"Are you saying that John Blymire was one of these morally superior Christians?"

"It's not clear if he thought of himself that way, but these were the trends that were going on at the time. When you put those things together — mysterious Appalachian folk, *The Long-Lost Friend* grimoire, Emma Knopp's promises of a curse, and the fear of any practice not considered Christian — isn't too hard to see how Blymire ended up murdering Nelson out of fear."

Max sipped at his wine. "This is fascinating. I love it. But what's it got to do with our granny witch?"

Sandra shrugged. "I didn't say it did. I just thought you'd be interested in it, and you looked like you needed a distraction. Plus, the title of the book kept coming up in everything I've researched about authentic witchcraft in the Appalachian people. If nothing else, we might be able to find whatever folk remedy she used to help your mother."

Max looked at the book again with new appreciation. "Then we're really going to need this."

He told Sandra how the afternoon had gone, managing to speak of his mother's request without crumbling into a vacant stoicism. An improvement.

When he finished, he slumped in the kitchen chair feeling more exhausted, more used up. His muscles had weakened with the telling as if each word spoken aloud manifested a reality absent his mother. More than ever before, Max gleaned the power of a word uttered and how these things, over time, became spells and incantations. But those academic thoughts would not free him from the shackles his mother had placed upon him.

"That's not fair to you," Sandra said. "You didn't make the witch deal, and the fact that you're trying to get her out of it, that we all are taking risks to do so, should be enough."

"She's in a lot of pain. I don't think she meant it other than a plea for help."

"Then let's get her some help."

"What? Like therapy?"

"Absolutely, therapy. A professional trained to deal with

suicidal thoughts — why not?"

"I doubt she would agree to go."

"A few days ago, you would have doubted that she would ever go off to the mountains to make a witch deal. A few days ago, you would have laughed at the idea that she would come close to being arrested for any crime. A few days ago —"

"Okay, okay, I got it. Point made. Once we get her through all of this, assuming we succeed, then we can talk to her about therapy."

Sandra reached over and rubbed Max's hand. "There is another possibility to this. We never heard the exact language of the deal she made."

"You think her desire to end it all is not really her? A spell or a curse?"

"It could be. Might be indirect. It's possible that for breaking the deal, her pain not only returned, but came back twicefold or worse. She might have been told that the pain would continue to grow for each day she failed to fulfill the deal. Or it might be a direct voice in her head urging her to take herself out of the picture. Plenty of other nasty possibilities, and if any of that is the reason, then when we stop Granny Witch Westra, your mother should return to her normal, oh-so-cheery self." Sandra sipped her wine. "But I'm getting the sense that there's more."

"It's just — when I left her apartment and drove around, after I cleared my head a little, I started thinking."

"That's never a good thing."

He grinned. Only for an instant. Then: "Seeing my mother in that state, knowing that even if we fix this problem like she asked, it doesn't change anything. Even if this all is caused by a spell, even if she goes to therapy and no longer wants to kill herself, she's still going to pass away. Eventually."

"Honey, you've seen what happens to those witches that try to overcome dying. It isn't pretty."

"I'm not suggesting that. I'm just saying that thinking about her mortality, well, it got me thinking about how we're all going through such changes. PB and J are grown up. PB is out in the wild, and J is soon to follow. My mother won't last forever. So, pretty soon, it's going to be you and me and that's it."

"True, but I thought you worked through all this already."

"This isn't me feeling an empty nest. Not really. It's more like … well, it's like we built up a life together, and now I feel as if I'm on one of those spinning wheels at an old playground. I'm holding on tight to the metal rails while Life itself is shoving that wheel faster and faster, and it's pulling at me, trying to rip me right off. Somedays, I'm barely holding on. But the thing is, while I'm still on the wheel, it seems like everybody else is flying off, like everything else is coming apart."

"Not to sound too sappy, but you're forgetting the most important part."

"What's that?"

"I'm the railing. You're clinging to me, to our love. And unlike the railing at the playground, I can cling right back. I'll keep you spinning with me."

He reached across the table and laced his fingers with hers. She tightened her grip on him. With a cleansing breath, he said, "There are days I think I really don't deserve you."

"Those would be the days you are right."

Clearing his throat, Max sat straighter and scanned over the research on the table. "Tell me more about all of this."

"Not tonight."

"No?"

"We can deal with this case in the morning. Right now, I'm suddenly feeling the urge to take you up on all that bedroom time."

Max didn't need to be told twice.

Later, as he drifted into sleep, he thought about the last thing Sandra had said — that they could wait until morning to deal with the *case*. That word — *case* — struck him. This wasn't only a personal matter, not only handling a difficult situation for his mother, but it was also a *case*. Thinking of it in that context altered everything for him. With that one word, he could take a step away from the deep familial connection and inspect the details as he would for any other client. The Porter Agency dealt with witches all the time. This should be no different. And that meant he had the full resources of The Porter Agency, too.

Closing his eyes, feeling a surge of freedom, Max composed a mental list on how to proceed with this new case.

Chapter 9

WHEN MORNING ARRIVED, Max hopped out of bed with youthful vigor. He prepared a full breakfast of eggs, toast, bacon, and a serving of assorted berries. Coffee, too. He knew Sandra would need that.

To answer her questioning expression, he said, "Seems to me if I'm going to stop my mother from committing a drastic act from which she cannot return — not without some witchcraft, anyway — then the only way is to solve this case. That means we don't have room for making mistakes from brain fatigue or physical fatigue or anything else detrimental. So, eat up. We've got a lot of work to do."

After filling their bellies and washing up, they agreed on a plan of attack. Sandra called her apprentice, Brenda, so the two of them could dig through the mound of information about Appalachian folklore, granny witches, and anything else they might find useful. She would also attempt to identify the hairball that was meant to be left at the Vellmer's house. Sandra even suggested that if they couldn't find the answers they wanted, they would go to Haven House. Max bit back his objection. He didn't have to like it, but he had just finished saying they needed to do everything they could — if that meant Haven House, then so be it.

For Max's part, he and Drummond had an appointment to meet with Montgomery Dun. The man still used a landline which made it easy to find a number. He answered on the first ring. Having learned well from Drummond, Max made sure to have a story prepared when the inevitable question came as to why Max wanted to meet. Max tended to go with pretending he worked for a magazine and wanted to interview the subject as part of a profile on the local area. Most people liked being interviewed, made them feel important, and often they gave up critical information without realizing they had said anything at all. However, Montgomery Dun never questioned Max's reasons. He simply agreed to meet. He suggested a time and insisted that they do not meet at his home.

"I'll feel much more comfortable at the Wallburg Baptist Church. It's on the corner of 109 and Wallburg Road. You know how to get there?"

"I'll find it."

The section of Route 109 that connected Winston-Salem to Wallburg consisted mostly of a two-lane road that snaked through residential areas and a few built-up crossroads. The drive did not take long, but Max still had enough time to tell Drummond all that had happened the previous night.

"Don't worry," the ghost said with a click of his tongue. "Believe me, lots of people wish that death would come take them out of a bad situation, but it's two very different things — the wishing and the dying."

"She looked pretty serious to me."

"I'm sure she did. They all do. But when the moment arrives, it suddenly becomes a different proposition. Doesn't matter how old you are or what kind of condition you're in. Most people do not welcome the end. Even if they've been hoping for it to come for years."

"I'm not sure I believe that in this case. I'm not sure that's true for anybody suffering like she is. This MS stuff is no joke."

"The only people I've ever seen that this doesn't hold true for are those who have lost all hope. There's no chance that they'll get better or that they'll find even a little joy left in life. Otherwise, if there is even a sliver of light shining towards them, it's usually worth holding on for. Right now, you're working to be that light. Besides, we're talking about your mother. She is not going to die over some witch."

Nobody paid much attention to the various speed limits posted along the winding road — until he reached Wallburg. After a 55 mile an hour burst, passing a Mexican restaurant, a bunch of homes, and a thickly forested area, the road inclined up a large hill and curved off to the left where the speed limit dropped to 35, and everybody obeyed. Apparently, the locals knew where to expect a speed trap. Or perhaps they simply cared about this little section of their town. He drove by an elementary school as well as some small mom-and-pop stores. On the left, he came to the corner of 109 and Wallburg Road.

Max pulled into a mid-sized parking lot that wrapped around the back corner of the Wallburg Baptist Church — a classic church design with a tall steeple out front, plenty of gray stone, and a letterboard sign in the grass promising *Got problems? Pray. It works!* On the other side of the lot, the creatively named Wallburg Diner shared a building with a US Post Office — white, single-story structures that looked well-cared for, though old.

The breakfast crowd — if there was one — had gone, leaving the cracked lot mostly empty. Early morning, midweek — Max didn't expect a lot of public attention. In fact, the cars cruising along 109 created the most traffic. A surprising amount considering the size of the town, but then 109 served as a backroad conduit between a lot of towns.

A one-lane street acted like an alley connecting Wallburg Road with the main parking lot, and Max chose to park there. On one side, he had the church. On the other, a small cemetery plot filled with gravestones. A black Dodge Ram pickup took up a chunk of space, but Max managed to get in behind it. Less eyes would be on him, not that there were any eyes about, but he figured safest to follow best practices. The approving nod from Drummond bolstered this opinion.

As he walked toward the front entrance which faced Wallburg Road but also provided a good view of 109, he saw a man sitting on the stone steps. Long thin legs and jeans, black T-shirt over a trim frame, and enough salt-and-pepper in the man's hair and beard to properly season a porterhouse. If Max had been told that this man played bass in an Allman Brothers tribute band, he wouldn't have doubted it for a second.

Spotting Max, the man sat up and offered a single wave of the hand. "You're Porter?" He had a strong, gritty accent that outsiders tended to mock or fear while those who knew better found it warm and endearing.

"Nice to meet you, Mr. Dun."

"You can call me Monty."

"Then call me Max. Want to go in the diner? Get a cold drink?"

"I'm good here."

Max would rather have been in the air conditioning, but he would make do.

Drummond tipped his hat back and gazed up at the sun as if he could feel the heat beating down on him. "I like this guy. He agreed to meet with us, but he doesn't really know us. Doesn't want to meet at his house and prefers to sit in front of a church by a busy road which has plenty of cars going by. About as public as you can get in a town this small. He's smart."

Monty scratched under his beard. "I'm curious — are you going to be playing some little games to try and get to whatever it is you want from me or are you more of a direct and to the punch kind of man?"

"What is it you think I'm trying to get out of you?"

"Games then? That's a shame. I like men who are upfront about what they want."

Drummond said, "He's given you an opening. Take him at his word."

While Max agreed with his partner, he also knew that there was the truth and then there was the whole truth. No matter how upfront Montgomery Dun wanted his information served, Max didn't think the man would appreciate tales of witches, witchcraft, and witch deals. Some of the story, however — the more mundane, realistic sounding parts — he could provide.

"Your foreclosed house is what I'm interested in. Do you know any of the history behind it?"

Monty's bushy eyebrows lifted. "That old place in Olin? Well, well. Not much to tell you about it, really. Don't know the people who bought it 'cause I didn't sell it. My end of the story itself is as boring as a visit to the DMV."

"Feel free to bore me, then."

That got a grin. "Well, it's a typical sad luck story. I lost my job and fell behind on payments. Only two, really, but apparently that was enough. After that, the bank came in and the government screwed me over. I wanted to fight it, but fighting costs money that I didn't have for lawyers that I didn't know. It's a shame, really. I was hoping to buy the place back, but I guess that's done for. Let me tell you, the politicians and the bank people will take everything from a good hard-working man. They sweep in and destroy all around them without a care. Long as they get their money." He angled his head up and squinted at Max. "I can't tell if you're a cop or a lackey for the banks or what."

"This guy isn't going to help us," Drummond said, bending closer to Monty. "Not unless you can get him talking without realizing it."

Max strolled to the corner, surveyed the parking lot, and wiped at the sweat on his face. A few cars had come, and others had left. He made sure to put his back to Monty and waited for Drummond to float around. Nobody paid them any attention, so nobody noticed when Max mouthed *How?* to the emptiness.

"And here I thought you finally started learning from me." Drummond lowered the brim of his hat. "You get him talking the usual way — go straight at him, see if you can get a rise out of him. You hit the right nerves and he'll spill it all before he knows what happened."

"That all you want?" Monty called out from the steps.

Turning around as a semi rumbled along the street, Max paused, then returned with a defeated smile. "I appreciate your time. I had hoped for more, but I guess you really don't know why an Appalachian granny healer is so interested in that property. Doesn't matter, I suppose. I'm scheduled to interview her tomorrow, so she can explain it all."

Monty snickered as his lip curled. "I wouldn't trust a thing that old crone says."

"There you go," Drummond said. "Got him on the first shot. I guess you've learned a thing or two, after all."

"You know who I'm talking about?" Max asked.

"Granny Witch Westra. And you can cry on and on about anything you want, but the one thing you won't ever get from that lady is the truth. Not from her or anybody in her family. Bunch of snakes and weasels. Anybody good in that family pops up, they cut them out right away. All they want around them are the obedient and the stupid."

"I take it you've had some dealings with her before."

"Duns don't trust Westras, and we got generations of history to prove that's a right way of thinking." He sniffed hard as one hand pressed against the church step. "You see her, you tell her from me that I ain't got that house no more. She don't need to bother some innocent folk who bought it. If she really wants to have it out, she can come on down to Wallburg. I'll be here. It's about time she and I deal with the hard truths of all the wrong she's done."

"What happened between you all?"

But Monty clammed shut. Swiping at the dust on his pants, he stood, then tipped two fingers off his brow. "Nice to meet you, Max Porter. You have a good day, now."

"Not even a handshake goodbye," Drummond said. "You really pissed him off."

Before Max could saunter back to his car, Drummond put out an arm. Max could have walked straight through it and endured the cold, but habit caused him to stop. With a piercing ghostly stare, Drummond watched as Monty swaggered toward the black Dodge Ram pickup.

"A new lesson for you to learn," Drummond said. "Once you have shaken up somebody you interrogated, you'll want to stick around and see what they do."

"Then shouldn't I be going to my car so we can follow him?"

"Sometimes, that's exactly right. But tell me, out here in this small town in this small parking lot, how are you going to tail him without him knowing?"

The big truck fired up, growling as Monty pumped the gas pedal like a teenager trying to impress anybody within earshot. As he pulled onto the road, he went to the corner and headed south on 109, Max got a clear view of the man. He had one hand on the top of the steering wheel and the other holding a phone. He did not look happy about the conversation.

"Well, well," Max said in his best imitation of Monty.

"Time to see if you've gotten any smarter. What have we just learned?"

"For starters, his house is in that direction. He's probably going home."

"We already know his address, and he could be going anywhere. Even if you're right, knowing he's headed home doesn't really help us. What else?"

"We know I really got under his skin. Not only because of the way he acted, but he immediately called somebody. He looked ticked off."

"You're getting warmer."

Before answering, Max paused to think it over once more. Obviously, Drummond thought they had seen something of greater value. The fact that Monty had a pickup truck meant nothing — half of North Carolina's population owned a pickup. Apparently, his direction of travel did not tell them anything, or at least, anything important. All they really had seen was Montgomery Dun on the phone talking ...

"Who was he talking with?"

Drummond clapped his hands once. "Bingo. Now take it a step further."

"What do you mean?"

With his hands thrust in his long coat pockets, Drummond looked every bit the 1940s detective he had once been. "He's talking with someone, and that means there is someone worth talking with. Whatever his connection to all this, he's not alone in it."

Walking off towards his car, Max said, "I guess it's time to look into the Dun family."

When they turned the corner into the alley where he had parked, Max saw the large bald man from the library. He leaned against Max's car door. When he spotted Max, the bald man pushed off and cracked his knuckles.

Drummond must have picked up on Max's instant fear.

Without asking for details, the ghost said, "I'll take care of this."

Rolling his shoulders, he swooped ahead. But a second large man appeared from behind the far corner of the church — presumably, the same man that had visited Mrs. Porter. As Drummond descended on the bald man, the big guy in the back stomped toward them all. He lifted his left hand, and in it, Max noticed a wooden token painted red. From this distance, he couldn't make out the finer details, but he had no doubt some version of witch symbols had been carved into it.

Drummond must have noticed, too, because rather than strike the bald man, he backed up a little. "Looks like they came prepared with a ward."

Both men's eyes locked on Max. Of course. They couldn't see Drummond. But as the big man came alongside his partner, smoke seeped out of the wooden token in his hand. Drummond glanced back at Max, confusion across his brow. As Max started to shrug an answer, the wooden token snapped in two, the sound louder than it should have been for a small piece of pine. Gray-blue smoke spewed out. It did not billow in all directions like normal smoke, though. No, this moved with purpose — straight for Drummond. It enveloped him with the speed of a python wrapping around its victim.

Seconds later, the smoke dissipated. Drummond was gone.

"Hey!" Max stormed towards the two men.

The bald man raised his hand flat and blew hard enough to puff his cheeks out. Dust flew into Max's face.

Coughing, Max tried to rub off the powder. He recalled taking the next step, and the next one, and then it all ended. His head grew heavy. His vision clouded. Until he lost consciousness.

Chapter 10

THE DARK FOG LIFTED, beginning with muffled sounds that came from a far distance and over time grew louder and more distinct, followed by aching limbs, a pasty mouth, and a throbbing head that made a college hangover feel like a fond morning practice. Max awoke. Even as he squinted open his eyes, with a weakness in his limbs and a crick in his neck, his brain struggled to comprehend his situation. The sounds his ears transcribed, the objects his sight informed — they were noises and objects he had encountered all the time, yet he could not get his mind to connect everything into a coherent picture. Until the smell hit him.

Lexington barbecue.

He sat in a restaurant booth with his head pressed against a large plate-glass window overlooking a parking lot on a hill. He couldn't make out the name of the place, but he saw the steep, high angled roof of a business next door called *Granny's Donuts*. Hopefully, not *that* kind of granny. Across a busy road, he spied a Little Ceasar's Pizza, and turning his head slightly, he could make out a hardware store. Looked like a small town. Not Wallburg, though.

Pushing to an upright position — his head a few seconds behind and jeopardizing the entire operation — Max discovered the brutes from the church sitting across the table. The bald one watched him with curiosity while the big one paid more attention to the dining room — probably making sure nobody took notice. Dry-mouthed and tasting licorice on his tongue, Max followed the big one's gaze.

He didn't recognize the restaurant. North Carolina had a lot of barbecue joints, and Max had a long way to go before he had tried them all. The sparse crowd suggested the lunch rush either had yet to start or had recently concluded. Or the food would be awful, nobody ever came, and the restaurant would be out of business soon.

A young, curvy waitress arrived with three heaping plates of pulled pork sandwiches, slaw, and fries. She set one in front of each man before asking if she could do anything else. Her eyes drifted to Max with a questioning glance.

Max opened his mouth, but the big man said, "Maybe some coffee. He overindulged last night."

"Sure thing." The waitress inched closer to Max. "Don't feel bad about it, sugar. We've all been there."

Despite the tangy aroma of the barbecue, her candy perfume cut through with a nauseating result. She strolled away with the sway to her hips that came with youth while his stomach swayed to an older, less rejuvenating beat. But a few breaths, a sip of water, and a few sniffs of barbecue cleared away that candy scent. Drummond was going to hate finding out he missed this waitress. What she lacked in taste for perfume, she made up for in curves. *Drummond!*

Trying again to speak, Max managed, "D-D—"

The big man said, "You should eat. It'll get rid of that nasty taste."

The bald man took a large bite out of his sandwich, pulled pork and slaw dripping out the back, and while chewing, he said, "Best food ever, too."

"That's true," the big man said. "We live up in the mountains, and they got what they call Lexington barbecue up there, but it isn't quite right. Not the same."

"Not like this." The bald man chewed a second bite while still trying to swallow the first.

Max swished water in his mouth. "What did you —"

"Trust us with this. If you're going to eat barbecue, it's Lexington all the way. Whenever Granny says we can come down to Winston with her, she knows to make sure we got time to get somewhere close to Lexington. We've got to have our barbecue."

Pointing to Max's plate, the bald man said, "You should eat

it. It's good."

"Don't force the guy. Besides, if he don't want it, that's just more for you and me."

"Oh, yeah. Forget what I said. This stuff is awful. You don't want any of it."

Max's head still reeled, but the desire to eat could not be ignored. He picked up his sandwich and took a bite. Damn, it was good. He didn't want to love it so much, not at this moment with this company, yet the combination of his grumbling stomach, his aching body, and the deliciousness of the food produced a pleasant groan.

The bald man chuckled. "Told you it was good."

Before either man could get talking again, Max finally found his voice. "What did you do to Drummond?"

"Don't know who that is," the bald man said.

The big one elbowed the other. "I think he's talking about the ghost." To Max: "That's a powerful ward, isn't it? Granny worked on that a long time. She knows how to be patient with things like a ward."

"Took her six months."

"That's right. I only wish a ward could get rid of a ghost for good. We could clean up the mountainside in no time with something like that."

Max tried to channel his inner-Drummond, tried to pay attention to the information given below what they thought they had said. He knew that they were aware of ghosts and witches. No surprise, there. But he also learned that the ghost ward they had used took a long time to create, and since Max saw the thing break apart, it could only be used once. Most importantly, the ward didn't kill Drummond. Probably tossed him miles away.

Tapping a napkin over his lips, the big man said, "Do you understand why we're here?"

Stifling a belch, Max said, "Really good barbecue?"

"Nobody likes a smartass. This here is simple — don't make things difficult."

"I get it already. You're both big tough guys, you're the muscle, and you're here to deliver a message. But I don't even know your names."

"I'm Billy. This is my brother, Luke."

Max raised an eyebrow. "Never would've pegged you for brothers — except for the same jawline, same build, same — well, not the same hair."

Luke continued shoveling food into his mouth, picking fries off his brother's plate. Though he didn't say anything, Max could feel the man's aggression seething off him. Every sarcastic remark Max made, Luke's fingers tightened, the desire to punch palpable.

Perhaps sensing his brother's need for a violent release, Billy pushed his plate to the side. "Have the rest," he said, and Luke piled into the leftovers. "Okay, Mr. Max Porter, this is how we go forward. Either you or your mother honors the deal you made with my granny."

Max waited for more, but it didn't come. "Or what?"

"There is no *or what*. You will do it. You already saw her ghost ward in action. You know she's the real thing. If you think that failing to honor your end of the deal will send me and Luke down here again to rough you up, no."

Luke snickered. "No, no."

"We're here as a courtesy. We're here as the only warning you'll get. You will follow through on the deal. Not to do so — do I really need to explain what a bad idea it would be to go back on a deal with a witch?"

Max wanted to continue his sarcastic defiance, but his heart dropped. He suddenly felt like a boy who had messed his pants at school. Embarrassed — embarrassed and ashamed and not sure how to get out of the situation. Even his barbecue started to turn his stomach.

Billy folded his hands on the table exuding a gentleness his muscles did not support. "I'm sorry we're having this conversation. Truly. Your mother seems like a nice lady, and I don't enjoy being mean to nice ladies. I can even forgive your attitude because you're only looking out for your mother."

"If you don't like this, then why do you do it?"

"Even if Granny wasn't Granny, I'd still do what she asked.

She's family. Without that, you got nothing."

"Got it. Message received. Only one thing — I didn't make the deal. My mother made it, and she hasn't been too clear on all the details."

"That ain't my problem. And I promise that you don't want it to become Granny's problem. I wouldn't dare cross her. You shouldn't, either."

Luke said, "Yeah, look at our Aunt Mary, and you'll —"

"Shut up. He don't care about our family."

Max wanted these brothers to leave. Treading water in this conversation had grown exhausting, and he needed time to digest everything. But they showed no signs of being done with him. It didn't help that Billy had just admitted to being afraid of Granny. All this talk of family and —

Family. That gave Max an idea.

"You know, you're not the first one to talk to me about a mountain family today. The way I hear it, the Westras and the Duns don't like each other too much."

Luke froze. A shred of coleslaw dangled from his mouth. Billy unfolded his hands and reached over to grip the edge of the table.

"You really don't want to get involved in that. You've got enough trouble with Granny."

Max raised his hands. "I'm only saying what I heard. Montgomery Dun told me —"

Spewing food, Luke said, "Don't listen to anything that bastard says. He's a liar. All them Duns are liars and thieves. They're not even proper mountain folk."

"They're not from the mountains?"

Before Luke could say another word, Billy slid out of the booth. "We're finished here. You want to live through this? You want your mother to live through this? Stop worrying about things that don't concern you and focus on finishing your end of the deal."

Max said, "Hold on. You can't just leave me here. I don't even know what town I'm in."

Luke slammed Max's car keys onto the table. "You'll figure it out."

As the two burly men thumped away, the candy-scented waitress returned. She ripped off the bill from her pad and placed it on the table. "You can pay up at the register."

Max patted his pants — still had his wallet. At least the Westra brothers didn't screw him over. He waited five minutes to make sure they had left before paying the bill and finding his car parked off to the side. Only when he walked out did he learn the name of the restaurant — Bar-B-Que Shack. He was in Thomasville. About fifteen minutes from Lexington. Not a bad choice.

No more than a minute after sitting in his car, a cold chill rolled over his skin. He looked to the passenger seat and watched as Drummond appeared.

"You okay?" Max asked.

"I'm still dead. But I don't think that ward did anything lasting."

"What did it do to you?"

"Threw me into the Other. Kept me there, too, until now. I've never seen a ward that powerful. Didn't even know one could be made like that. Maybe Sandra has some idea because I don't know how I'm going to break through it."

"You won't have to. It's a one-use thing, and apparently it takes half-a-year to make."

"Yeah? Except Granny Witch probably started making these things when she was young. She could have tons of them."

"But she can't make any new ones — not easily."

"Great. I'll tell my sore head to count its blessings."

Max checked the time — nearly two o'clock. His phone also notified him of several messages from Sandra. He figured most wondered where he had gone. Without bothering to listen to them, he called her.

"I'm okay. I'll tell you all about it later. You got anything good?"

He could hear Sandra's joy when she said, "I certainly do. The Porter Agency needs to have a meeting."

Chapter 11

SANDRA HAD SURPRISED MAX plenty of times throughout their life together, and that night proved no exception. When he entered the new office space — after shouldering the door twice before it gave up with a disheartened whine — he questioned holding the meeting there when the place was nothing more than a glorified warehouse at the moment. But in addition to researching Appalachian witchcraft with Brenda, the two women had arranged for the office to be furnished. Not completely — they only had a few hours at hand — but enough to get a sense of how the space would be used and to hold that night's meeting.

A desk for Sandra occupied their claimed locations as well as two large filing cabinets. Max's desk from the house had been transported over, and he wondered if he might miss his little kitchen alcove. It had been a snug fit, but he had grown accustomed to having walls crowding him while he delved deeper into research of one kind or another. Plus, working hard built up an appetite, and he had enjoyed the convenience of having the kitchen right there at his disposal. Then again, seeing his desk in a space designated for their work, seeing a real office to call home for their business — he could get accustomed to that once more.

In one of the yet to be fully-furnished areas, a circular rug had been rolled out to cover the space where Sandra's casting circle would eventually be set. Boxes of files had been stacked next to Max's desk while a large portion of Sandra's witchcraft library formed piles against one wall. A gray, somewhat ratty couch had been found — they saw it on the side of the road with a sign reading FREE — as well as two wooden chairs.

"Not the most comfortable," Brenda had pointed out, "but until y'all get the real furniture, this'll keep us from having to stand all night."

Sandra had used blue tape to mark out where Drummond's bookshelves would eventually go, while Brenda hung several pictures on the walls. Among them, one of Max's favorites prints — a rather famous black and white photograph from 1934 depicting Grand Central Station with shafts of sunlight cascading into the cathedral-like building.

Drummond swished around the office as if experiencing it for the first time. "Doll, you've outdone yourself. I know you've got a lot planned for here, but it's already looking great. Just like you."

J's 2010 Fiesta pulled into the parking lot, and as he helped Mrs. Porter out of the car, Max observed from one of the office windows. She moved in short, frail steps, and J made sure to always have a hand on her elbow. Once they left his view, Max turned back to the office.

"We should make sure to have a spot for J's desk," Max said. "That is, assuming he still wants to join us after college."

Sandra said, "We've got about four years to figure that out."

By the time J and Mrs. Porter made it into the office and settled on the couch, Brenda and Osorio had arrived. They all spent a few minutes looking over the new office with plenty of admiring comments. Max couldn't help but wonder if Sandra had asked Brenda and Osorio to be a little more vocal in their approval — Max's mother would certainly take a cue from their reaction — but he decided he didn't care. If hearing others state that Max and Sandra had done a good job meant his mother would be satisfied, then that meant one less bit of trouble on his plate.

One of those troubles came in the form of his mother's presence at this meeting. Several members of the Agency — all of them, actually — objected to having Mrs. Porter attend. Max argued that she was the client and deserved to hear what they had learned. However, others pointed out that, unlike regular clients, she did not believe any of what she had experienced. She denied the existence of the supernatural, and as a result, she might find the meeting either ridiculous or terrifying. Max pointed out that he hoped for the latter. He wanted to scare her into understanding this stuff was real and she was in real danger — not simply from the roughnecks wanting to enforce her deal but from the reality of her deal with an authentic witch. At length, those who debated against her involvement backed down, but Max could tell that Mrs. Porter's attendance made the rest of the Agency uncomfortable.

After a short time, Sandra called everyone together around the couch. Max rolled over his trusty office chair. It hadn't had the chance to move on those wheels since being relegated to the kitchen alcove, and he liked the feel of it.

Sandra stood in front of the group, her notes on her phone in one hand, and she gestured to Brenda. "Aren't you going to join?"

"You don't need me."

"But I couldn't have done all this research without you."

"It's okay. This is your agency. You get to play the bigshot. Besides, I'll interject whenever you get something wrong, don't worry."

The women shared a grin before Sandra rolled her shoulders to face the rest of the group. "To start with, you have to know the reality of the Appalachian people because they are not the backwoods, banjo-picking freaks Hollywood and much of the world likes to depict them as."

Max thought about his experiences that day. Both Billy and Luke had been polite in their threats and generous in not leaving him abandoned without his car. Even stiffing him for the bill showed a level of civilized behavior that did not match with the ignorant, tooth-gapped oddities seen in many films.

Sandra continued, "Way back, the Appalachian Mountains served as a conduit between many from the North and South, and because of this, the Appalachian people are an amalgam of all the cultures that passed through. They learned to live close to the land, reaping its benefits and surviving its dangers. But too many outsiders have come in and raped the land for its wealth. These outsiders are everything from speculators to corporations to governments to you name it. They come to the mountains with promises they never intend to keep. Coal, wood, property — the Appalachian people have watched as outsiders took it all away, destroying what is left behind, including lives. Many of the mountain folk are poor by our standards, and they know it. So, they distrust anybody that doesn't come from the mountains."

"I didn't do any of that," Mrs. Porter said, avoiding eye contact with everybody. "I didn't destroy anything or lie to anybody. This granny has no reason to bully a little old woman like me."

In a gentle tone, Osorio said, "I think she's mad because you didn't follow through on your deal."

"Oh, crap," Drummond said. "Did nobody warn him not to say stupid things like that?"

Mrs. Porter's nostrils flared as she turned a stern gaze upon the unwitting policeman. "I don't know how you were raised — I certainly hope your mother tried to teach you proper — but you should not speak so rudely to an older, wiser person. We all make mistakes. That's natural. It is how we learn. For a young man like you, making a mistake about daily living or how to speak with your elders — that's a bit understandable. You're still learning. So, let this be your lesson. And while I'm sure you see all old folks as the wisest people in a room, I am not too proud to admit that there are things still for me to learn. At my age, you should be more understanding when a mistake is made about such things. Like dealing with our deaths. Nobody has answers for us about death, and we have to figure it out through our mistakes."

Suppressing a laugh, Max swiveled to face away from his mother. He also bit back the urge to argue. Not only because many in the room knew some of what happened after death — particularly the ghost floating by the soon-to-be bookcase — but also because Max's mother appeared to find and lose religion whenever it suited her. One day, she might praise the Bible and claim it had the answers she sought. The next day — well, she made a deal with a witch.

"Brenda and I could talk about their culture for days," Sandra went on. "It's fascinating stuff, but that's not why we're here. So, witchcraft and the granny witches."

Max peeked back at his mother. She had her arms folded over her chest and her chin tucked down. The only thing missing from this petulant image was a pouting bottom lip, and he thought that might come soon.

"Like their culture, Appalachian witchery is also an amalgam of the various groups that traveled through the mountains. Hoodoo and Wicca mixed with herbalists and even Christian lore. Because of this, we've found things such as tasting the wind — a lovely, naturalistic magic in where the granny witches supposedly can taste changes in the wind that reflect changes in everything from the coming weather to good or bad fortune for a person to whatever you want to predict in the future. Doubtfully effective and mostly harmless, yet it reflects their connection to nature and their surroundings. But then, we have this disturbing explanation on how a granny witch becomes a granny witch. One of the regular methods was to go to the top of a mountain or at least a hill, somewhere that you'll be close to the sky, and you do this at dawn —"

Drummond said, "I've heard this one. It involves a loaded pistol."

"That's right. You would take a gun with you and a handkerchief, and you would have to curse God's name three times while holding the handkerchief in the air. Then you shoot a bullet through the handkerchief. If blood pours out of the hole, it meant you were accepted as a witch."

"Does that even work?" Osorio asked.

"Not at all. Not in any sense they think it does. But it does work as any initiation rite would work — it's a ceremony for the person; a moment that marks the change from one point in life to another. But as off-the-wall as that one might sound to us, we've also found versions of it that involve taking somebody to the top of the mountain under a full moon until the Devil appears. The wannabe witch would then sign away her soul. In fact, this shows you how Christian beliefs mix with these other forms of magic. Almost every Appalachian method of becoming a witch involves giving up your soul to the Devil."

Without lifting her head, Mrs. Porter said, "Then Granny Witch Westra is soulless as well as evil."

Perhaps trying to help avoid conflict or simply keeping things on track, Brenda said, "You should explain the witchballs to everybody."

Sandra offered a relieved nod. "The witchball is considered to be one of the most terrifying weapons a granny witch has at her disposal. They can be thrown at something living and cause great injury or even kill. They tend to be made from a variety of strange and often disgusting objects like the bladder of a black cat, a dead baby's toenails, the fat from a corpse, and such. All of that would be weaved into a ball with matted hair. The best witchballs included hair from the intended target."

Osorio said, "Excuse me, Mrs. Porter, but am I correct that you broke into that house to place one of these witchballs in one of the walls?"

She nodded and made a grunting affirmation.

"Then it seems to me that the easiest thing to do would be to take the witchball and put it in the wall. Now that I know about it, I might be able to get the police to look the other way for a moment."

Max cocked his head over. "Doesn't that put the Vellmers in danger?"

Sandra said, "I doubt it. This is about the house and that door. The Vellmers haven't even settled in yet. Granny Witch probably thought the place was empty."

Looking back at Osorio, Max said, "You can get the police to ignore this?"

"I'll end up owing more than one favor, and I —"

"But when I picked my mother up in Yadkinville, you said you couldn't be a part of this. You said you were working on a promotion."

"A pay raise. Different thing."

"I thought you were doing us a favor being here tonight. How come you can suddenly pull strings so we can break into a house?"

"Because if I were to suggest that by helping you out, we

could solve the issue and ease Mrs. Porter's worried mind, thus helping keep the peace in the area, they might listen. Like I said, I'll end up owing a favor, but it's a far different ask than when I had them ignore an arrest."

"You sure? I don't want to hurt your chances for getting better pay."

"I wouldn't offer if I didn't mean it."

"Good man," Drummond said.

Mrs. Porter smacked her knee. "No."

Max looked to his mother. "Why not? It's a good idea. You want to be done with this, right? You wanted us to fix it, well, this could complete the deal. And once you complete it, Granny Witch Westra might still honor the original agreement — you could return to feeling whole."

She tightened her arms around herself. "It's not that I don't want to, it's that we can't. I — that is — I don't have this witchball thing anymore."

"What happened to it?"

Raising her voice a notch above Max, she said, "I don't know exactly. I had it in my hand, I went into the house, but I was nervous. I was scared. What do you think happened? I heard the police, so I ditched it."

"Then it might still be in the house."

Drummond said, "Not likely. Otherwise, Granny wouldn't be upset. It may not have made it into the exact wall she wanted, but it would be doing — what exactly would it be doing?"

Sandra put out her hands to calm everybody. "We don't know exactly what Granny Witch's purpose in doing this is. Clearly, it has something to do with the trouble between the Westra family and the Dun family. Beyond that, we're still grasping at straws."

Mrs. Porter said, "This doesn't matter. I lost the witchball."

"In the house you were supposed to deliver it."

"Maybe *lost* isn't the right word. When the police sirens came, well, I panicked."

Max's gut dropped. "You didn't. Tell me you didn't."

"Isn't that what you're supposed to do when you have illicit contraband, and the police show up?"

Drummond smacked his forehead. "She flushed it?"

"I flushed it down the toilet."

In the stunned silence that followed, a bad idea struck Max. One that he knew he would share. "Seems to me that this all has to do with whatever's behind that locked door in the Vellmer house. Osorio, you said that you could arrange it so that we could break into the house without getting police problems."

"I can. I'd rather not."

"I'd rather not have to do any of this. But if Sandra and I and Drummond can go into that house, maybe we can figure out what's happening with that door. We'll do it tomorrow while the Vellmers are at work, and we'll be fast. Won't disturb anything. Nobody will know we were ever there. With a little luck, even if we can't get through the door, we should have a better idea of what the Dun family had going on before they lost that house. We learn that, and we'll know why Granny Witch Westra is so adamant about putting a witchball in the place. Because it sounds to me like a witchball is a jacked-up version of a hex bag, and we've all seen how bad those things can get."

Waving J over to help her, Mrs. Porter stood and headed for the door. "I don't understand what any of you are talking about. And who is Drummond? Never mind. I don't care. It sounds like you have a plan to help, and I don't need to understand it. I'm going home."

"Not a bad idea," Max said. "Sandra and I need to get a good night's sleep, too. What about it, Osorio? You think you can make this work?"

"I can, but like I said, I'm going to end up owing them big time. That means you might end up owing them big time, too."

"If that's the way it's got to be. Brenda, I suggest you also get some rest. You never know when we'll need you."

As the group broke up, Max waited until everyone had left except Drummond and Sandra.

The ghost said, "You sure this is the best plan?"

"I think this is a horrible plan," Max said. "You got any better ideas?"

"I guess not. At least, the three of us will be together."

Gathering her things, Sandra said, "Brenda is proving to be an invaluable resource and help. She's a good researcher, too. Maybe we should see if she's good at researching more than just magic. I was thinking of asking her to look into the Dun family. Or the Westras. Or both and their feud."

"I was going to do that," Max said.

"And you should. You're the best at it. But tomorrow, we're going to be breaking into that house. You're not really going to have the time, are you?"

Grumbling, he said, "Okay. Give her a call on the way home. I'm tired."

With that, Max and Sandra stepped into the hallway. Despite the scattered bits of information, despite the looming criminal activity planned for the next day, Max had it within him to feel a little thrill as he closed the door to The Porter Agency office. It had been a long time since they had to drive home from work, and a part of him happily admitted that it felt good.

About the only thing feeling good at the moment.

Chapter 12

SANDRA TREMBLED as they strolled up the walkway to the Vellmer's front door. The morning sun had risen a few hours ago, and the day's heat already pressed upon them. One look at her, though, and Max knew her prickling skin came from the house. She felt the building's uneasiness as much as he had — probably more.

No cars in the driveway. That was a good sign. Still, to be certain, Max asked Drummond to sweep the house.

"Not a soul," the ghost said upon his return. "At least, not in the parts of the house I can enter."

Max called Osorio. "The house is empty. Do we have the okay to go in?"

"I hope you understand how unusual this request is."

"I get it. I've never asked for it before, and I don't see why I would in the future."

"Because people are like that. Once they learn that a way of doing things is an easier option, they want to use it all the time. Except this isn't easier. Not for me."

Of course, Max heard the concerns in Osorio's words, but more, he heard it in the uncharacteristic quake beneath the words. It occurred to Max that this might be more than owing a big favor to another officer. In fact, it definitely was more. After all, they were about to commit a crime, and Osorio had convinced the local authorities to look the other way. If The Porter Agency was caught, a lot of people might lose their jobs, Osorio would certainly lose his, and those that survived would be punished in other ways.

Taking a quick survey around them, Max didn't see anybody watching. Mostly farmland, anyway. "We'll be as fast as possible," he said.

"And you're sure you can do this without leaving any signs of forced entry?"

"That part is easy. I promise. I know what you're risking. Don't worry."

Sighing, Osorio said, "Okay. You've got about ten minutes. Fifteen at the most, but don't push it that long."

After ending the call, Max gave Drummond the thumbs up. The ghost slipped through the wall to unlock the front door from the inside. As Max and Sandra entered, Drummond winced from touching a real-world object, but he knew not to waste time getting caught into a round of banter. They had a job to do, and a tight timeline to do it in.

"Where is the door?" Sandra said.

"This way." Drummond led them down the hall.

Two feet before reaching the strange door, Sandra halted. Her brow tightened.

"If you ask me, doll, I still think it's a spell lock. Not that I'm an expert — really only dealt with the one spell lock at Madame Ti's — but this feels too much like that on me."

"It's not a ward," she said. "You're still here. A spell lock is a good guess."

As they continued to inspect the door, Max strolled back to the living room. They didn't need him hovering over their work, and the longer he remained standing in the hall, the worse he felt. Not because of the spell or spells on the door, but rather, he didn't like what they were doing.

He had broken into homes before. Offices and apartments, too. But those had always been investigating people they suspected of magic wrongdoing. In Max's view, if a person breaks the rules, then they can't expect everybody else to follow those rules when it comes to that person. It was like the fallacy of tolerating the intolerant. If a person chose to be intolerant of others, that person broke the social contract, and in doing so, had no right to be tolerated themselves. Same thing.

Except this time, the house did not belong to the suspects. Wyatt and Callie Vellmer were good people who didn't deserve to get caught up in this. Heck, they didn't even rise to the level of a foolish kid messing with a Ouija board. They simply bought the wrong house.

All the more reason to get answers. If The Porter Agency succeeded, they could send Granny Witch and her family back to the mountains. This could end without any harm coming to the Vellmers.

"If we fail," he muttered to the empty room, "then the Vellmers might end up as the Agency's next clients."

From the hall, he heard Drummond. "What if it's just a series of curses?"

"Could be," Sandra said. "Might even be some curses atop a spell lock. See if you can feel out where the energy is concentrated strongest."

Max wanted to remind them that a strict time limit had been placed on ignoring this break-in. They had to focus. But admonishing them for taking too much time would also take up more time, and it was too precious to waste right now.

Instead, Max snooped around the unpacked boxes that had been left open. His curiosity urged him to open a few of the boxes still taped, but they had promised Osorio there would be no sign of the break-in left behind. That included disturbing the moving boxes.

A weird sensation coursed through his blood as he pulled back the open flaps of one box. Part of him, he realized, wanted to find evidence of witchcraft. If the Vellmers were involved, then there would be no reason to feel guilty about sneaking into their house, no need to feel wrong at all.

Instead, he found a *Virginia is for lovers* mug, a few wedding photos, and a framed copy of their wedding announcement — complete with a Richmond, Virginia address for the ceremony. If not for the weird door, Max would have objected to this invasion of privacy. He would have been objecting to his own idea, but he would have objected nonetheless. Glancing through a second box, he found several old gaming systems — a PS3, an Xbox 360, and even an old GameCube — as well as a hodgepodge of controllers, cables, and batteries. Looked like Wyatt and Callie liked their video games. Not very witchy.

With a guilt-ridden huff, he called out, "You almost done in there? We're short on time."

Sandra and Drummond joined Max in the living room. Her face looked both frustrated and tight with excited concentration. "There is definitely a spell lock on that door and the room. But there might be more."

"Curses," Drummond said. "From the outside walls, I can feel these odd pulses of energy even with the spell lock. Seems like a curse to me. Probably more than one."

"I might be able to break the lock, but it'll take a lot of time."

Max said, "Maybe we should come back when the Vellmers are here. Explain to them that —"

His phone rang — J again.

"I'm sorry," J said, his upset voice jolting through Max. "What's wrong now?"

"It's Grandma. She's in the hospital. She's gone blind."

Chapter 13

THE NEXT SEVERAL HOURS WHIPPED AROUND, twisting Max's sense of time, leaving him spinning, desperately seeking anything normal to latch upon. It started with J's call which took Max several minutes to comprehend. Then, a nerve-wracked drive to Wake Forest Baptist Hospital. A frenzied search through that labyrinth facility resulted in two wrong turns and Max's tension straining to its edge. Finally, they found the correct nurse's station and after a few confused minutes of a nurse tapping away on a computer, they met with Dr. Rodriguez.

She explained that Max's mother had suffered a flare up, an attack, of her MS. Often, flare ups like this one were caused by sudden or prolonged stress. The doctor mentioned MS patients that had flare ups while giving birth or simply had an unusually stressful week at work. There seemed no clear pattern to it all and little consistency. It varied between people, too, and like MS itself, a flare up could manifest in numerous forms. In the case of Mrs. Porter — blindness.

Thankfully, J had reacted fast and got her to the hospital right away. They pumped her with steroids, and so far, this flare up appeared to have caused no permanent damage. Her eyesight would return, the doctor promised, though it might take a few days. For the moment, Mrs. Porter needed rest and a stress-free environment until she recovered. Dr. Rodriguez wanted to keep her in the hospital for a day or two — until her eyesight fully recovered — and then Max needed to bring his mother back for several follow-up visits.

"This was a warning shot," Dr. Rodriguez said. "It's not the kind of thing you want to get worse. There may be a lifestyle change needed. Is your mother's routine life filled with a lot of stress?"

If he hadn't been in shock over the entire incident, he would have laughed. His mother could create stress out of anything and share it with ease. Should she ever visit Buddhist monks meditating on a mountaintop, she would leave them shaking with her anxiety.

"We're treating the MS-induced blindness, of course, but I've also ordered monitoring of her heart. She's an old woman, and I don't want the strain on her body caused by the flare up to lead to a cardiac trauma, too."

Standing in a hospital and discussing MS and trauma, Max's mind jumped back to the last thing his mother had said in her apartment. "Can you tell me what a normal amount of pain is for somebody with MS?"

Dr. Rodriguez gave Max an odd look. "Pain is not a measurable thing like that."

"I mean for my mother. She claims that her pain from MS is so terrible that she'll do anything to get rid of it, and I'm wondering how bad it normally is for a person."

"Are you worried about drug addiction? I don't see any signs of that with her."

"No, no. It's only, well —"

Sandra said, "His mother is a born complainer. It's hard to tell fact from fiction with her."

"I see." Dr. Rodriguez offered a relieved nod. "It is difficult to know. The amount of pain varies from patient to patient. But so does a person's tolerance for pain. That's one of the reasons we ask patients to tell us on scale of one to ten how they feel. Not everybody's eight feels the same. If your mother tells you she's in a lot of pain, unless you have solid reasons to doubt, I would believe her."

Max and Sandra thanked the doctor for her efforts before hurrying through the halls to find his mother's room. Drummond floated nearby the entire time. He stayed quiet, and Max thought part of that came from respect for the living. But he also knew Drummond and Sandra both could see all the ghosts in the hospital — on par with a cemetery when it came to the numbers of dead still hanging around. It could be an unsettling place, and Max appreciated how they both prioritized him and his mother over their own discomfort.

Entering his mother's room, Max felt as if he had stepped through a magic portal. The world around him slipped behind. He saw only the woman who had raised him. In this sterilized environment, the place smelled off and sounded odd, too — beeps and warbled voices lost in the distance.

Mrs. Porter slept. The hospital bed — with its safety railing and tubes sticking out of her arm and monitors connected to her fingers and her chest — looked both like something out of science fiction as well as some torture device from the Dark Ages. Bracketed near the ceiling, a television flashed a commercial for denture cream, and Max had thought that with all her troubles, at least his mother still had her teeth. He slumped into a chair, let out a held breath, and shuddered. She looked small. Weak. She lacked all the fighting spirit he associated with her. While he knew losing her eyesight, suffering from a debilitating disease, and struggling under the pressures of a witch deal gone wrong all contributed, he didn't think any of those things — even combined — had enough power to weaken her so much. No, this came from within. This was her giving up.

He wanted to leap over that hospital bed, grab her by the shoulders, and shake her. He wanted to demand that she fight to live. But a smaller voice within spoke ideas he didn't want to acknowledge — that he might be better off letting her have her way. Let her be done with it. Forcing someone to go against their wishes exhausted the mind and body. And who was he to impose upon her? How could he demand that she live when he would not have to be the one spending each day in pain and anguish? Laws and religions spoke out against such action, but neither had to face the body breaking down after a long, full life.

Max pressed his hands against his face and fought his tears. There was no shame, but Sandra and Drummond would soon enter, J would return from wherever he had gone off to, and they all had their own emotions to sift through. They didn't need the added burden of his emotional stresses. At least, that was what he told himself. It didn't stop his body from convulsing as he swallowed down his sorrow.

"I'm really screwing this up," J said from the doorway.

Max rushed over and hugged his son. "It's okay," he said, but his voice shook. That sound dropped whatever gates he had locked. Tears flowed.

He did not recall the next several minutes. Not so much like waking up from surgery and having no memory of the experience, but more, he felt as if he had been punched in the side of the head. Dazed. Aware of things around him but lacking the processing power to do more than stumble through it.

At length, he sat in a chair with Sandra on the arm, rubbing his back. Drummond floated on the other side of the room, acting like an agoraphobe stuck on a busy city street.

Max placed his hand on Sandra's knee. "I'm okay," he said. With a deep breath, he turned to J who stood nearby the hospital bed. "Nobody's blaming you. Can you tell us what happened?"

J nodded, and Max knew the full report would soon come. But the young man's shoulders sagged forward as he held Mrs. Porter's hand. No amount of kind words or encouragement would help J. Max had encountered this type of thing before. The hardest lesson any parent had to learn — that there were many things a child simply had to work through on their own.

Yet as J launched into an explanation of events, as the reality of his words helped bring the reality of the situation into focus, Max's anxiety washed away as if each word had transformed into the rain. The doctor had said his mother would be fine. The flare up did not kill her nor did it damage her forever. More of a scare than anything else — *a warning,* the doctor had said. Equally important — J was okay. Not only okay, but going through the story appeared to have a similar effect on the young man. The telling helped relieve even deeper worries that Max held. J would be okay. Eventually.

The story as it related to the case provoked a mixed reaction. On the one hand, Max expected as much. On the other, it enraged his building fury toward Granny Witch Westra.

According to J, the morning had started off with Mrs. Porter in good spirits. A little surprising considering her attitude at the end of the previous night's meeting, but J found comfort in her ability to bounce back. He already had missed a few days of school, but this was his senior year. Classes were easy, and despite the strict policies of the school, he figured calling in sick a couple more times wouldn't cause him trouble. Provided that Max would do the calling.

"Besides," he said, "Grandma needed me."

The morning meandered on without incident. They ate breakfast, played card games like Gin Rummy, and watched a few sitcom reruns that she liked.

A knock at the door broke their peace.

When J answered, he found Billy Westra taking up most of the doorway and his brother, Luke, filling up the rest. Using one hand, Billy pushed J aside, and the two men entered the apartment. J had done his best to make a spell under the welcome mat that would repel anybody with harmful intent, but it had no effect.

Sandra said, "There's a reason witches are women. It's very difficult for a man to cast spells, so don't feel bad. It's good that you tried."

J shrugged, but clearly, her words mattered. Max thought she might say something more, and maybe she had intended to do so, but J coughed his throat clear and continued with his detail of Billy and Luke's visit.

The Westra brothers forced their way in, shoving J aside with ease — a point that clearly rankled J since he repeated it. Mrs. Porter glowered at them, but this lacked the chilling effect it usually had on others. Instead, Luke turned off the television while Billy pulled a chair in front of her. All this time, J stayed against the wall. At first, he pushed off, but a warning scowl from Billy set him back.

Once more, Max wanted to let J know he had acted smart and brave — even if he felt cowardly — but those words would have fallen to the floor. J knew danger. He had lived years without a home, without safety. He knew the difference between courage and cowardice. At least, he knew the difference as understood by a young teen struggling to survive.

Max opted for the best he could offer, the only thing he knew might get through. "When you're ready, we'll be here to listen about it all."

J hesitated, visibly processing the offer, and finally made a short motion of his head. Not quite a nod. Not a rejection, either. Max took it as encouraging.

Leaping back into his recounting of events, J explained that Billy hunched forward, his thick arms on thicker legs, and he dared to smile at Mrs. Porter as if they had a deep and full friendship. Much like the previous night at the office meeting, Mrs. Porter crossed her arms and looked away. But just as before, she heard everything.

Billy apologized for barging in and promised that he knew she had not meant to break the deal with his granny. That pulled Mrs. Porter's focus. She looked at him with hope.

"But that man had no intention of letting her off," J said. "I've known his type. PB and I had to deal with bullies like that most of our lives. They act all sorrowful about what they say they have to do, but it doesn't change anything. They still punish you, and they still enjoy it."

Billy had said a similar thing in the Bar-B-Que Shack — that he regretted the things Granny required him to do. Like the Sandwich Boys, Max had a few experiences with people claiming sorrow yet still going through with their harmful actions. Mostly, he had heard it from witches, and J's final statement on the whole idea plucked at the truth in a way that resonated with Max. These bullies enjoyed it.

Luke certainly did. He snickered and sneered, grinned and growled, while his brother had chatted with Max's mother. But two incidents changed matters, shifting them from a frightening meeting to a hospital-inducing trauma.

First, Billy put his big hand on Mrs. Porter's shoulder — not in a friendly gesture, but rather to impress his strength upon her. J shouted at the big man, stomping forward. He didn't get far. Luke spun around and slammed a fist into J's stomach. J dropped to one knee, all his air gone and his lungs having difficulty functioning for several moments.

Second, Mrs. Porter confessed that she no longer had the witchball. J didn't think she meant to say anything, but her rising fright combined with seeing her grandson bashed to the floor thrust the words from her. Billy and Luke froze.

"I thought they had been pushed too far." J looked at Mrs. Porter in the hospital bed, and his shoulders quivered. "On the streets, PB and I were in fights. We'd been hurt before. I never thought once that we were going to die. Not really. More like an expression. Not true death, but a beating so bad, you'll end up here in the hospital. I've been through that. But this time. Seeing those two big guys look at each other and knowing what they thought. I mean I *knew* it. I could read in their faces that they were afraid of what their granny would do when she found out the witchball was lost. I thought this was it. I thought they were going to kill us."

Apparently, Mrs. Porter thought much the same. She started hyperventilating, started whimpering, started clutching her chest. Billy asked her if she was okay, sounding like a decent, concerned man instead of an enforcer. Luke whined, worried about the witchball and the old lady on the couch. He paced near the front door, wiping his hands on his sides, and asking Billy question after question. The entire time, J remained still. He wanted to stand, to help his grandma, but hard-earned experience promised that if he moved at all, more punches would follow.

J had to wait. He figured that either they would be killed or the men would panic at Mrs. Porter's distress and leave. Thankfully, they chose the latter. Billy said he thought she was having a heart attack, and he told Luke they needed to get out. Granny Witch didn't want it to happen like this.

Once they were gone, J rushed to his grandma's side. She had rolled to the floor, her eyes bugged toward the ceiling. Her hands waving in front of her.

She cried out, "I can't see. Oh, J, I can't see."

He called 9-1-1.

Sidling next to him, Sandra put an arm around his shoulder. "You saved her life."

* * * *

Mrs. Porter weaved in and out of consciousness over the next several hours. Though her eyesight returned, it lacked clarity. Dr. Rodriguez said that Mrs. Porter's vision should be as good as before, but it would take patience and care. Each time Max's mother awoke, her eyes darted straight towards Drummond. The first time, Max thought it nothing more than a coincidence. But it happened time after time, and he could no longer deny it. He had to wait, though, for an opportunity to discuss the matter.

He finally got the chance while having a mediocre meal in the hospital food court. After pointing it out, though, Sandra said, "It's not surprising. When people have a near-death experience, some see the dead afterwards."

"She went blind. She didn't come close to death."

"The doctor has been monitoring her for a heart attack, and J said the Westra brothers ran off afraid they had caused one."

"You think that really happened? That she had a heart attack?"

Sandra shrugged. "A little one? Or maybe not. Regardless of what actually happened, I think it's safe to assume your mother thought she was dying."

"That's enough to get her seeing ghosts?"

"In people who are sensitive to the supernatural but never quite opened themselves to it, absolutely. The true belief, like down to her core, that she would die may have triggered a latent ability."

"Permanently?"

"Depends on the person. Most reject what they've seen. That usually causes the ability to fade away, get suppressed like it had been all along. Others will believe their eyes, and they'll hold onto that ability."

Max did not like that. Then again, he did not like any of this.

As the day wore on, Sandra decided somebody needed to get back to work. Max agreed. She meant it, but he knew that really all the dead roaming the halls, trying to get her attention, taxed her. Plus, she wanted to check in on Brenda, see the state of her research, and help if possible. Drummond took the opportunity to also leave. He said that other ghosts didn't bother him, but those found in the hospital were lost, confused, and sometimes in pain.

"It's depressing. And I'm dead," he said before vanishing into the Other.

At length, Max told J to go home. He should get some rest, catch up on some homework, and have a break from all this madness. "I'll watch over my mother. Don't worry."

He couldn't tell if J took the request as a punishment, but trying to clear that up would probably backfire. Stumbling over words would only invite scrutiny, and if J was determined to see the worst in the moment, nothing Max said would alleviate that. But J had done a fine job. Nobody could have stopped those two big Westra brothers — at least, Max couldn't have done any better. When this all finished, he promised to take J out somewhere for a long talk. Because while he believed a young man like J needed to figure this out for himself, a little fatherly input would do no harm. Might even help a little.

Max startled awake. His neck ached from being tilted down and to the side — fiery stabs ran straight up to his ear. He doubted it would feel normal again for about twenty years.

Stretching his arms, he sat up. His back didn't feel much better. A decade of witches and ghosts had started to take its toll.

He glanced at his phone — 3:02 am. One of the more powerful witching hours.

"Good, you're awake."

Max jumped in his chair, his feet splaying outward, bordering on a Jerry Lewis comedy bit. He was about to admonish his mother for startling him, saying she had come close to giving him a heart attack, but then thought better of the comment. Instead, he moved closer and held her hand.

"You're going to be okay," he said. "The doctor said everything's going to be fine."

"Of course. Why? Were you worried? Just the stupid MS doing its thing. Got a little blind when that man came to my home, that's all."

Max squeezed her hand. "You're the toughest."

"Is J okay?"

"He's fine. I sent him home to get some rest."

She looked around the room.

Max followed her gaze, and though he loathed the question, he knew he had to ask. "What are you looking at?"

"I keep seeing these blurry blobs."

"The doctor said it'll take a while for your sight to clear like normal."

"My eyesight is clear again. Mostly. Certainly enough that I know what I'm seeing and not seeing. This is not blurry vision from the flare up. This is something else. Maybe I should have my eyes checked. Cataracts starts with what they call floaters. Maybe that's what I'm seeing."

Trying to hide his relief, he said, "Once we get you back on your feet, I'll arrange an eye doctor appointment."

She frowned and rolled her lips in. Then she shook her head. "It's not cataracts."

"Let's wait for a professional to take a look."

"I know what it is, and it is not cataracts."

"But you're the one who said —"

"I know what I said. It was a lie." She lifted her head and stared straight into him. "I need to share something with you, and I'm a bit scared, but that's no excuse. I shouldn't have lied just now, and I shouldn't have lied before."

"Before?"

"You listen to me. I need to tell you the truth."

Chapter 14

PRESSING THE CONTROL PANEL built into the side railing, Mrs. Porter raised the head of the bed until she sat upright. The whine of the bed's motor roared in the late-night quiet, and Max thought a nurse would certainly race over to check on things. But nobody bothered. The sound only roared for him. The dim light behind her that cast her in stark shadows, making her loom like a witch emerging from a firelit cave. This shrinking, frail woman regained some of her strength, and though it dried Max's mouth, a thrill surged through him. She still had the fight within her.

"I want to thank you and Sandra and J and all your friends who work with you."

Max lifted her hand and kissed the back. "I appreciate that, but we still —"

"Don't interrupt your mother. I've had a hard enough time lately. I don't need to be reminded of my failings in raising you with proper manners."

"Yes, ma'am. Sorry." He sat back, placing her hand gently on the bed.

She glanced around the room yet again. "I wanted to say thank you to all of you for taking this seriously. I know what I said last night, but it wasn't because I don't believe any of this. Not exactly, anyway. Not completely before today. I don't know if you believe in ghosts, but from everything I heard last night, your little group certainly knows that others believe deeply in a lot of odd things. Well, as silly as it may sound, you should start believing because ghosts and witches are real. Your father knew this."

"My father?"

"Ever since you were little, I've told you many stories about your father. I know you've wondered why sometimes those stories didn't always line up. Tonight, I'm going to tell you."

Having faced witches, having been cursed, having been forced out of his body to live a half – ghost existence, Max thought he understood fear. But the jagged rock lodged in the middle of his chest promised he had barely broken through the surface.

His mother went on, "Don't misunderstand me. The stories I told you were true — mostly. They were pieces of your father. I told you once that he had been a mechanic, and he was. Only for five months. I told you that he worked with teenagers abandoned by their parents. Also true — technically. He had been a counselor for several years at a sleepover summer camp."

"Holy crap."

"Watch your mouth. I'm still your mother."

"You lied to me?"

"I protected you. It's the one thing all mothers are required to do at all times."

"From what? Was Dad a murderer? Is he in jail somewhere? Is that what this is?"

"Murder? No. That would be easy."

Max bounded to his feet and rushed across the room. His mouth opened and closed but no sound came out. This had to be a spell from Granny Witch. That made more sense. A spell cast during a witching hour had forced his mother to spout lies. After all, if Granny Witch's broken deal could push his mother towards suicide, then why not this, too?

He peeked back at her. Not a hint of disorientation. Not a glint of struggle against saying things she did not believe. Nothing but calm acceptance. This was real.

And what did that say about all the suicide talk?

He needed air. He needed space.

"Sit back down. This is important, and I can't tell you everything with you pacing about like a frightened chicken."

Max stopped. "A frightened chicken?"

"I don't know. It doesn't matter. Don't start nitpicking. That's what you do when you're trying to avoid something, and you can't avoid this. Now, sit down so I can explain to you about your father."

"I think I should get the doctor. You're not making much sense."

Digging deep into her motherly repertoire, Mrs. Porter spoke in a voice Max had not heard since he had been in kid. More than simply being in trouble, that voice signaled an end to all her patience. "Max, sit down this instant."

Heart racing, lips drying out from an open mouth, Max shambled back to the chair. As he watched his mother rally the courage to speak onward, he thought that perhaps a curse launched during this witching hour wouldn't be so bad. Better than having his brain spun like a child's toy.

"Your father was not around often."

"I know that. Is that why everything went bad between you two?"

Mrs. Porter slapped her hand on the bed. "Please, this is hard enough."

"I'm sorry." And he was. With his nerves bouncing around inside him, his mouth just opened and spewed out words. He had not intended to interrupt. He hoped she understood.

"Your father was not around a lot when you were little because for a time, he drove trucks. He would be gone for days, and I was left to raise you like a single mother. Quite an embarrassing thing back in my day. What you don't know is that his job as a truck driver ended when he fell asleep at the wheel. He jackknifed — I think that's what it's called — and ended up going off the side of the road and flipping over. He nearly died that night. Sometimes I think it would've been best if that's what had happened."

Max could not decide which shocked him more — the revelations about his father or the fact that his mother admitted to wishing him dead.

"Everything changed after the accident. He came home, and he was different. He started seeing things — strange, scary things — like the things I'm telling you now that I'm seeing. We had his eyes checked. We took him to specialists. I even dared broach the idea that he should see a psychologist — that did not go over well." She cringed at the memory. Then: "One night, your father told me no more tests. He said he knew exactly what was going on with him, and no amount of testing would ever come up with a different answer — or any answer. Of course, I asked him what he thought those the spots were. He said they were ghosts. I laughed. I actually laughed at him. But he said he could hear them talking. Make out some of their words. It frightened him at first, but then, he started reading about ghosts, watching movies and documentaries, anything he could get his hands on. It became an obsession. That led him to darker, darker places."

"Like witchcraft."

She shied from the word. "Initially, he shared with me everything he found. Until I had him committed."

"You what?"

"I didn't know what else to do. It was becoming hard for him to keep a job because he would talk incessantly about the witches and the ghosts. Nobody wanted to hire him. He couldn't be a truck driver again, or a driver of any kind — not with the accident on his record."

"One accident shouldn't have meant —"

"It wasn't his first accident. Just the one that nearly killed him. It was all falling apart, and I was scared. You were just a little boy. I had to take care of you, and he had been the main source of income in this family. Besides, it wasn't permanent."

"This can't be true," Max said to himself.

His mother snapped her eyes at him. "I have never lied to you. Sometimes a mother is forced to reshape the truth so that her child can understand a difficult concept. When you were little, what else could I do? How could I possibly explain about this supernatural nonsense and how it changed your father? But I have never lied to you. I was careful. I made sure. But you are not a little child anymore. Right now is the most truth you could ever possibly get."

Max knew better than to attempt parsing out that last statement. Instead, he decided she had been right — he shouldn't interrupt. Better to let her get this over with as fast as possible.

"When your father was released a few months later, I thought everything would be fine. He acted normal and in control. He still read about witches and the supernatural, but it no longer filled every thought in his head. At least, I believed so. But he had not changed at all. He had told the psychologists and psychiatrists exactly what they needed to hear, and he learned to put on an act at home. Then he started traveling again. You see, he got a job as a salesman for a vacuum company. Well, that was what he told me, and I believed him. Why wouldn't I? The dutiful wife expects the truth from her husband. But the truth turned out to be the lie. He had no job, and he bled into our savings so that he could take trip after trip after trip. Not simple visits to another state, either, but to other countries. He went to Romania and Bermuda and Zaire. Anywhere he thought he could meet with people that dabbled in different forms of magic. I only found out because — well, it doesn't matter. I found out. That's the point. I hated all his lying and the stealing of our money, but I could've pushed on through it. I would've found a way to make it work."

Max couldn't stop his mouth. "Why?"

"A lot of reasons. I don't like to give up, that's one. I loved him. That's a very good reason. But to be honest — and that's what I'm trying to do tonight — the ugly truth is that I had been raised to see a divorce as failure. Not an option. And back then, even though divorce was more common than when I was a child, I still felt like people would look down upon me and upon you. I couldn't do that to you."

"But to go on like that. I mean —"

"It all changed when I found a book. He had gone off to some country in Africa or the Middle East or I don't know where, and I started looking through his things. That's when I found this little book. It scared me just looking at it. When I picked it up, it felt even worse. But the most horrifying thing was when I opened it. It was a book of spells. I told myself it was ridiculous, but I'll tell you right now that part of me was shaking. I didn't think any of it was real, but I knew he believed in all of it. Reading those spells listed like recipes made me want to throw up. That's when I fell upon a page that described a spell which required the heart of a firstborn son. Nothing could have scared me more. I had you packed and out of that house before sunrise. I'm sorry we had to do it, but you must understand — we left your father to protect you."

She paused as if expecting him to respond. He held still. Max felt stoned — not the pleasant feeling from smoking a plant but rather as if an angry mob had picked up rocks and chucked them into his head. Every sentence she spoke was another rock battering him about. He tried to make logical sense of it, tried to connect it with the life he had lived, but the pieces did not fit. No, that wasn't true. If he squinted and cocked his head to the side and rearranged his memories, he had to admit that perhaps this version could snap into place, fill in the gaps. Besides, if she had wanted to lie to him, why would she pick such a bizarre lie?

"I worried he might try to find us. I even looked into changing our names. But your father never returned from that trip. I don't know what happened to him. I tried to find out — no, that's not true. I *thought about* trying to find out, but I wasn't sure I wanted to know. The moment it became legally acceptable, I had him pronounced dead. I raised you from that point onward, and let this all become some faded part of my past. Even when I moved down here, and I saw the things you and Sandra had got involved in, I ignored it. I didn't want to think about any of this happening again. As truthful as I have always tried to be in my life, I've found that we can lie to ourselves very well."

"You certainly can."

"I didn't believe in any of it. I thought he was mad, and I only watched you closely to make sure you didn't suffer the same illness."

"But then why would you go to a granny witch?"

"Desperation mostly. Maybe a little defiance — trying to prove to myself and the world that your father had been wrong. But also — I hate to admit this — I hoped maybe I was wrong. I hoped maybe she would be able to help me." Leveling her eyes upon him, making sure he saw a clear-minded lady, she said, "Witches are real. Ghosts are real. Magic is real. You must believe me. Because it's all very dangerous. You and your friends have been treating this like I treated your father. You act as if you are investigating somebody's superstitious beliefs, but it's much more than that. I don't want you to get hurt. I don't want any of you getting hurt."

Taking a deep breath, Max stood. He pressed the button to lower his mother into a resting position. As numb and stunned as he felt, hearing her admit the truth lightened him. A freeing sensation swelled from deep within and rose into his chest. He kissed her forehead.

"I do believe you. I know these things are real. And I promise you, we'll take care of this. You've got nothing to worry about."

Just as her strength had fed him, he could see his own strength feeding her. She grinned, patted his hand, and closed her eyes.

During the remaining hours until dawn, Max sat in that chair, watching his mother sleep, and he strategized. Granny Witch Westra, Billy and Luke — they had no idea the trouble Max could cause. He planned to cause all of it.

Chapter 15

A SHORT BURST OF RAIN rushed across the city, and as the sun lifted, Max looked upon the wet roads from the hospital window. The cool waters may have lowered the temperature slightly, but weather reports promised another scorching day. That was typical of North Carolina summers which had become a cycle of rising heat for days followed by blasts of rain that returned the world to being bearable, only to start the pattern over again. But they had yet to finish with spring. J still had a few months before graduation. Yet the world seemed bent on moving Max faster and faster through this cycle.

He wondered if, like his father, he had begun a familial cycle — discovering the reality of the supernatural, delving into that world, becoming seduced or obsessed with it, watching it destroy those he loved without the ability to stop it. If Max continued the vicious circle, then he would pass it to J. Eventually, J would pass it to the next generation of Porters.

But Max rejected the idea with a whip of his head. This wasn't a legacy of abuse. He hardly knew his father. To think that the man influenced his life so greatly gave his father far too much power.

Saving Max from going down his whirlpooling thoughts, his family returned to the hospital room. Drummond appeared first. Max checked his mother for a reaction, but she still slept. Hopefully, she would not wake for hours.

Sandra and J entered looking refreshed and in good spirits. In particular, J's attitude had taken a positive boost. Even as he smiled warmth and affection for everyone, Max noticed the determined way J repeatedly checked the room door. He acted as if Granny Witch Westra might enter at any moment. This time, however, the young man wanted to be ready.

It helped that Sandra had made him a ward. "It won't do much — sort of a minor flash-bang — but it might get you out of a tough spot."

To make an effective ward in just a few hours was not easy. Max embraced his wife with a kiss.

"I'm impressed," he said.

"Don't get too excited. It only has one use in it. But I figured it was better than nothing."

Looking at how J wore the oblong pendant around his neck, Max agreed. As the young man set up in the chair for his turn at Grandma watch, Max could see he meant business. If anybody that didn't belong showed up, J wouldn't need that ward. He would launch in with aggression, fists flying, making up for what he probably saw as previous failures.

The night had also brought news from Brenda. She continued researching the Dun family but had limited success. "Don't get a big head," Sandra said, giving Max a playful squeeze, "but this isn't as easy as she and I thought it would be. She's been able to get pieces of a family tree but there are a lot of gaps. She doesn't know all of your tricks."

An arrogant flush coursed through Max's chest, but it did not last. Partly because he tried not to be cocky in general. Mostly because he could still see the hard look in his mother's eyes when she told him about the reality of the supernatural, told him during the witching hour.

Drummond said, "Not that anybody has bothered to ask, but I've had a good night myself."

"I don't want to hear about your dating life," Max said.

"I'll listen," J said.

"Is that all you people think goes on in the Other? There's more to the afterlife than romantic encounters. For crying out loud, do you think it's one big orgy out there?"

"Please, stop. The last thing I ever want to do is put your image next to the word *orgy* in my head."

"You're doing that on your own."

Chuckling, Sandra said, "Well, now that we know ghosts are more platonic than we had been led to believe, what did you do last night?"

Cinching his collar, Drummond said, "I may have had a date with a waitress, but afterwards, I had a quiet evening alone. That's significant. You see, my time in the Other hasn't been the most pleasant lately. It's taken me a lot of work to build up some new contacts, new snitches, and a network of people who aren't mad at me for handling cases that involve witches. But I was able to pass last night in peace. I think those that spend most their time in the Other have started to forgive me — heck, maybe even accept me."

"That's good news. We're glad to hear it."

"What about you?" Drummond asked Max. "Anything happen here last night?"

"A little," Max said. "Come with me, we've got work of our own to do. I'll explain on the way."

As Max stormed through the hospital corridors, Sandra rushed to catch up. Floating by his side, Drummond said, "What's the hurry?"

"This needs to end."

Dodging a nurse wheeling a cart with a laptop and medical equipment, Sandra said, "I think we all agree, but we won't succeed if we die on the way out of the hospital. Slow down."

"My mother doesn't have time to wait."

Drummond cocked an eyebrow. "Did you hear something new from the doctors?"

"It's not her immediate health. It's the more magical side of things."

Sandra said, "Rushing off like this is a bad idea. How are we even going to do it? End this? We still don't know how anything fits together."

On the elevator to the parking garage, Max said, "There's only one part that is truly a mystery — that door at the Vellmer house. Everything else we can find out in time. The Westra-Dun feud, according to Montgomery Dun, that's been going on for generations. There must be some written trace of it. The full history of that house — all it takes is more research time. Even the spell lock and ward and whatever else is on that door — you'll figure it out eventually. The only thing that matters, though, is what's behind that door. Once we learn that, everything else will fall into place. So, we're going to the Vellmers, and you're going to pick that spell lock."

Drummond said, "Not a bad idea except that Osorio can't help us out again. If we break into that house, we're on our own."

"We won't. This time, we'll go about it much simpler. We knock on the door and ask for their permission."

As they walked towards their car, the sounds of other cars and other walking echoed throughout the garage. Not far ahead, coming in their direction, Max saw Billy and Luke Westra. The fire that had lit Max into action, raged into an inferno.

Billy put out his hands against this heat. "We're not here to cause trouble. Luke and I feel very sorry about —"

Max decked the big man. Caught Billy in the jaw — hard enough to send the lug to his knees.

Luke said, "You son of a —"

He said nothing else. Drummond swiped a hand through Luke's bald head. Held long enough, Drummond could incapacitate a person. In this case, he merely gave Luke a migraine-level brain freeze — enough to stop any threat the man posed.

Red-faced and breathing heavy, Max said, "The two of you are never to see my mother again. I don't want you stepping foot near her. I have been patient and forgiving with your actions, but you've gone too far. Scaring an old lady into the hospital is not going to get you or Granny Witch any closer to fulfilling the deal. In fact, you can go tell Granny Witch that the deal is over. She returned my mother's MS pain, and you caused her to go to blind, almost have a heart attack. That's plenty enough payment and punishment. You come around us again, and you better have more than one little ward to protect you. We'll destroy you, your granny, and anyone else remotely connected to you." He leaned closer to Billy. "You're afraid of your granny. Well, we've taken down some of the strongest witches in North Carolina. You should be ten times more afraid of us."

Sandra tugged on Max's arm until he relinquished. As they walked toward their car, he knew Drummond hovered back with those two men. If either of them made a move, Drummond would freeze them for hours.

Still, Billy said in a loud voice, "I'll let your sucker punch go. You're upset. But this doesn't end until Granny Witch says it ends. You'll see us again."

Without looking back, Max raised his arm high overhead and flipped his middle finger.

Chapter 16

DURING THE DRIVE OUT TO OLIN and the Vellmer house, Max related the witching-hour conversation with his mother to Sandra and Drummond. They stayed quiet — an amazing feat for Drummond — and Max wondered if they were in shock over the short confrontation in the parking garage. If anything, though, hearing the story should have made his actions clearer.

When they reached Statesville, Sandra convinced Max they should grab some breakfast and call the Vellmers rather than appear on their doorstep unannounced. They stopped at a diner filled with the morning wake-up aroma of eggs, bacon, pancakes, and coffee. Hardworking, bleary-eyed folks filled the seats, each trying to fuel up and face another day.

Drummond chose to float around outside. The delicious scents in the diner tortured him since he couldn't eat. Plus, Max suspected, the pretty and living waitresses tortured him in another way.

While Max visited the restroom, Sandra had made the call to the Vellmers. He returned to find mugs of coffee and a waiter ready for his order. His stomach rumbled. Hunger attacked him with the speed of racecars on the final lap. He asked for waffles topped with strawberries, hash browns, toast, sausages, and bacon. More food than he could possibly eat.

"I spoke with Callie Vellmer, and she said they would make time this morning for us," Sandra said over sips of steaming coffee. "Apparently, today's Friday and —"

"Really? I've lost all track of time."

"I feel the same. But it is, and they took the day off to give themselves a long weekend so they could make a dent into moving in. She said if we didn't mind them opening boxes or doing some painting while we talked, they didn't mind a little company."

"Great. What time are we going there?"

"After we eat. No rush, though. They're not planning on being anywhere else today."

Hot food did its magic. Max's anger loosened. Though nothing would make him relax until he knew his mother's safety had been achieved, he could see the sense in finding a better approach than barging down the door. He picked up Sandra's hand and kissed the back. By slowing him down and getting him to eat, she had saved him from ruining their easy entrance to the house and that door. Possibly, she had saved his mother's life, too.

About forty minutes later, they sat in the Vellmer home with more sweet tea service and a bright Southern smile from Callie. Many of the boxes had been opened, some of their contents segregated into different piles, while the emptied boxes had been broken down and stacked in the back of the living room. The stink of fresh paint wafted in from their bedroom. All the windows stood fully open to air out the harsh odor, but without any breeze, it merely contributed to the stifling heat already building up to another brutal day.

After all that had happened with his mother's revelations, Max's brain had frayed into cotton candy. While breakfast had helped, it had also been quiet. Sandra tried to engage him in a discussion about how they would approach the Vellmers, but he couldn't think clear enough for the purpose. He simply said they would be fine. They had dealt with all sorts of bizarre conversations in their career. This one would be minor compared to some of the things they had handled. Sandra did not like that answer, but she gave him the space to recompose.

Wyatt entered from the hallway, aqua paint speckling his white t-shirt, and he brushed his hands on his jeans. "Doesn't matter how many times I've done this job, I can't paint anything without wearing as much as I put on the walls."

Snickering, Sandra said, "That's one reason I won't let Max paint our rooms."

"We all have our talents," Max said. "I happily admit that

house painting of any kind is not one of mine."

"That's good to hear, hon. Then I won't have to argue with you about painting our new office."

Callie said, "You have a new office? Congratulations. What exactly do you do?"

"That's kind of the reason we've come today."

But before Sandra could speak, Max blurted out, "My mother's in a cult."

Wyatt and Callie exchanged a look, and Sandra said, "Um…"

From the ceiling, Drummond said, "Huh. That's an unusual tactic. Can't wait to hear the rest."

Part of Max's mind joined the ghost in doubt, while part supported the sudden maneuver. Anything would be better than trying to convince the Vellmers of the supernatural and that their door had magic spells on it. They would laugh Max and Sandra straight out of the house. A cult, however, might sound outlandish but plausible.

"My mother has been sick for several years now." The words tumbled out of Max's mouth like an avalanche launched by the sound of his previous outburst. "Multiple sclerosis. Nasty stuff. The doctors can't do anything for her, so she has taken to seeking out alternative medicines and such. Recently — and, I swear, we knew nothing about this until she was arrested — but recently, she joined up with this old leader of a small group."

Drummond snapped his fingers and pointed at Max. "Not bad. Keep doing that. Keep staying close to the truth. It'll make everything sound more honest."

Unable to spin around and tell the ghost that he knew what he was doing, that this wasn't his first time, Max kept his attention on the Vellmers. Callie expressed sympathy and concern. Wyatt, however, sat back with his arms folded. He would be harder to convince.

"We don't know much about this cult. They don't even really have a name. But we're trying to learn what we can. At first, when my mother was caught in your house, we thought like you did — that dementia had taken hold and that she ended up here out of confusion. But the more we've looked into it, and once we discovered some papers about this cult, that view changed."

Callie's hand rose to her chest. "Did she come here to harm us?"

"No, no, nothing like that," Sandra said, picking up Max's lead. "In fact, it had nothing to do with you, at all. Not with you as people."

"What else is there?" Wyatt asked.

"Your house."

Drummond said, "Hats off to both of you. This is turning into a good bluff."

Wriggling to a different position in his chair, Wyatt said, "You're saying that your mother is in a cult?"

"What else would you call a small group of people loyally following a charismatic leader to do all kinds of crazy stuff?" Max folded his hands with a studious air. "In this case, it's believing in witchcraft and magic spells. She was a perfect candidate. She's been depressed for a long time since she got diagnosed. She's felt like she didn't have a purpose anymore. She's lost and desperate to find some kernel of hope."

Max saw the uncertainty in the Vellmers, and Sandra must have, too. She said, "We know it sounds ridiculous. We didn't believe it at first, either. We thought she was part of a support group that often read some obscure and disturbing kinds of books. Like a reading group that focuses on horror."

"But when my mother got arrested, that had us looking through some of her things. We found these weird books and other witchy stuff, and when confronted with it, she told us the truth."

Callie said, "She admitted she was in a cult?"

"Not exactly. People in cults don't think they're in cults."

Sandra said, "But she did tell us that her group knew there were these magic doors."

"Magic doors?" Wyatt scoffed as he looked to his wife for support.

Drummond said, "Keep on this. I think Callie's starting to believe."

"Please, we know how crazy this all sounds," Max said,

directing his energy towards Callie. "It is crazy. That's the simplest way to say it. It's sad and pathetic and crazy. But unfortunately, it's also the truth. Not that you have actual magic doors in your house — now that would be nuts — but her group believes in these things."

"They think we have a magic door?" Wyatt again.

"Exactly. I have no idea how they pick their houses, but they must have known you had this door that wouldn't open. Maybe one of their members is a handyman and word gets around."

"Or a real estate agent," Sandra said. "I used to be one, and you learn all the little quirks of the houses in the area real quick. It wouldn't be hard for somebody like that to keep an eye open for doors that fit what they wanted to find."

"Whatever the case, my mother learned about this place, and that's why she was here. She was trying to fix your magic door." Max made an act of laughing. "It really is quite absurd. You people are being so kind to even listen to this nonsense."

Wyatt said, "How come I get the feeling you've got more to ask of us?"

"Don't be like that." Callie gently slapped her husband's arm. To Max: "Is there something we can do to help?"

In the next few minutes, Max explained that a simple bit of proof given to his mother might solve all their problems. Sandra had come equipped with instructions from Mrs. Porter on what magic spell to perform upon the door. If the Vellmers would allow it, Sandra could draw the spell out and Max could take a picture of it as evidence for Mrs. Porter.

"It's really easy," Sandra said. "Should only take a few minutes. Oh, and Max needs to pour some salt outside around the edges of the property to protect you all. At least, that's how we understand it."

Max said, "I have to take pictures of myself doing this, too."

"Of course, none of this is real. It's all for show."

Digesting this, Callie said, "When your mother sees these pictures, she'll know the magic door has been fixed? Is that the idea?"

"That's right. We hope it'll stop her from ever trying to come back here again. More importantly, it will stop anybody else from this cult trying to do so, either."

Wyatt looked as comfortable as a man sitting on a knife. "You're saying that not only do we have to worry about your mother, but this cult might send other people, too. We should call the police. They can take care of this cult."

Callie said, "Stop it, honey. The Porters have come here looking for help. They're obviously trying to avoid their mother from getting arrested again. Besides, this is all rather interesting."

"It's a nuisance."

With demure bashfulness, she said, "You have to forgive my husband. We have a rather traditional way of doing things in our house. Not a lot of room for magic spells and cults." She dismissed it all with a giggle. "If it won't take too long and it won't damage the house, I don't see the harm. Besides, it's the right thing to do to help ease the mind of a poor, old lady. If there's anything else we can do, just ask. Oh, and if you don't mind, would it be okay if I watch? The whole thing sounds remarkable."

Despite a scowling Wyatt, Max could see the decision had been made. He promised they would be as fast as possible and no trouble to the Vellmers. Sandra explained they needed nothing extra, that they had everything in the car, and thanked both husband and wife profusely.

As Max and Drummond headed outside to get Sandra's case of paraphernalia as well as a large bag of salt, Drummond said, "I've got to hand it to you, partner. I didn't think that would work, but it played far better than we would've gotten trying to explain the truth of ghosts and witches."

"It did with Callie. I don't know how long her husband's going to allow Sandra to work."

"True. I mean these things can take hours, but once Sandra gets started, I think Callie will find it so fascinating that she'll shut down any objections from Wyatt."

After delivering Sandra's case, Max walked the property line along the side of the house, casually spraying salt about like grass seed. Though a true salt line helped prevent ghosts and some magic, his actions at the Vellmers were performative. Sandra did the real work.

Drummond floated close by, careful to avoid getting hit with salt. "Are you doing okay?"

Max's face scrunched at the blazing sun as much as the question. "Yeah. Why?"

"You got hit with quite a blow last night. Your mother knowing that magic exists. Your father and all she had to say about him. Then you cold-cocked Billy Westra and raced off to do this. Not your usual line of behavior."

"Since when did you start wanting to have heart-to-heart conversations?"

"I don't, really. But either Sandra gets that door open or we'll end up facing Granny Witch Westra again. Or both. Either way, you need to be at your best. Just because I dislike these kinds of chats doesn't mean I'm not going to engage in them when it's what has to be done."

"I think that might be the sweetest thing you've ever said to me."

"Let it go to your head and you see how sweet my fist is."

Max tossed some salt in Drummond's direction. He licked his sweaty lips and wished for some of that cold sweet tea. Southerners might drink themselves into diabetes with that stuff, but they sure knew how to beat the oppressive heat.

Wiping off the salt sticking to his hands, Max said, "I don't know what to think about any of it. It's only been a few hours. My mother — well, she can be duplicitous to herself. So, even as she's telling me that she knows these things are real, she could turn around and convince herself it's all a made-up fairy tale. I wouldn't trust anything out of her mouth anymore."

"Don't go down that road."

Max stopped. "What road?"

"Keep walking. You don't want to chance Wyatt checking on you from the bedroom window and see you talking to yourself."

Max started up again, spraying salt around with harder throws. "I'm walking as slow as I can, but the back corner is coming up. You got something to say, you better say it."

Adjusting his hat as he stared off into the distance, Drummond said, "You forget that my mother died in a mental hospital. I know exactly what it's like to think your parent is one thing and have her turn out to be something else. I also know what it's like to have the supernatural face you every day and be in denial about it. All I'm saying name when is that you should cut your mother a little slack. Family's important — maybe the most important. You need to be there for family — even when you hate them."

At the back corner of the property, young forest stretched the distance. Tall grass and thick brambles covered the ground. As Max let Drummond's words settle within him, he noticed a stone sticking up — flat on the front and back but curved at top like a...

"Is that tombstone?"

Drummond slid through the trees and approached the odd-shaped stone. "It is, indeed. The markings are all faded and covered with moss, but it looks like *Dun*."

"That would make sense. This house did belong in the Dun family. Can you read the years?"

Drummond lowered into the ground so that he could read without bending. "Looks like they were born July of 1854. Can't make out when they died."

Max's phone chimed — Brenda. He answered, "You've got great timing. We've just found something that'll help with our research."

"I've got something you'll want to hear right now. I tried Sandra, but she's not answering."

"Slow down. What's going on?"

Talking even faster, Brenda said, "I was looking into Montgomery Dun — figured you hadn't had the time to do that one yet — and that led me to the foreclosure on his house. I know you already looked at the foreclosures, but I thought since you're trying to put together a history of the Vellmer house, I ought to check even further back. And since Sandra showed me how to look up some of the real estate details, I found that the loan came from a small bank and was approved by Cynthia

Denmark. Not too many years later, that bank folded. First Community took over the building and picked up the loans. I decided to check on Ms. Denmark, see if that led me anywhere, and that's when I saw her photo — she's Callie Vellmer."

"Callie went by a different name?"

"I know. Strange, right? But it gets even stranger because that got me thinking about her being married. People change their name when they get married. So, I checked for her maiden name."

Max's heart dropped into the pit of his belly. "No."

"Her name was Callie Dun."

He looked at Drummond, then back at the house. He started running.

Chapter 17

IT HAD BEEN A SET UP FROM THE START. Maybe not during that first meeting with the Vellmers when Max apologized for his mother. Maybe they didn't know then that the Porters were connected to Granny Witch Westra. But since that moment, Callie Dun Vellmer had to have been aware. She must have been amused as Max and Sandra spun their story of a cult. And Wyatt — Max thought he had to convince the man, but Wyatt's discomfort probably came from not wanting to play this game.

These thoughts flashed through Max's mind as he sprinted across the yard. The thick, humid air fought each thrust of his legs, and his lungs cried against the sudden action as worry constricted his chest. Drummond tried to ask why Max ran, but Max waved him forward, uttering one word that got the ghost soaring. "Sandra."

Yanking the back door hard enough to slam its hinges, Max burst into the house, stumbled into the living room, and pulled up sharp. Sandra was on her knees with her hands laced on the back of her head. Callie stood behind. In one hand, she held an ampule of brackish liquid.

With an arm stretched out in front, Wyatt gripped a basic ghost ward. "Not an inch closer, Drummond."

The detective pushed back a foot. "You can see me?"

"Hear you, too."

"Well, crap."

Making sure she had all the attention, Callie said, "I'm holding a little concoction of my own creation. It's a special formulation that will melt a witch. Dissolve her far better than acid." She nudged Sandra with her toe. "A little *Wizard of Oz* humor from one witch to another."

Max took a slight crouch like an athlete waiting for the gun to go off, allowing him to blast into motion if he saw an opportunity — any opportunity. His eyes darted from Callie to Sandra to Wyatt, and he wasn't the only one. Wyatt also watched with anxious care. The stillness, the quiet in the room grew stranger with the chirping birdsongs floating in through the open windows. Sweat burned in Max's eyes and trickled into his ears.

"We know you're the one who handled the loan to Montgomery Dun for this house," Max said. He didn't know what else to say, but experience had taught him that as long as they kept listening to him, they weren't killing his wife. "I suspect if we look deeper into the history of this house, we'll find lots of people in your family working in the banking industry. Isn't that right? You all kept handing this property down generation after generation through different names and banks."

With a devilish smirk, Callie said, "Something like that."

"All for whatever's behind that door. Well, you should know that no matter what you do to her or me, Sandra is never going to unlock the spells for you."

"I'm not asking her to."

That wasn't good. Either Callie was confident in her own witchcraft abilities, or some other member of the Dun family could handle the task. Either way, they didn't need Sandra. It should have been obvious. If they had wanted her to open the locks, they wouldn't have stopped her. Heck, if they had needed Sandra, they would have played these last couple days differently, maybe even hired The Porter Agency spinning a story to get them to do the job. It all meant one thing — Max had lost his leverage.

Time for desperate plays. Opening himself into a wide target, he said, "If you don't need Sandra for the door, and you obviously don't need me, then let us go."

Callie snorted a laugh. "You're serious?"

"Why not? This whole thing is between you and Granny Witch Westra. Duns versus Westras. Westras versus Duns. The Porters don't factor into it at all."

"Your mother factored into it."

"Granny Witch used her like a pawn, and she didn't even

succeed. That's all over now. We have no stake in your feud, so let us go."

Wyatt moved forward, leading with the ghost ward like a blade. "Just because you're not part of the Dun–Westra feud, doesn't mean you don't hold value."

"That's right," Callie said. "Being from the mountains don't make us stupid. We know who you are. We know all about The Porter Agency. How could we not know about you when the Porters helped start the witch war? We know everything. Since the moment you set foot in North Carolina, you've destabilized our world. I suppose we should thank you."

Wyatt pointed off to the left — at Drummond. "I've still got my eye on you. You drift any further, and my wife dumps that liquid."

Drummond put up his hands. "Wasn't trying anything. We ghosts naturally drift with the air currents. I'll stay right here."

Max knew the drifting thing was a lie, but he had no idea how far Callie's education went concerning ghosts. However, given that they knew far more than they had let on, Max decided not to push for an advantage based on presumed ignorance. After all, making assumptions about the Vellmers' ignorance toward the supernatural got them in this mess in the first place.

Callie said, "Listen to my husband, ghost. He won't hesitate to let me know what you're up to. Getting rid of you would be every bit as beneficial as getting rid of the Porters. Alive or dead, all three of you have value. Alive, you're bargaining chips. Dead, our reputation goes through the roof."

"She's overestimating your value a whole lot," Drummond said.

To his wife, Wyatt said, "The ghost doesn't think so."

"With the Hulls destroyed," Carrie said, "and all the older, most dangerous covens either disbanded or in disarray, you are the major reason for this war. Look at all the disorder you introduced to a once stable system. Now, this war may have been inevitable. Doesn't matter, though. It's given us the opportunity we've wanted for a long time. The Duns are going to take over. It's our time now."

"Not quite," a crackling voice said from the front doorway.

A small, old lady bent over a gnarled wood cane. Behind her, Billy towered.

"Well, well," Callie said. "Welcome to my home, Granny Witch Westra."

Chapter 18

SHE STEPPED OUT OF A DEPRESSION-ERA PHOTOGRAPH — an elderly, bent, and wrinkled woman designed in every facet to appear hardened by a rough life and create sympathy from her meek yet sturdy countenance. She wore a black skirt held by a belt of faded scarves, a gray sweater buttoned at the bottom with wood pegs, and a dour babushka over the head. Her wrinkles deepened the lines of her face, forming puffy cheeks and a pronounced chin. Everything about her portrayed age in balance with strength. Her eyes, buried behind numerous folds of leathery skin, sparked with resolve. Her hands, boney and crooked, gripped her cane with vigor. And her voice, creaking and slow, resounded through the house with terrifying threat.

Callie blanched for a second, and Wyatt visibly shivered. Even Drummond flinched. As for Max, he finally understood why a man as big and dangerous as Billy Westra feared his little, old granny. She was more than a witch. She projected the immeasurable power of the mountains and the endless centuries that made them. This was a woman connected to the earth below and the past within her.

Max's fear of Callie Dun, however, grew when he saw her roll back her shoulders and lift her chin. In the face of the formidable old witch, Callie did not shrink. He knew enough from Sandra and from experience that witches rarely played chicken. If Callie stood against a witch, she firmly believed she could win. True or not, her confidence and audacity spoke of her abilities with witchcraft far greater than anything Max had seen yet.

His fears for Sandra compounded.

While everyone else watched Granny Witch and Billy, Max turned his attention to his wife. With her head bent low and her arms winged out, he had a hard time seeing her mouth. This wasn't the first time they had been in a similarly perilous situation, and they often relied on Sandra quietly casting a spell. But he could not see any movement. That suggested she believed Callie Dun capable of creating a witch-melting potion. Far too dangerous to risk any kind of spell.

"You need to let these people go," Granny Witch said.

Though Callie put on a cordial mask, she fooled no one. Not that she tried. "You seem to be a little confused. Understandable considering your age. Billy, would you please explain to your granny this isn't her house. This is Dun property, and you've made a grave mistake coming here."

Granny Witch folded her one hand atop the other on her cane. "Dear, it's true that I'm old, but I haven't forgotten where I came from. You seem to think you were born somewhere else. Where the Duns and the Westras come from — the mountains — we have tremendous respect for our elders. Not only because those who have come before you have seen more, know more, and have true perspective on what is important, but also because an old witch like me could be a powerful adversary."

"All you Westras are the same. Talk, talk, talk. You like to think you're some kind of chess master, moving people around so that you keep your hands clean. We Duns — we don't mind getting dirty when it's necessary."

"Even when it's not necessary."

As this back and forth continued, Max searched for any sign that one of the witches in this room worked on a spell. As far as he could tell, nobody did. Perhaps Callie Dun had more respect for Granny Witch Westra's power than she showed. Perhaps Granny Witch had far more power than she projected. Because if Callie held back, it was out of fear. If Granny Witch held back, it was because she knew she could cast a spell far stronger and far faster than anybody else in the room.

Wyatt's focus had turned to Billy Westra. The two men stared off, sizing each other up, waiting as the tension between the witches rose, readying for the instant they would have to clash. But if Wyatt paid attention to Billy, then he didn't pay attention to Drummond. Moving his head slightly, Max looked to his partner. Drummond returned a slim nod — he saw the advantage, too.

"You listen to me, dear," Granny Witch said.

"I'm not your *dear.*"

"You'll be whatever I decide you'll be. Right now, you're behaving like a foolish child. A little girl upset she hasn't gotten her way. Wants to be a powerful witch but isn't willing to work for it."

"I've worked my whole life for it."

"You have yet to live the beginning of a whole life."

"You can yack on and on, but it won't change that this house belongs to the Duns. It always has. The power that resides here is for the Duns. For me. Sending in the Porter family to stop us — first, the mother; then the son and his wife — pathetic."

"Every word from your mouth proves that you are not ready or worthy of the power you seek."

"I suppose you think you deserve it. You wrap yourself in this noble attitude as if you are fighting some great evil, but the truth is that we both want the power here. We both recognize that now is the time. All those who controlled magic in the state are gone, and I think you would agree with me that it's time for somebody from the mountains to run things for a change."

"Somebody from the mountains? Yes. You? Never."

Assured that Wyatt no longer paid close enough attention and bolstered by Drummond now drifting further away from the Westras, Max inched towards the back wall. This would give him an unencumbered angle at Sandra. He had no plan for what do with that advantageous position, but better to be ready than unprepared.

Granny Witch Westra's constant frown darkened. "You stole this house, and we allowed it because it wasn't worth fighting over. You've attempted to break through that door — yes, I know what you've been up to, and I know all that your family has stolen from us, too. We allowed these things because we know you aren't strong enough or talented enough to succeed. But threatening the Porters is not allowed."

"Are they some special pets of yours?"

"Threatening anybody outside our families is not allowed. This has always remained within, and if you violate that, you show the Westras and the whole world that the Duns have no honor and truly cannot be trusted."

Another few steps and Max would be in the best position he could find. As he maneuvered, he kept a close watch on Callie. The more she argued with Granny Witch, the less awareness she had of her surroundings. One of many unwise ideas popped into Max's brain, and he started giving it serious consideration.

Callie snarled at Granny Witch. "You're a big talker, but it comes out both sides of your mouth. You say we can't threaten outsiders, but you're the one who brought the old lady Porter into this. These two here would never have been in danger if you hadn't caused it."

"I didn't know the lady who visited me to make a deal was one of the Porters."

"Doesn't matter. You knew she was an outsider when you forced her to break into my home."

"It's not your home, really. And I didn't —"

"You want to twist words around like the old witch you are, it won't change anything for me. I don't play semantics."

Max didn't know how much longer these two could trade barbs, but he noticed that both Wyatt and Billy had grown impatient. They puffed their chests and nudged their chins at each other. Silent boasting and silent threats. Soon enough, there would be no stopping them from charging the other like two rams butting horned heads.

But before either man sprang forward, Max caught Drummond's narrowed focus on Callie. He followed the gaze — not just Callie, but Callie's twitching hand that held the foul concoction. No. Max saw now that it wasn't her hand that Drummond noticed, but rather the drop of liquid that had run down the side of the ampule. The drop that touched Callie's skin. No burning, no smoke, no cries of pain. Nothing.

Her potion was a lie.

"Now," Max yelled, and Drummond dashed forward.

The ghost ward flashed bright as it went off. Not what Max

expected. A well-made ghost ward rarely did anything noticeable in the non-ghost realm, but when he thought about it later, it was another sign that Callie's witchcraft did not match her boasting.

Drummond cursed a few words as the ward flung him straight through to the kitchen. Billy pulled Granny Witch back as he used his body to protect her. His fists whipped across at Wyatt.

Whatever happened next between them, Max did not see it. The moment he had yelled out, he lunged along the clear line for Sandra. While he thought Callie bluffed with the potion, he wouldn't call that thought a certainty. He tackled his wife to the floor, covering her body with his own.

A liquid stinking like wet dog splashed onto his back. Why would she dump the potion if it wasn't effective? Unless it wasn't a bluff. His heart rate shot up as he waited for a burning pain.

Nothing happened.

Either the potion had no effect on non-witches or Callie had no idea it wasn't going to work. Glancing over his shoulder, he saw Callie pressed against the wall. Granny Witch held her gnarled cane out like a Tolkien wizard as she mouthed her spell.

"Get off me," Sandra grunted, pushing at Max with her elbow.

He rolled to the side in time to catch Billy clock Wyatt in the jaw. Wyatt's head thrashed to the right and his body followed. He went down onto one knee, and Billy pressed forward. But he came in too fast, assuming Wyatt no longer posed a threat. One step too close and Wyatt twisted his torso as he rose to his feet. His fist caught Billy between the legs. Stunned and gasping for air, Billy couldn't stop the follow-through punch to the temple. He dropped to the floor and curled into a ball.

Drummond twice tried to enter the living room, but Callie's ward proved strong enough to keep him out. If he wanted to — if he needed to — he could have knocked himself silly bashing against the ward until he broke through it. He had done so before. But the situation wasn't bad enough to require such drastic measures. At least, not yet.

As if hearing Max's thoughts, Wyatt stomped across the living room and shoved Granny Witch against the front door. Air huffed out of her. She dropped her cane. Showing no mercy, Wyatt slammed his hand upside the old witch's head. A loud rumble like thunder ripped through the house and the spell broke. Callie slid to the floor, drenched in sweat and fear.

"Get ready," Sandra whispered.

Max checked on her. Licking her finger to use her saliva, she had sketched a quick casting circle. A tiny one, but Max did not to question it. Sandra knew more about what she could accomplish than anybody. He listened. He got ready — for what, he didn't know, but something was about to happen.

Waves of hatred pulsed off Wyatt as he slapped Granny Witch. "This is our house. This is our time. You go home and tell all the Westras in the mountains that Callie Dun is here. With the power she's already getting from this house, she's growing stronger every single day. You tell them. She will rule magic in the Triad, the Piedmont, the mountains, everywhere. And not you or any Westra will get in our way this time."

Whatever Sandra planned to do, Max wished for it to happen fast. Billy had made it to all fours but stopping Wyatt wouldn't happen. In fact, stumbling out of the house might be a challenge. Blood dribbled down the side of Granny Witch's cheek. Her shock at Wyatt's animalistic rage kept her from retaliating.

But worst of all, Max saw Callie rising to her feet. She wore the same hatred as her husband but appeared far more in control of her actions. When she cast her next spell, it would be focused and fierce.

Sandra spoke one word — a command from an ancient language — and thick, black smoke jetted from her casting circle. In seconds, the room became obscured in dark, choking fog. It was the result of a fire without flames and offered the perfect cover to escape. Max held Sandra's hand as they staggered across the living room.

Wyatt blocked the front door, so Max led his wife into the kitchen. Following behind, he discovered Billy. The large man carried his granny over his shoulders. Max wanted to ask how that happened, but they didn't have the time. He guessed she had cast a spell to escape Wyatt's notice. As Max opened the back door onto the yard, he realized that not a sound had come from Callie or Wyatt nor had they tried to block the escape. That had to be Granny Witch's doing. He knew Sandra was a strong witch, but creating the smokescreen *and* somehow freezing the Vellmers in place all on a tiny circle made of spit stretched credulity.

Once outside, Max ran for the car, never letting go of Sandra's hand. He had a lot of questions, but that could wait. He didn't waste time with talking or even glancing back at the Vellmer house, though he did notice a blue Ford F-150 parked across the street. With no other vehicles nearby, he assumed it belonged to the Westras. By the time Sandra hastened around their car and settled in the passenger seat, Max already forgot about the pickup and had his car's engine running. He slammed the gas, screeched the tires, and left a smoke trail behind.

A few minutes later, when they reached a stop sign and paused, Max finally breathed. He looked to Sandra, touched her cheek, and smiled. They were okay.

"Don't freak out," Luke said, his bald head popping into view from the back seat.

Max shrieked and jumped. Sandra whipped around, raising her hand as if she had a spell at the ready. Max didn't think she did, but Luke didn't know that. The man coward back.

"I'm not a threat! I'm not a threat!"

"What are doing in our car?" she said, her voice rasping from the smoke.

"Granny sent me. Not a bad thing, though. I promise. She and Billy went into the house to help you. She said I was to wait for you, that things had gone too far. She said you'd both come out while she and Billy finished with the Duns, and I'm supposed to tell you to meet with Granny later, that she'll explain it all."

"Then why were you hiding in our car?"

"The door was open, and it was still cool inside from your air conditioner. I guess I fell asleep. What happened in there? Why you driving crazy like that?"

Max adjusted the rearview mirror. "No, no. You answer us. You say Granny wants to meet with us? Tell me where to go right now, or my wife will do something awful to you."

Luke gulped and with a shaking finger pointed. "Make a left here."

Chapter 19

LUKE DIRECTED THEM TO THE WINSTON-SALEM MARRIOTT on the corner of 5th and North Cherry Street. Max thought they would take a table at the Butcher & Bull Steakhouse, a restaurant inside the hotel, but Luke walked them to the elevators and pushed the button for the top floor. Turned out the Westras had a suite composed of two bedrooms connected by a large room with a couch, television, kitchenette, and a dining table.

Granny Witch Westra and Billy sat at the table as if nothing noteworthy had occurred only a half-hour earlier. Her bruised cheek had a small bandage on it, and her hair had not been reset from her scuffle. The only signs of any activity. Still, she carried the authority and threat that always permeated her presence. The only thing undercutting her strength — she looked tiny sitting next to Billy, and when Luke took the seat on her other side, she became a toothpick sitting between two bowling pins.

As Max and Sandra settled on the opposite side of the table, he surveyed the room, noting that the kitchenette and the area around the television appeared unused. The trash cans had been emptied and a glimpse through one bedroom door revealed none of the mess usually left around. Housekeeping could have taken care of everything, but there would still be some evidence of three people living in the suite. For Max, this oddity only made him more uncomfortable.

Underscoring the seriousness of this meeting, Drummond hovered behind Max, causing a chill. Max could not stop his instinctual human response at feeling the cold of the dead, but he could consciously feel comfort as well. His partner had his back, and he needed it. Sitting there, waiting for Granny Witch to begin, Max clasped hands with Sandra under the table — another comfort.

After a full minute of silence, Max had enough. This was not a negotiation, and power dynamics caused by who broke the silence first meant nothing to him. Not in this situation. Allowing his voice to boom into the quiet, he said, "Luke told us that you and Billy entered that house to protect us from the Vellmers. Do you expect us to be friendly towards you? Is this a game of enemy of my enemy?"

Granny's deep wrinkles in her hard-worn face made reading her expressions difficult. When she spoke, Max couldn't tell if she meant to convey amusement, appreciation, or threats. Her tone gave no clues, either. Just a steady, weary, creaking voice.

"You and your family were never meant to be this involved," she said, staring ahead at the table, never making eye contact with Max. "Your mother had a simple task to do, and when she failed, things spun out of control. Not the way we like to handle matters. We prefer quiet and unseen."

Max said, "It's far from that now."

"I'm going to tell you the story that you need to hear — why we Westras must accomplish our task, why the Duns are an abomination. But first, I must apologize for the harm that has come to your mother."

"You should do more than apologize," Sandra said.

Max stopped himself from blurting out a comment about Sandra defending his mother — something he considered a rare occasion; something he found both encouraging and disturbing.

Granny Witch went on, "I intend to. I have already started. After your husband brutally assaulted my grandsons, they finished their assigned task at the hospital. Your mother's medical bills will be paid for by us. Billy should never have scared her so badly. He sometimes forgets how intimidating a man of his size can be."

Drummond said, "That's awfully kind of her, but don't forget she still made the witch deal with your mother in the first place."

Max had not forgotten. He would never forget. But hurling recriminations would not help this conversation. Even so, he couldn't hide the snarl in his voice. "You called us here. What do you want?"

Granny Witch pulled her lips in, creating another wrinkle around her mouth. When she didn't speak further, Billy said, "It's hard for her to tell all this to strangers. Even when it's what she wants to do."

Luke said, "This is the kind of story that only gets told within the Westra family."

"Enough," Granny Witch said. "They don't need to know how things work in the mountains. They need to know why the Duns are horrible people." She lifted her head slightly, not quite looking at Max but peering in his direction. "For well over a hundred years, different groups of people have come to our home in the mountains and taken from us things that were rightfully ours. In the late 1870s, it was the wood that they wanted. Timbermen from all around the country arrived to cut down our trees, pay us a pittance, haul it all off, and make a fortune elsewhere in the world. This feud between the Westras and the Duns started back then, while the trees fell. Like a lot of feuds, this one began because of love. It's the way so much of the world moves — love and destruction."

Drummond clicked his tongue. "I wouldn't have pegged her for the poetic type, but she knows how to draw in her audience."

"Back then, there was a young woman — Rosie Mae Westra. She was a pretty gal. The kind of girl that never had to struggle to find some man interested in her. Her mama warned her many times to watch out who she looked at and who looked at her. It won't shock you that this story does not come with Rosie Mae making any good choices. Pretty gal, but none too bright. She fell in love with a handsome young man known to turn a few heads. His name — Gil Dun. Now, ordinarily it would be celebrated that two beautiful people found each other and would soon be making beautiful babies to liven up our little town. But unfortunately, Gil Dun worked for one of the timber companies."

Sandra said, "That can't be the whole reason for this rift. Surely, lots of people in your town were employed by those companies."

"There's a difference between getting paid by them to do

some work and working for them. Gil Dun sought more than earning an honest wage. He wanted to rise in the ranks of the company. He wanted money and power, and the only way to get that in a company devoted to destroying our land was to help them destroy us. I'm sure you can see that this did not make him popular. Before he met Rosie Mae, nobody paid Gil Dun much mind at all. If he showed up in a bar, at a dance, or anywhere, people politely ignored him. The Dun family wisely chose not to bring his name up at a Sunday social, and I suspect most of the Duns hoped Gil would leave when the timber company finished and moved on to other mountains. The Duns could forget he existed and still hold their head up."

Max said, "But falling in love with Rosie Mae meant he might stick around."

"That idea caused a rift through the town. People started taking sides. It got ugly. You see, I'm not the only Granny Witch Westra. We've had Granny Witches stretching back for centuries. The family Granny Witch back then met with Gil Dun and made it quite clear to him that he was to break it off with Rosie Mae, to be on his way. He ignored her. In fact, if the story hasn't been exaggerated — and considering the types of people the Duns are, I believe every word of this — well, the moment Gil left Granny Witch, he ran straight to Rosie Mae and asked for her hand in marriage. That bastard knew he would be ruining her life, knew he would be causing harm to the town and its people, to his own family, and yet he did it anyway. Selfish, self-centered — these are the Duns. The Granny Witch at the time had no choice. She could not allow this marriage to happen, but nobody would physically stop Rosie Mae, either. Not because they weren't capable, but it's simply not the right way to do things."

"What is the right way?"

Sandra turned her head to Max like he had said something inappropriate. "You're talking about a witch."

Wheezing out a short chuckle, Granny Witch said, "Your wife understands. My ancestor, that ol' Granny Witch Westra, she cursed Gil Dun. Not only because he defied her and took Rosie

Mae as his wife, but also because he allowed the timber company to move him down here into the Triad. The rest of the local timbermen would only work the land, take their wages, and then quit their jobs when the company left, but not Gil Dun. He got a promotion and a new assignment. Rosie Mae was thrilled. She thought it would be exciting to go see the rest of the world — to her, moving to the Triad was the same as going to Paris or London. But this curse — the night before they left, Granny Witch met with Gil Dun and explained to him that he had been cursed, explained to him that all his good fortune and good looks, the things that had served him well and brought him the attention of a beauty like Rosie Mae, those things were over. Misfortune would follow him the rest of his life."

A knock at the door caused everybody to hold still. Luke scooted back his chair and went to answer. Drummond flew ahead. Before the ghost reached the door, however, a voice from the hall called out, "Room service."

Granny Witch frowned. "Who ordered room service?"

Billy raised his hand an inch off the table. "It's been a long day, and we needed to eat. You should, too."

"It's expensive. They overcharge."

Luke took the tray of food from the bellhop, gave the kid a twenty-dollar tip, and never let him inside the room. As Luke carried the tray into one of the adjoining bedrooms, Max caught sight of plates with burgers, fries, a salad, and an overstuffed baked potato. His stomach rumbled.

Drummond raised an eye at Max. "Been a long day for you, too?"

Max placed a hand over his belly and returned his attention to Granny Witch. "You were saying that your family cursed Gil Dun."

Holding her disapproving eye upon Luke as the man returned to his seat, she said, "The curse took effect fast. They bought a house — same property the Vellmers are on — and the day Gil and Rosie Mae moved in, they found a family of raccoons living in the attic. While attempting to remove the critters, one attacked Gil. Scratched his face up deeply. Scarred him for life. No more beautiful face. Then his precious job went sour. Mismanagement led to a troubled company, and Gil learned that few companies are more loyal to their workers than to their money. They had no trouble firing him."

Sandra said, "But that wouldn't stop Rosie Mae, would it?"

"Unfortunately, no. If she had left him, returned to the mountains, none of this would be going on today. But she still had Westra blood in her, and we Westras are loyal people. We certainly don't betray those we love. She never left him. She died giving birth to their third child. But a curse like this one lasts longer than the grave. Even with the Westra-Dun union dissolved by death, that Granny Witch's curse would not let go. Punishing Gil Dun was never meant to end."

Leaning her elbows on the table, Sandra said, "She cast another spell, didn't she? Another curse."

"A most powerful curse. It happened on February 19, 1884. Took her hours to get the spell working properly, but during the third witching hour on the 20th, she struck."

Max's jaw opened. He knew that date. "Are you telling me that she caused the Enigma Tornado Outbreak?"

"No witch is that powerful. Least, none that I've ever known of. But she did take advantage of the storm. The moment it started, she could feel the shift in the winds. Taste the change in the air. She created a tornado to divert from the rest. It veered off towards the town of Olin, and it destroyed Gil Dun and his home. Razed it to the ground."

"And his children?" Sandra asked.

With a dismissive sniff, Granny Witch said, "They survived. It is unclear if the spell had been intended to wipe out the entire family or allow the young safe passage. One of Gil's brothers went to Olin to raise those children. He couldn't afford the property, but through some clever and deceitful practices — very like the Duns from the beginning — they managed to transfer the land into the brother's name. He built the house that now stands there."

Drummond said, "It's clear why the Duns hate the Westras, but Gil Dun is long dead. Why are the Westras still keeping this feud alive?"

Max asked the question on behalf of his partner.

Before she could answer, Billy put his hand on Granny's shoulder. "You told them enough."

Shrugging him off, she said, "It's important the Porters understand."

"Why? They've done nothing but cause us trouble."

"Trust your Granny Witch." Then she looked straight at Max, and a lump lodged in his throat.

"It's that power," Sandra said. "You and Callie argued about a source of power. Is that what's behind the door? Whatever's left of Gil Dun?"

"Perhaps. When the curse was cast upon him, and then the spell cast that killed him, they required a lot of anger and a lot of hate. The Dun family has witches of their own, and they have sought to gain control of all that was put into those spells so that they could use it to harm the Westras. But we Westras are smart, too. Every few years, we have been able to secretly stash a few witchballs in the house. Sometimes in the walls; sometimes in the attic. We even had one of our family members help pour the foundation of the house and put some witchballs in there."

"You're using them to suppress the power emanating from Gil Dun."

"Oh, yes. And since the Dun witches are not as honest or formidable as the Westra witches, they require whatever power they can siphon from him in order to be anything resembling a threat."

Max said, "But with this witch war creating a leadership vacuum, Callie Dun thinks she can unleash that power. She thinks she can take over the whole state."

"So it would seem."

Max did not know how many more shocks he could take, but his mind put together a new one for him. "You're telling us all of this because you want our help."

Granny Witch nodded. "I thought, perhaps we could make a deal."

Chapter 20

NOBODY IN THE PORTER AGENCY wanted to make a deal with a witch, but they all agreed to discuss it further. Granny Witch Westra acknowledged that such a deal should not be taken lightly and provided them access to one bedroom, the bedroom without the food, so that they could come to a decision in private. Max thanked her, making mental notes — that the witch must be more desperate for their help than he realized (otherwise, she would never have allowed them to discuss a deal in private), and that she must respect the Porters, or at least, respect Sandra (otherwise, she would never have asked to make the deal in the first place).

Max and Sandra entered the bedroom — the witch's room based on the use of only one bed, the floral suitcase, and the eucalyptus scent from a muscle relief cream. The Westras retired to the other bedroom — presumably, to eat their ordered meal. Max's stomach gave one final protest.

To open the discussion, Drummond slipped through the wall and went straight to Max. "I'd remind you that this is a stupid idea to even consider, but that hasn't stopped you before."

"You say that like I *want* to make a witch deal."

"I say that to point out that this is a stupid idea. I'd also remind you that until an hour ago, Granny Witch Westra was the enemy. I say she still is."

Sandra sat on the corner of the unused bed. "She was never an enemy. She's a witch, doing what a witch does, and she's been acting to protect her family. No different than us. Max's mother is the one who created this problem, and while we obviously have larger issues to deal with now, let's not lose sight of our client's needs. She needs to be protected."

Lowering his chin, Drummond said, "Sorry, doll. You're

right. But a witch deal?"

"If we go down that road — *if* — then we'll have to be extremely careful. Just because Granny Witch is not our enemy doesn't make her our friend. We shouldn't trust her."

"Then the first question we need to answer is do we believe her story."

Max considered poking around that floral suitcase. Not that he had any desire to filter through an old woman's undergarments, but rather, a witch like her probably packed a few interesting books, wards, or other items of her trade. Then again, perhaps Granny Witch allowed them use of this room to tempt him into such a brazen action. Perhaps the suitcase had been rigged to curse any unauthorized snooping.

"Honey, don't." Sandra spoke in a harsh tone that pulled him back.

"The story," Max said, his words fumbling at first. "If she's making it up, she's basing it on a lot of truth. If not, she could replace Meryl Streep. The details are both too specific and too vague to be the kind of tale handed down for generations. That's not an easy thing to fake."

"Plus, if she lied in order to get our help, then she could have come up with a better lie."

"Or not bothered with a lie at all," Drummond said. "All we needed to know was that Callie wants to be head witch in North Carolina. Granny didn't need to explain anything else for that."

"Except we knew about the feud — just not what caused the feud."

Max's researching instincts caused him to leap forward. "She told us what happened because we need to know. She said that to one of her grandsons — that we needed to hear the story. These Westras are a private people, so she wouldn't have told us anything she didn't absolutely have to."

Drummond tapped his hat as he stared in the direction of the other bedroom. "She must have thought we wouldn't help otherwise. Or she always intended to offer a deal."

"Maybe. But I think she knows the threat is more than simply Callie Dun Vellmer. It's the power behind the Duns. She's not making a deal simply to destroy a rival or strike a blow in this old feud. I think she needs our help in shutting down this power source." He pointed at Sandra. "You said she wants to protect her family. You're right. But not simply to protect them here and now. She wants to fix this for the future. Make sure no other Granny Witch is stuck having to handle this. Probably, my mother's screw up made Granny realize the danger this feud has caused."

"Partner, it sounds an awful lot like you're arguing to make another witch deal."

"No," Sandra said. "If we're going to make a deal, then I'm the one that should make it."

Max grimaced. "Hon, I've had plenty of experience with these deals, too."

"But I'm the witch."

"But my mother caused the problem."

Drummond said, "You ask me, neither of you should do this."

"Guess we'll have to settle this the fairest way possible." Sandra put out her fist. "Rock, paper, scissors. Two-out-of-three, or do you want to risk it all on one?"

Bringing his fist to meet hers, Max grinned. "You are one-of-a-kind, so I guess we do it all on one. Ready?"

Max went with paper. Sandra chose scissors. "I'd say you won, but I'm not sure that's true. You get to make the deal, though," he said. "But I'll be there with you, and if I hear anything suspicious, I'll speak up."

"Wouldn't have it any other way."

A quick kiss, and they headed back into the adjoining room. Drummond drifted through the wall, grumbling about risk and idiocy, but Max knew the ghost would pay close attention. Sandra could handle the deal, but even with her knowledge and experience, tricky wording or simple mistakes could lead to disastrous results. Neither husband nor ghost intended to let that happen.

Granny Witch sat at the table while Billy and Luke cleaned dishes in the kitchenette and disposed of their meal remains.

Once Luke placed the tray in the hall and returned to the table, everyone else had already seated. It all looked so normal. Max found it disturbing.

To a stranger, of course, it appeared like an old grandma with her darling grandsons and some family friends washing up after a delightful afternoon meal. Even if an observer knew that the two women were accomplished witches, the situation would still appear benign. Only knowing the truth revealed the dark tension underscoring each gentle movement, each subtle sound, each breath, and the moments between the breaths.

Granny Witch Westra rested her hands flat on the table and looked straight at Sandra, the wrinkles widening enough for everyone to see her gray eyes. Max pursed his lips, trying to hide a swift rush of jealousy — Granny thought Sandra worthy of a look, but earlier Max barely earned a glance. He then remembered that garnering the full focus of a witch was not something to be desired. In fact, seeing those old eyes lock onto Sandra brought both a wave of worry through him and the confidence that she was the right one to lead this deal.

Tenting her fingers, Sandra leaned back in her chair. "I have a suggestion for how to begin."

"Please," Granny said. "I would love to hear your idea."

Even those two simple statements threw ice water over Max and the Westra brothers. Luke visibly shivered. Heck, Max guessed even through the cold of death, Drummond felt it, too.

Sandra offered a nonchalant flick of her hand. "Nothing bold or dangerous. Simply that it seems to me we have two things to consider at the start. First, we have a bit of a time issue."

"I agree with that. Callie Dun and her husband are not sitting at their house waiting for us to do something. I'm sure they've doubled their efforts to open that door."

"Second, you're the one who proposed making a deal."

"I admit, I did that, too."

Max wanted to clap and cheer. Getting a witch to admit anything during a deal negotiation could be near impossible, yet Sandra pulled it off in the opening minute. His chest puffed with pride for her.

"Well, then, I suggest we begin with an offer from you outlining what you hope this deal to look like."

Pulling her lips back into a grotesque smile, Granny Witch said, "Naturally. But you already know the answer, and it's awfully simple. We want to stop Callie Dun. The real question is what do you require from me to give your aid."

"I wish it were as simple as that. We could make this deal quickly and be on our way. But you're more than aware how specifics are the key here. I'll ask again — what *specifically* do you hope for this deal to look like?"

Over the next five minutes, Max watched his wife duel with Granny Witch, each woman launching surreptitious traps, each woman parrying the other, each woman picking apart subtleties and insinuations, each woman fighting brutally hard while neither moved from their chairs. He wondered how he would have handled this if the Rock, Paper, Scissors game had gone differently. The answer hit him at once — poorly. Sandra would have been forced to intervene early on or risk Max agreeing to a curse that would ruin his entire family without him realizing he had agreed to anything at all. Within the first few words between them, these two women, these two witches made clear their negotiation occurred on another level. They mesmerized as they parsed each other's phrasing like contract lawyers of the highest order. They weaved around their intentions, their deeper goals, their hidden agendas, each smiling at the other, each moving little more than their mouths, and even then, barely curling a lip as they spoke. Max felt as if he watched Michaelangelo and Da Vinci competing to see who could produce more masterpieces.

Even Drummond sounded impressed. "I've never seen anything like this," the ghost whispered.

Lost thinking about how much he admired his wife, Max missed several exchanges, but he did not miss the results. Silence. Like two samurai facing off, neither speaking but each making slight adjustments as they envisioned the next clash, Sandra and Granny Witch glowered at each other. Billy and Luke's reticence to move a single muscle, to even shift in their seats, put Max on higher alert. All involved held vigilant to the moment. All watchful for any indication which of these women had won. From the corner of his eye, Max caught Drummond sliding toward the head of the table — within reach of the Granny Witch should she attempt anything. Max worried more about Luke and Billy, but as long as the ghost kept close by, he figured they would be okay.

Whatever transpired between the two women, Max could not tell. However, nobody missed Sandra standing with her fists pressed against the table.

"I'm sorry we couldn't work anything out," she said. "Good luck, and I sincerely hope your family can resolve its issue with the Duns. Vicious circles like that are so hard to break."

With a toss of her head, Sandra indicated to Max that it was time to leave. They walked towards the exit with Drummond right behind. Granny Witch remained motionless. Billy, however, rose to his feet and hastened to open the door.

"Thank you for coming," he said, glee painting every word.

From the table, though muttered, Luke said, "Good riddance."

Before they could break the threshold into the hallway, Granny Witch called out. "Stop." Less of a command and more her bitter acceptance.

Sandra turned back. "Yes?"

Focusing on the chair where Sandra had been sitting, Granny Witch said, "I don't like to admit shortcomings, but it was clear from our latest encounter with Callie Dun that she has already grown stronger than expected. Her display may not have seemed impressive to the likes of you who have dealt with far more dangerous witches, I'm sure, but believe me, she has shown strength tenfold from the mewling kitten I knew her to be only a year ago. At this rate, even if she never opens that door, even if she never succeeds in taking over North Carolina, she is gaining enough power to become a formidable threat to the stability in your witch community and mine." She gestured to the empty seats. "Please. I state now, in the most honest way, that I need your help."

Acting more Southern than Max had ever seen, Sandra

painted a broad smile. "Why all you had to do was ask."

The remaining negotiations progressed with ease. No more posturing. No more power plays. No more bad faith phrasing. While a few minor quibbles over defining specific words faltered the conversation, in the end, they struck a deal that served both their immediate purposes and their longer-term concerns.

Simply: The Porter Agency agreed to help the Westras take down Callie Dun and her husband, Wyatt. In exchange, Mrs. Porter's deal ended immediately, and once they resolved the Dun situation, the Westras would return to the mountains. Unfortunately, Mrs. Porter's pain from her MS would not be alleviated. That required magic, and Granny Witch refused to continue those services free-of-charge. But at least Max's mother would no longer be beholden to a witch. The Westras agreed to stay out of the witch war and the power struggle it surrounded. Granny Witch made it clear the mountain folk had no interest in this war. Keep it out of the mountains and the mountains would keep to themselves. The last matter concerned the suicidal urges of Max's mother. While Granny Witch promised she had not invoked any such mental state upon Mrs. Porter, she conceded that it may be a by-product of the spells she had used and removed. When this deal concluded, if those thoughts were an unintended result of a spell, they should disappear.

"That is the greatest witch deal I've ever seen," Drummond said taking his hat off and placing it over his heart. "Specific, with no wiggle room, and you got her to back off another deal. Doll, you've outdone yourself."

As Max and Sandra prepared to leave, Luke said, "Where are you going? You just made the deal, and you're going to break it right away."

"Nobody's breaking the deal," Max said.

"The first part is that you got to help us fight the Duns. So, let's go fight her."

Billy said, "Don't be stupid. We got beaten by that witch, beaten bad, and you want to go run back in there? What do you think Granny and the Porters have been dealing about all this time?"

"I just meant that —"

"If you were listening, Granny made it obvious that this Dun witch is getting stronger and stronger. Even if we could go back tonight, don't you think she'd be ready and stronger?"

"Yeah, but the Porters are supposed to be helping us and they're leaving."

Max said, "Helping you all is exactly what we're going to do. But we'll do it the way The Porter Agency fights all witches. Starting with the research."

Chapter 21

RESEARCH SOUNDED LIKE A GOOD IDEA, but nobody, not even the witches, had a solid plan for how to win against Callie Dun. Instead, a plan to come up with a plan was put into action. Granny Witch Westra and Sandra would work together on various spells designed to combat Callie and Wyatt. They would stay in the hotel room and work through whatever they thought a witch like Callie could cast. Then, they would try to counter it. In addition, Sandra insisted they work on spells to break through the spell-locked door in the Vellmer house. Meanwhile, Billy and Luke were assigned to recon the Vellmer house and alert Granny Witch should anything important develop. Finally, Max drove out to The Porter Agency office to do his research. Drummond joined him.

Though Max needed to stay focused on the task at hand, he permitted a few minutes to enjoy the newness of the office one last time. Sitting at his desk, he surveyed the space like a feudal lord admiring his acreage. He might have wasted more minutes than he intended, but Drummond snapped him back.

"I'm no fan of watching you hit the books, but a growing number of people are counting on you. So, hit the books." Drummond flicked the brim of his hat and floated into the wall that soon would become his bookshelves.

Opening his laptop, Max started with two broad questions he wanted to delve into — he needed to learn all he could about the Vellmer house, its history, and most importantly, its layout. If the current building had an attic or basement or crawl space, they needed to know. The second issue would be more difficult information to attain. After hearing Granny Witch Westra's version of the family history, he wanted to verify everything she had said and possibly expound upon it if he could uncover any further avenues to research.

The first part proved simple enough. Public records for construction permits gave him most of the information. Often when applying for such permits, blueprints had to be submitted, and most of that information had been digitized over the last few decades. The current version of the Vellmer house had a crawlspace underneath and a crawl attic above. Nothing large enough to walk through but certainly large enough to hide a body. Most intriguing, in every version of the house he could find, Max saw no area marking out a room behind a door at the end of the hall — spell-locked or otherwise. In all the blueprints, the hallway simply ended with a small window for sunlight. Best he could think of, the door had been placed in the hall so that it opened into the alcove it created. In other words, there was no room on the other side, simply the last bit of hallway — essentially creating a glorified closet. But a lot of magic could be placed inside a small space. Even the remains of a man cursed a century-and-a-half ago, buried in the backyard, and then dug up at some point.

Next, Max turned to researching the Dun lineage. Though Brenda sent over an email providing all her work on the family, teasing out the final connections tracing from Gil Dun to Callie Dun would be difficult. Delving into the individual lives to learn if anybody mattered to the current predicament would be far worse. It would take longer, too. A lot longer. Then again, Sandra would be working on spells all night and J would be protecting Max's mother as well. Max could put in the effort to uncover whatever waited in the dusty history of these quarreling family lines.

Though early records could always be incomplete, and early records in hard-to-reach places like the mountains even more so, Max still managed to put together a rough family tree of the Duns — at least, one going back to Gil Dun. Gil had several siblings, but only Dale Dun mattered. He was the brother who raised Gil's children and continued living on the property in Olin. His wife had been training to be a granny witch in the mountains. She loathed the idea of moving down to the

Piedmont, away from her parents and her friends, forced to become mother to children not her own — worse, the children of an unholy union that had already started a feud between the Westras and the Duns.

But Dale coaxed her with a simple promise. She could do whatever she wanted with Gil Dun's body. At least, that is what Max surmised had happened. It made sense, given Callie's assertion of the magical power from Gil's body, that such an offer would lure Dale's wife and lead to generations of Duns owning, controlling, and profiting from the magic power on this property. However, Max had to admit that most of this story was conjecture based on the movements of different family members, the scraps of stories he could find connected to obituaries or marriage announcements in old mountain newspapers, and basic gut instinct.

No matter the particulars of how it all went down, the result stayed the same. Dale and his wife raised the children while having a few of their own. By the turn-of-the-century, Gil's family line led to a man named William, then in the 1920s to Frederick and John, then in the 1940s to Colin, then in the 1960s to Nicholas, Beth, and Bo, then to another John in the 1980s and his sister Sue, and finally to Callie. Dale's family line followed a similar trajectory though off a decade, resulting in the April 12, 1970 birth of Montgomery Dun, Callie's uncle.

Max also uncovered a photograph of Gil and Rosie Mae Dun taken a year before her death. Like most photos of the time, the subjects stared at the camera with grim, stoic faces. Gil had a thick mustache and beard that gave him a stern yet warm quality like a favorite uncle who had seen war or some other horror yet managed to retain the charm that endeared him to others. Next to him, Rosie Mae's dark eyes pierced through the decades, lacking all sense of love, all sense of empathy. Instead, Max saw a defiant woman. The kind of person who focused solely on her own desires and damn the consequences. Not simply the family consequences — though she had no qualms about starting a feud that would last over a hundred years — but all consequences. She stood with her husband, but in her eyes, Max saw a woman who could have been standing alone. Perhaps she didn't care about her neighbors, her friends, her husband, her own children.

Max sent the photo to Sandra.

With that done, he decided to take a brief stretch before diving into the Westra lineage. He strolled down the short hall to their new breakroom. The refrigerator hummed away in the corner. They never had a full refrigerator in the office before. One previous office had a mini-fridge and the other had nothing at all for much of the time they spent there. He opened the door to find mostly empty shelves. However, a sixpack of cola awaited him. He popped open a can, tipped back the cool beverage, and returned to his desk.

He could get used to this.

Max jolted awake, sitting up on the couch. His tongue stuck to the roof of his mouth, and his teeth felt fuzzy. The back of his head ached.

Looking across the room, he saw three crushed soda cans sitting on the corner of his desk. The sugar-caffeine combination had helped him finish tracing out the basic lineage of the Dun family and peek at the Westras, but the resulting crash sent him headfirst into the couch. He had intended to only close his eyes for fifteen minutes. By the stream of moonlight coming through the window, he guessed it had been several hours, at least.

Stretching his arms overhead, Max clambered to his feet and strolled toward the bathroom. He checked the medicine cabinet for a toothbrush and toothpaste. No such luck. Instead, he bent over the sink and filled his mouth with water. After spitting it out, he ran his finger over his teeth and rinsed again. Returning to the main office, he sat at his computer, flicked on his desk lamp, and planned to get back to work. But when he tapped the keyboard to wake up his computer, he saw the time — 3 am. The witching hour. One of them, anyway.

His skin prickled. Had the temperature dropped? Or perhaps the simple connection of the hour with witches caused a psychosomatic reaction.

All in my head?

Holding stone still, Max listened for any sound that did not belong. Nothing but quiet and crickets. No odd smells, either.

"This is ridiculous," he said, hoping the sound of his voice would break the illusion he had cast upon himself. He strode to the front door to make sure nobody walked in the halls. Never mind that nobody would be walking in an office building at three in the morning — especially an office building on the outskirts of the city. But when Max tried to open the door, he found it locked.

He turned the deadbolt as well as the knob lock, but they were already in the open setting. He pulled on the door a few more times. Nothing. Remembering that the door could often stick, he gave it a final sharp tug. No luck.

His heart beat faster. His breath grew shallow. He surveyed the office once more, searching for any sign of activity. He waited. If a ghost from some long-forgotten case had caught up with him, it did a poor job of scaring him. Sure, he felt tension, but nothing really had happened. Not yet.

Still, no sense in being reckless. As casually as he could manage, he ambled toward Sandra's desk. He considered whistling but dismissed that thought — too much of a show.

Sitting in her chair — one that felt much nicer than his — he opened one drawer after another. Though he found a few expected items like pens and paper clips, she had yet to put in the more useful tools of the trade. Not a single ward for him to pick up. No salt, either.

And still, nothing had happened. No attack. No frightening screams. No pounding walls. Certainly, no manifestation. If this ghost wanted to exact revenge on Max, it sure took its time.

Unless it wasn't real. Could he be dreaming? He didn't think he was dreaming. He had read the time clear enough, and he thought he heard somewhere that most people could not read words or numbers while dreaming. But that wasn't true for all people, and he had never bothered to figure out which camp he fell into — to read or not to read.

Vivid dreams, ones that felt so real he couldn't be sure when he woke, had only happened to him a few times in his life. Usually, though, the sensation faded fast.

He decided he had to believe this was real. If it turned out to be a dream, then no problem. He would wake up, have a good chuckle, and get on with the day. But to assume he dreamt and then to find out this was real — that could have devasting outcomes. Especially for a member of The Porter Agency.

"Okay. I'm not dreaming," he said, the sound of his voice now adding to the concrete of reality. "But where is this ghost?" And then another question hit: *Why now?*

Max paused at the thought. Any case involving ghosts that would still be around and sought to harm him or anybody in The Porter Agency would have been dealt with ages ago. Most of the recent cases involved witches, not ghosts. Those concerning ghosts had ended with the ghosts moving on. Besides, though Drummond insisted that ghosts had eternity to plan, Max found it hard to believe that some ghost had been watching and waiting for this opportune moment when he would finally have his own office again, be there late at night, have fallen asleep, and awoke at the witching hour. For that matter, ghosts don't care about the witching hour. It's called the witching hour not the ghosting hour — suggesting this was a matter of witchcraft. And that brought the focus back to his current case.

Recognizing this, however, only brought up more questions. Why go through the trouble of casting a witching hour spell for it to simply mimic a ghost's presence? Given the nature of The Porter Agency's casework, having the office haunted once or twice in the coming years would not be a surprise. In fact, if the spell had been done at a different time, he might never have considered a witch's involvement.

It was possible that Callie Dun cast the spell simply to delay Max. After all, he had spent the last several minutes dealing with this seeming paranormal experience instead of continuing his research. But again — what a waste of effort and time to cast a witching hour spell for such meager results.

Max walked to the center of the room. "I don't know what you want, but if you're listening, I'm here. If you've got something to say, then say it. Otherwise, I'm getting back to work."

He waited.

Like a squall appearing out on a calm sea, lightning flashed in the office, thunder roared, and a wall of wind blasted Max off his feet. His heel caught the back of the couch, tumbling him to the floor, smashing his shoulder into the coffee table. Pain jolted straight through to his fingertips as his nerves misfired.

Grousing a few choice words, Max rose to his feet. "That wasn't necessary. Not if you wanted to have a simple conversation. No need for all this."

"After yesterday's unfortunate turn," a voice said from behind, "I thought you should respect how dangerous I can be."

Max whirled around to find Callie Dun standing on the spot he had previously occupied. But she had the pale glow of a ghost.

Chapter 22

MAX WATCHED CALLIE'S GHOST and tried to calculate how this would impact the larger situations. Unable to walk through the landmines of this discussion, he decided barreling through would be best. Or at least, it would be the Max Porter way. "What happened to you?" he finally said. "Granny Witch accidentally kill you when she tossed you against the wall?"

Callie laughed, and the sound of her voice doubled on itself as if projecting through a PA system but slightly delayed. "I am not dead. Not in the slightest. In fact, I'm sitting in my house. Wyatt is here with me, and we're enjoying tall glasses of sweet tea."

"You sure love that stuff."

"That and a bottle of Cheerwine is all a Southern gal truly needs for refreshment." The ghostly visage winked. "Maybe a shot of whiskey once in a while."

"If you're not dead, what's with all this?"

"It's called a witching projection."

Rubbing his shoulder, Max risked a few small steps towards his desk. "That like astral projection?"

"It's far more complicated and takes a far stronger witch."

It appeared Granny Witch had undersold that Callie would be gaining more strength from that house. This did not seem like the same woman from earlier. "If you wanted to talk, you didn't need to cast a difficult spell. Cell phones work wonders."

"But the witching projection is so much more impactful."

A few more steps. "I see. You want to do this kind of astral — excuse me, witching projection — and throw me across the room to show me that I'm not safe. Is that it?"

Her pleasant expression strengthened. "Sometimes a relationship starts out all wrong. That's what has happened with us. Wouldn't you agree? It's not your fault. Granny Witch Westra set your mother up to fail. The Porters and the Duns had no choice but to meet each other at some point. It was inevitable. No way around it considering I'm going to be the Queen of North Carolina's magic. But it should never have been like this. We could've started on much friendlier terms."

"You're not here to threaten me then? You simply threw me across the room as a way of welcoming me to the neighborhood."

She giggled, covering her mouth as she watched him move closer to the desk. "I came here tonight to make you an offer. I threw you across the room so you would know I'm serious, that I truly will have the power I claim is in my house. You can forget all about the Westras. They are inconsequential. They don't want to expand their control beyond the mountains, and as long as you let them be, they'll scurry back up there and never bother you again. Heck, if your mother hadn't gone and made that witch deal, you would never have known the Westra family at all. I would have introduced myself to you properly as I took power, and we would be having this conversation under less strenuous circumstances."

Gesturing to his chair, Max said, "You mind if I sit? Think I've got a broken rib. Or maybe just a real bad pulled muscle." She tilted her head — he took that as a nod — and as he sat, he closed his laptop. If she saw her family line traced out, he figured she would do a lot worse than bang his side up a bit. "I'm listening. What's this offer?"

"I'd say it's quite obvious. Take my side of things. Help me get rid of the Westras. Then, when I have control over magic in North Carolina, you'll have a steady source of income. The Porter Agency can continue doing what it does best — protecting the mundane world from rogue witches and bad curses and all of that."

"You want me to become your enforcer."

"Isn't that the work you did for the Hulls? Isn't that what you did for Mother Hope?"

"Not remotely."

She laughed again, once more covering her mouth. "Bless your heart. They really got you thinking you had autonomy."

Max did not know how to take being insulted by a witching projection. Insulted by a ghost — sure, happened all the time. But this was new.

Callie's smile stopped right below her eyes. "I'm fixing to take over the whole state, and you are worried about semantics. Not smart."

"You're new around here, so I guess you haven't heard. I never do the smart thing."

"If you won't do it for yourself, think about your wife or your mother or your children. Now, don't get all upset. I'm not threatening their lives — not much, anyway. Rather, I'm asking you to think of the opportunity for those you love. Your wife would have access to all the books on magic she could possibly imagine. She's a strong, capable witch. Think of the great things she could accomplish when given real resources. As for your mother, I don't think she has much time left. But with the Duns on your side, her final years could be peaceful, pleasant, maybe even joyful. As for what comes to your boys, well, a bright, prosperous future is what I see. And all you must do is what you had set out to do from the beginning. Stop Granny Witch Westra."

Max scratched the back of his head. "I've got to say that's a nice offer. Only problem is that making an offer and then accepting the offer — well, that's called a deal. Witch deals are never to be made lightly. Certainly not quickly. My guess — without looking at the fine print — this deal is rotten to the core. With all respect, I'm not interested."

Her smile switched off. "Last chance to reconsider."

"I've reconsidered already. Answer is still no."

Callie planted her feet firm, put her hands on her hips, and leaned forward with a broad smile. "Well, I certainly do apologize for being so unclear. I gave you the impression that you had a choice. I mean I suppose you do — you can either accept the offer or I can kill you."

Max shot to his feet. He had no idea what he would do, but

sitting behind a desk seemed the worst idea. She never gave him time to think beyond that.

Her eyes rolled up as he lifted off the floor. When his feet became level with the desktop, an unseen force wrapped around his chest like an enormous snake. And it tightened.

"You don't want to do this," he said, barely getting the last word out as the constricting force made breathing difficult.

She didn't respond. That gave Max a glimmer of hope. He imagined the effort it would take to perform a witching projection on top of the location spell she would have had to use to find him in the first place, and then on top of those spells, she now performed this attack. No wonder her eyes rolled into her skull. She didn't respond to him because she couldn't. She needed all her concentration, all her energy, to keep the spells going.

He only had to figure out how to break her focus.

Unfortunately, she had him floating in the middle the room, and she diminished his air with every second. Soon enough, even if he had an idea, he would lack the oxygen to see it to fruition. He had to think of something.

Think, think, think.

He tried kicking at his desk. If he could get a toehold, perhaps he could push himself in her direction — maybe collide with her. But as he wriggled his leg, the invisible snake tightened again. He coughed out what little air he had, and that motion pushed him further away from the desk.

Circles of gray formed around the edges of his vision. He needed help, and he knew how to get it. He opened his mouth to call for his partner, but no sound came. With the wheezing inhalation, he tried again.

"Dru … Dru …"

The clouding narrowed his vision further. His fingers and toes tingled as the grip on him reduced his circulation. He still needed to think. Before the blood left his brain. How else could he stop her? He needed to find a key to —

A key.

He slapped his left leg and felt the metal mound of keys in his pocket dig into his thigh. Unable to inhale, he strained to get his hand around those keys. He yanked them out and threw them at Callie Dun's pale apparition. Though the keys sailed right through her, the jangling noise distracted her enough.

The snake around him uncoiled. He gasped in a breath, and before she could regroup to attack again, he screamed, "Drummond!"

Pale ghost light flashed in front of him. Max's vision blurred and clouded. The spell that held him aloft disappeared, and he collapsed onto the floor. He gasped, and the air entered his lungs, scratching down his throat. Tears trickled along his nose as he concentrated on taking the next breath. And the next. And the next.

Last thing he recalled before he fell unconscious — Drummond floating over him.

"You're okay, pal. I've got you."

The remaining few hours of night passed without further life-threatening events. Max returned to the couch, stretched out, and slept. Drummond promised to visit Sandra and explain what happened.

At some point, Max awoke to find Sandra sitting beside him, patting his forehead with a washcloth. Her worried face smoothed into happiness when she saw him looking back at her. She leaned over and kissed him gently.

"Why are you always fighting witches who can murder you?" she said, and it sounded like the sweetest declaration of love he had ever heard.

"Wasn't what I planned for."

She babied him for a few minutes until he assured her that he felt fine. He wanted her back with Granny Witch. "If we're going to stop Callie Dun, and after tonight, you bet your beautiful face I want that woman stopped, then we're going to need all you can bring. The longer this takes, the stronger she's going to be."

Within minutes of Sandra leaving, he dropped into a deep sleep. By morning, after Max had washed up in the bathroom sink — he really needed a toothbrush — Drummond told him not to worry about a return visit from Callie Dun.

"Not only did I show her that I can touch her without pain — she put herself in somewhat of a ghost form, after all — but Sandra said the kind of spells Callie used were draining when combined together. She might not be as beat up as you, but she's every bit as exhausted."

"I find that hard to believe."

"You know better than to doubt your wife. Anyway, the plan is still moving forward. Sandra and Granny Witch are out purchasing candles and other witch supplies they need, and you've got to finish your research. This thing is going down tonight. All the more reason because Callie won't be at her best."

Struggling to his feet, Max said, "I don't think I'll be at my best, either."

"That's no problem. You're never much help anyway."

Max laughed, sending a wave of ache through his muscles. As he worked toward his desk, holding his side against another bout of pain, he managed a serious look at his partner. "Thank you."

"Think nothing of it. You would do the same for me."

Once at his desk, Max opened his laptop with the determination of a warrior unsheathing a sword. He set his fingers on the keyboard, narrowed his eyes on the screen, and pushed himself into the final research.

Chapter 23

THE WESTRA FAMILY TREE proved far more difficult to uncover. Because Gil and Dale Dun's family lines brought them to the Piedmont, those records became clearer and more easily accessed, but the Westras had stayed in the mountains. Many of their births occurred at home, and many of their deaths were buried in their backyards. Not everything ended up being recorded in official government documents which meant that not everything had been digitized onto official government websites.

"You okay?" Drummond slipped out of the wall.

Unconsciously rubbing his shoulder, Max said, "I've been better, but yeah, I'm fine. It's frightening how getting attacked by witches is no longer frightening."

"You looked pretty shaken up to me when I saved your life."

"I don't mean I wasn't scared. But if this had been the first time, the only time, I would be shaking still. I would be a wreck for a week. Instead, I went right back to working."

"I saw a lot of that near the end of my life. Guys discharged from injury trying to find their way back into the civilized world. Some of them couldn't hack it. Became a real mess in their heads. But others — heck, you'd think nothing happened over in Europe. I knew one guy who made it through D-Day, Reggie Pezzoli, and I'm telling you, Reggie was the happiest, funniest guy I ever knew. Always had a new joke to tell you. Never let bad news bring him down. And the man had lost an arm. What can I say? People take things different. You've seen it plenty of times. We've had clients that are being haunted yet never admit that's what is actually happening. People encounter witches and curses and all of it, but they act like there is some other explanation, something that fits in with what they think is reality. Others accept reality right away. You never know."

"Guess I'm one of the lucky few who can get attacked by a witch and shrug it off."

"I'm not saying you're never going to feel it. Ol' Reggie put a shotgun to his head one night."

"Gee, what an encouraging story."

"Be careful, then. Don't think you're immune just because you can handle the aftermath."

Max nodded. For a few years now, he had considered getting therapy. Maybe he should consider it more seriously.

Pointing to the laptop, Drummond shifted his tone, clearly indicating he had enough personal talk. "What have you got?"

"That's a real good question." Max's office chair squealed as he leaned back to put his feet on the desk — something he never had room to do in the kitchen alcove comfortably. "On one hand, I've got tons of details that might add up to something. On the other hand, I don't think I've got much of anything at all."

"If your info is anything like that answer, I'd say you've got a lot of nothing."

"Look at the screen. That's as much of the Dun and Westra lineages that I could work out. Lots of names, connections, histories. But it doesn't get us any closer to an answer for, well, any serious questions about them."

"Other than who begat who."

"These families have spent so much of their time hating each other, they never do much else. At least, nothing notable enough to appear in a newspaper or online media or anywhere."

Drummond tapped his chin. "Appalachian folks are known for being private."

"But other people in those communities have a footprint in the world. I've found books of fiction by Appalachian writers, non-fiction about their lives in the mountains, and tons of music — recorded for sale, videos on YouTube and TikTok, historical music by old musicians, as well as young mountain bands playing everything from Taylor Swift to Pantera to classical to German polka. There's no shortage of Appalachian people reaching out to the rest of the world."

"Except for the Duns and Westras."

"Exactly. Ambition can do that. A person gets so focused on gaining power or attaining some level of wealth or however they define success that they lose sight of everything else. It's the kind of thing that destroys a marriage or turns the kids into brats who misbehave because Mommy or Daddy isn't around enough."

"Seems like both these families have had that attitude injected deep into their blood."

"It can be as bad as a parent that's physically abusive. At first, the child is victimized. Then, they grow up and repeat the abuse onto their own children. Duns raise their boys to seek out girls to be witches that crave the power emanating from that house. Westras raise their girls to be granny witches that'll fight the Duns. Nobody ever is allowed to dream of a different life. It's the family duty and their curse."

Drummond swept over to the window. "I've never understood people like that, families like that." He dropped his chin against his chest, deliberating one thought against another, until he finally nodded as if the verdict had been spoken aloud. "I'll say this much — there isn't a day that I don't wish I had taken advantage of the time I had been given with my mother. Before she got so bad that I had to put her in a mental hospital. Heck, even after that. I could have visited more, made her more part of my life — even if she barely responded — I could have had memories with her during the milestones of the little time I had left before being cursed. And these people fight each other for generations. This feud is robbing these families, wasting their precious time. That's not something they'll ever get back." He paused. Then cocked his head. "Hey, are you even bothering to listen to me?"

But Max typed fast as his fingers attempted to keep pace with his leaping mind. "I heard you," he said in a vague tone. "Some of it. The important part."

"It was all important."

"Yeah, yeah, but one part gave me an idea."

Drummond swished over to peer at the computer. "A birth

certificate?"

"Look at the name."

"Mary Westra? Don't recall that name coming up. Who is she?"

"She's the key to everything." Max snatched up his phone and called Brenda. "We need your help." After explaining what he wanted done and answering a barrage of questions, he then called Sandra. "I found it. How fast can you witches be ready?"

Before driving out to Olin, Max wanted to check on his mother. Her eyesight had still not fully returned, leaving J with the burden of taking care of her. He had outperformed what had been called of him. But at the same time, J needed to get back to school and to socialize with his peers. Max assured him that after tonight, their lives would return to normal — at least, normal for The Porter Agency.

Dr. Rodriguez promised to release Mrs. Porter once her eyesight had recovered enough for her to function with limited aid. Mrs. Porter was not happy. For once, Max was in total agreement with his mother. Not that he doubted the importance of the doctor's order, but he thought his mother would be safer in a more controlled environment.

Max chuckled. He had no doubt that was the exact same thought Dr. Rodriguez had. Only the doctor thought of a controlled environment from a medical standpoint, and Max thought of it from a magical one.

At the hospital, the visit went as smooth as sandpaper on a porcupine's back. One moment, Mrs. Porter would say, "You're such a good son for visiting me." The next moment, she would hurl off with, "What have you been doing to get me out of here? Nothing, apparently." Or even the more direct, "You don't love me. You never have."

Max surreptitiously watched the wall clock. He needed to have enough time to drive through the city, pick up Sandra, and head out to Olin. Somewhere along that way, Drummond would join them. He didn't blame the ghost for not being at the hospital again — not with all the dead around.

At one point, J took advantage of Max's presence so that he could grab a bite by himself and use the restroom. Alone with his mother, Max tried to say consoling things, little nonsense promises people made in hospitals to help with their loved one's morale. None of that worked. If J had said the same things, she probably would have listened. Max marveled at how deeply J loved his grandmother, and she clearly loved him equally. Reminding himself that he should not get jealous, that all sons have different relationships than grandsons, that it was inevitable, he tried to stay present, stay focused.

At length, he settled on a version of the truth. "When all this started, I promised you I would fix it. Sandra and I have been working hard on that, and I think tonight your problem with Granny Witch will be gone."

She reached out towards him, flailing her arm about — far more than necessary considering she had recovered a significant portion of her eyesight already. "Thank you. I'm sorry I ever spoke to that granny woman."

"It's okay. Just don't go making any witch deals again."

She hesitated, then winced as if anticipating a painful shot. "About that. I know I said some upsetting things, some strange things, and I want you to know that you can ignore it all."

It was Max's turn to hesitate. "What?"

"You can't believe anything I said then. They had me on so many painkillers, and I don't do drugs, you know that. I barely drink. So, you can't honestly believe what came out of my mouth. I don't even remember most of what I said, but I'm sure it was nonsense."

Max patted her hand before placing it gently on the bed. "Sure. I understand."

"Good. I wouldn't want you thinking anything bad of your father."

"Don't worry. I assumed it was the drugs talking. Anyway, I've got to go now. I love you."

Chapter 24

THE AFTERNOON SUN DESCENDED toward evening though hours needed to pass before dark could take over. The blazing day pretended to offer a cool night, yet the temperature would never drop enough to suffice. Standing outside the Vellmer house, across the street and in front of their vehicles, Max, Sandra, Drummond, Granny Witch, Billy, and Luke waited.

From the moment Max had called, Sandra pestered him for answers, but he asked that she concentrate on the spells and not worry about the rest. She did not like that. Drummond told her that he shared in her frustration; however, in this case, he had to back up Max.

"In my day," he had said while they drove out to Olin, "during the war, the idea was *loose lips sink ships*. I think Max is trying to make sure the Westras don't find out whatever he's learned. You and I can't slip up if we don't know anything."

All of that was true, but for Max, one other aspect kept him from sharing what he had learned — he wasn't sure. Not fully. He had discovered the piece of lineage that mattered — that information he knew to be true — but how it reverberated through this feud, he could only guess. Still, Max was a good guesser. Part of what made him good at research. That talent didn't reduce the risk, the gamble, in returning to the Vellmer house prematurely, yet he had enough faith that his team could handle it. Besides, if Sandra and Granny Witch lacked the proper amount of time to prepare every spell they wanted, that meant Callie also lacked the time. She only got the better of Sandra earlier out of surprise. Had they known Callie's true identity, she would never have come close to Sandra. Not without suffering a curse or two.

Drummond inclined toward Max. "Is your plan that we stand

out here admiring their house until somebody comes out, or are we getting on with this?"

"Everybody ready?" Max asked.

Sandra and Luke stood taller, Granny Witch Westra's grip tightened on her cane, and Billy shouldered a bag of casting materials. Ready as much as could be expected. Max took one step to cross the street when the front door opened. Wyatt Vellmer emerged wearing black jeans, black shoes, and a black shirt. Witch symbols had been painted white in vertical lines down his shirt. His serious expression, his tense posture, and his firm stride finished the grim picture. He had come to battle. Ready for war.

Heat pulsed off the pavement. The smell of hot tar blended with the earthy fragrances of the fields and forest. Each step closer to the edge of the Vellmer property strengthened the aromas. Maybe it was an illusion brought on by stress or maybe an act of witchcraft. Either way, part of Max wanted to turn back. He kept picturing Callie's ghostly appearance in his office, the twisted look of pleasure as she strangled him.

Wyatt moved like a hunter that had already bagged his prey, and as he came closer, Max understood why. Not only did he have the symbols painted on his clothing, but around his neck and both wrists he wore pendants made by his wife.

Max angled toward Sandra. "Can you tell what those do?"

"The one around his neck is basic protection. Probably big enough to keep us from reaching the house. Around his wrists — those look like strength enhancers."

"Witchcraft steroids?"

"More or less. They've been expecting us, and Wyatt is meant to stop the Westra brothers, in particular."

Together, Max and Sandra crossed the street and halted before stepping onto the Vellmer land. Waving his hand, Max put on a broad smile. "Good to see you again."

Wyatt stopped a few feet from the edge of the road. His protection pendant created an energy that Max could feel pushing against him. Warm and tingling like standing next to a generator. Sandra had cast similar spells in the past, but those spells had always created the barrier to protect them. It was strange to be on the other side of one.

"Thought you might have changed your mind." Wyatt jutted his chin at the Westra brothers in the back. "But you wouldn't be here with them if that were the case."

"What can I say? Their offer was better."

Wyatt's cheek twitched. "I doubt that. But I wouldn't trust anything they said anyway. Westras are proven liars."

"That's probably true. Then again, the same could be said about the Dun family."

"Now hold on —"

Max put up his hand. "Relax. I'm not trying to pick a fight."

"Then what are you doing here?"

"If we wanted to fight, we would have all come across the road together. But the fact is that my wife and I are here to make our own offer to you and Callie."

Wyatt kicked at the dirt and chuckled. "I've got to admit that is the last thing I thought you'd be saying." He folded his arms and snickered again. "Okay, Mr. Porter. Let's hear it. What's your grand offer?"

"Simple. Stop all this now. Sell the house, move away, give up this idea of winning the witch war and taking over control of magic."

"Is that all? And what do we get in return?"

Sandra raised her head so that Wyatt got a clear view of the power behind her eyes. "You get to stay together. She gets to continue being a witch. And neither of you risks losing your life tonight."

Squinting, as if truly debating the offer, Wyatt said, "Nah, I think I'm not going to accept that. In fact, I think you should turn around and leave before all this friendliness turns into something else."

Max and Sandra did the first half. They turned around and walked back toward their car. But they wouldn't be leaving. Wyatt had to know that.

Whirling back, Max pointed with exasperation. "What's wrong with you? Your wife is in a weakened state from attacking me, you're outnumbered, and you haven't been able to open that door in all the days since we've known you. Since before that, really. Are you so blind that you can't see you've already lost?"

Calm and cocky, Wyatt tossed a goodbye wave. "Thanks for the visit. Please don't bother coming back."

Max turned to his wife. "I didn't expect him to take our offer, especially the way we presented it, but I figured he might counter with something reasonable."

"Why would he?" Drummond said as they reached the car.

"Because his wife came to me with an unreasonable offer, and I returned with our own unreasonable offer. The next logical step is to stop posturing and start talking with common sense."

Sandra said, "Honey, they were never going to talk this out with us. They are too far gone for that."

She walked over to the Westras.

"This is it," Drummond said. "I understand why you tried, why you felt you had to try, but you knew the chances of it working were slim."

Max nodded. "With Callie, I figured the chances were nothing. But Wyatt's not a witch. He doesn't have any power. I guess I hoped too much from him."

"The man loves his wife. You'd stand by Sandra to your death. So will he with Callie."

"It's just so stupid. Such a waste."

Drummond gave Max a long look. "Is this because you visited your mother today?"

"What? No."

"I think it is. Before you left to visit her, you were locked and loaded, ready to rumble with these people. One visit to your mother, and suddenly you're trying to find a different solution. What did she say?"

"Nothing. Not anything about this. She wouldn't even admit to what she had said before. She denied knowing about ghost and witches."

"Not surprising."

Max glanced back at Wyatt. "He's denying reality, too. Just a different one."

"I know we've got the numbers, but let's not sing our praises until we've actually won. Callie has been getting stronger at a rate fast enough that Granny Witch and Sandra have both noted it. She won't be a pushover."

Max leaned back against the car and watched as Sandra and the Westras crossed to the Vellmer property. Nothing Max could do for the moment but wait.

Sandra and Granny Witch led the way with Billy and Luke towering a few steps behind. Max hated that he could not be next to his wife, that he had to trust the Westras, but Sandra had devised this part of the plan. He would honor it. If only Wyatt Vellmer had not come outside, this part wouldn't have been necessary.

No point in worrying. Wyatt did come out and made it clear that he intended to thwart every effort to reach his wife. In the end, that's what this night would be about. Wives versus each other. Families versus each other. Witches versus each other.

"Last chance," Sandra called out, and Max warmed. She had said those words, gave one final opportunity to end this peacefully, for him.

Wyatt replied with a vulgar gesture. He then set one foot back, bracing his stance as if holding a pike and expecting to repel a cavalry charge. But no charge came.

Billy and Luke spread to either side of the witches and passed small objects amongst them. From his view at the car, Max could not see what they looked like, but he knew exactly what they were — witchballs. Little globs of dirt and twigs combined with bones, sinew, muscle, and organs from small animals like birds and rodents. Max pictured Sandra and Granny Witch standing over a bowl of this mixture rolling out these mini-bombs like two generations rolling out meatballs. They chatted casually, placing each deadly spell upon the witchball before setting it on a kitchen rack to dry. Granny would stop Sandra to adjust her technique, patiently teaching the art that had been handed down from witch to witch. Sandra would make another ball and present it for inspection. Eventually, they both worked in a synchronized dance, relaxed and pleased with their results.

Wyatt said something that Max could not decipher from a distance, but Granny Witch did not bother to hear anything more from their opponent. She tossed the first witchball.

Chapter 25

WHEN THE WITCHBALL STRUCK Wyatt's protective barrier, blue flames burst from its muddy core with a distinct sizzle and streamed along the air like burning alcohol. They lasted a second before extinguishing. No trace of the witchball remained, though an odor like firecrackers lingered. Wyatt looked disappointed. He had prepared for a massive fight, a challenge to his wife's greatness, and only received a pitiful sputtering of magic.

But Granny Witch was not deterred. She gestured towards Billy, and the large man adjusted his position so that he stood sideways with his left shoulder facing Wyatt like a pitcher facing off a batter in a baseball game. And like a pitcher, Billy wound up, leaned back, and took one exaggerated step in the air. When his foot came down, his arm windmilled forward, and he released another witchball.

It slammed into the barrier with a drumbeat thump. As the blue flames spread across, sizzling in five directions like arms of a starfish, Wyatt staggered back. His arrogant grin faltered.

Luke jumped into the action, heaving a witchball at the barrier, and Sandra followed up with a throw. One by one in rapid succession, the team flung their witchballs creating a blue-flame fireworks display upon the protection barrier. The constant barrage continued to push Wyatt further onto the grass, and the team followed.

Billy and Luke put all their muscle behind each throw. Sandra opted for a more strategic approach, aiming each witchball at the locations that dissipated the flames slowest — the points that had weakened. Granny Witch, however, tossed out witchballs with barely a noticeable movement. Max guessed this came from practice — a witch using these projectiles in a small town had to do so without anybody noticing.

"You think that thing can last?" Max asked Drummond.

"They didn't have a lot of time to create the pendant. I'm guessing it won't be long."

Good, Max thought. The blazing sun had gone away, but the heat had not.

"You know what really gets me?" Drummond said as they watched witchball after witchball burn away, the air stinking with sizzling smoke. "Back when we started, nobody knew anything about us. Now, every witch in the state has heard of The Porter Agency, and they all know a ghost is part of the team. Seems like everybody's wearing a ghost ward."

"The price of your fame." Max gestured toward Wyatt. "At least, making a ghost ward takes time and effort. Not something they can throw together last minute."

"We can hope."

Billy finally took notice of Sandra's approach and its effectiveness — the weak spot she had focused on stopped cooling down; it now glowed a soft red. He whispered something to his Granny, and she placed four witchballs in his large hand. Bellowing an animalistic noise, he slammed his palm on the weak spot. And he held his hand there. Yelling as the flames burned between his fingers, his face turned red, but a moment later his hand slipped through the barrier. Knocked him right off balance.

Wyatt jumped back to avoid Billy's thick fingers. In one smooth motion, he removed his necklace and tossed it on the ground — out of Billy's reach.

"I'll see you inside," Wyatt said as he strolled to the front porch.

Sandra looked back at Max and raised her index finger. He nodded. He pushed off the car and turned toward the trunk.

"Guess we're up," he said.

Drummond swished around behind him. "Hold your horses. Wait until they're in the house. If Wyatt or Callie are watching you, the whole thing gets ruined."

With a huff, Max hopped onto the trunk. "Fine. You're right. Also —" he hopped off. "— that thing is burning hot."

Billy and Luke made quick work of expanding the hole of the

barrier. Within three minutes, they had a space large enough to fit through. Sandra entered first. She went straight to the pendant and stomped it into pieces. That brought down the rest of the barrier sounding like the crackle of several trees felled at once.

"Time to go now?" Max asked.

Drummond didn't bother looking at his partner. "I know you're anxious. I'm guessing part of you thinks we could stop this before Sandra has to even go in that house, but that's not the plan. We wait until all four of them are inside."

"I think they want to use all those witchballs and trinkets they put together. If we went —"

"If we do anything, we give up the entire plan. They are the diversion. Let them do their job and divert."

Max folded his arms and pouted, but he held still. At least, the Westra brothers had the decency to enter the house first. Once all four crossed the threshold and the front door closed, Max looked to Drummond like a dog waiting to hear the question *you want to go for a walk?*

Drummond paused as he scanned the front of the house. Finally satisfied, he nodded.

Max popped the trunk and pulled out a shovel. Next, he shouldered a backpack. "Let's go."

Keeping close to the property line, he scurried along the right side of the house, heading toward the back. Drummond floated ahead — turned around to face Max — so that he could keep an eye on the windows of the house. If anybody took notice of Max moving through the backyard, Drummond would find out.

From the sound of banging and grunting through the walls, Max didn't think it would be necessary. He guessed that Wyatt, strengthened by the pendants on his wrists, brawled with Billy or Luke or both. Hopefully, Sandra and Granny Witch had the sense to keep their distance. If they all acted as planned, the witches would draw a casting circle on the floor at the front door while the men tussled in the living room. This would hopefully draw Callie's attention. They all agreed that Callie would either be preparing more defensive measures or actively working on the spell locks.

"All a diversion," Max said, panting the words as he cleared the house. Pushing faster, he cut through the thick evening heat, angling toward the back of the property. "How are we doing?"

Drummond said, "All clear."

To stop Callie and the Dun family, they needed to destroy the source of power — namely, Gil Dun. While planning out their strategy, Max had revealed to the Westras that he had found Gil's gravestone in the back. His brother, Dale Dun, probably buried him on the spot where the original house had been. At some point, one of the Dun witches realized the power in those old bones. Gil's remains were then exhumed and placed in the end of the hall. The door was put in, the spell locks cast, and the Duns personal witchcraft battery had been created.

According to Sandra and Granny Witch, Max had to go back to the grave, dig up the casket, open it, and perform a simple spell — simple enough that he could do it — which would call back Gil Dun's soul. Once he returned to the site of the grave, Drummond would try to get him to move on. If he refused, then it was up to the Westras and Sandra to open the door, acquire Gil's remains, and bring them to the grave. At that point, they would have plenty of witchcrafting options to force the ghost to rest.

When Max finally reached the tall, dead grass fringing the forest, his shirt stank of sweat and failing deodorant. He slipped into the shadows of the trees, away from view of the house, and approached the decaying tombstone. If not for that carved rock, nobody would have known a man had been buried there.

Drummond swept through the trees, stopping directly in front of the tombstone. "Couldn't tell for sure last time, but I can see the faded letters better now — well, now that I know what it was meant to be."

Max came up next to the ghost. The *G* and the *I* had become ghosts themselves, barely indents against the weathered stone. Still, knowing the man's name, Max could see *GIL DUN* clear enough.

He let the shoulder bag slip to the ground and thrust the shovel in the dirt nearby. From his pocket, he retrieved a folded paper. Sandra had written detailed instructions. At the time, he had insisted that she merely tell him what he needed to do.

"Plenty of old ladies recall dozens, if not hundreds, of spells. I think I can remember one."

She touched his cheek, and with a look that screamed *Bless your heart*, she said, "I'm sure you can, but I'll write it down for you, too. Just in case."

He hated admitting failures of his mind, but she had been right. He had forgotten half of the details already. It had all been there moments earlier, leaning against the car, watching Wyatt get pushed back into the house. Yet now, after traversing the Vellmer property and reaching the tombstone, much of what he should have remembered disappeared.

"This place has power," he whispered.

"I feel it, too," Drummond said.

Allowing a single shaking of his torso, Max then rustled through the bag. He had four candles — two black, two white — and alternated placing them clockwise on the corners of the grave. With all the overgrowth, he had to estimate the size, but Sandra promised it did not need to be exact. Close, but not exact.

He lit the candles, and a soft breeze rose. Sandra had not mentioned that, so Max decided it probably was nature being natural. It felt good, too. Out of the forest, a breeze would simply push the stifling air around, turning the baking heat into a rotisserie. But in the forest, even the mere feet within that Max had gone, the breeze pushed across the shadows and leaves and bark, cooling — only slightly — but cooling nonetheless.

It eased Max's pounding heart. A little.

From the paper, he read off three long sentences. Thankfully, Sandra had written the words phonetically. They meant nothing to him, came from no language he understood, and felt hard upon his tongue. Dangerous, too. He had heard many witch languages over the years, and none of them ever felt pleasant to the ear. But in his mouth, these words left a sharp sting like alcohol on an open wound.

After completing the third sentence, Max picked up the shovel. "Hey, before I put in all this work, will you do me a favor and go check down there?"

"What for? You need the casket for the spell, and frankly, it isn't pleasant travelling through grave dirt. There's a reason ghosts don't go swimming in the ground of a cemetery."

"*Swimming in the ground?* You do that?"

"We can talk about that one later."

"Look, I just want you to make sure the casket is where I laid out the candles. Remember Graveyard Island? There were lots of gravestones and some did not line up properly with the bodies. Gil Dun was buried down there almost a hundred-and-fifty years ago and dug up at one point. If the stone fell over or was repositioned for any reason —"

"Okay, okay, I get it. You don't want to strain your muscles digging, only to find the casket is a little to the left."

"No. I don't want to waste time digging in the wrong place while Sandra is fighting for us in that house."

"Sure. Because you're so used to manual labor."

"What are you —"

Drummond lowered into the ground. "I'm on it. For Sandra, not you."

Once the ghost disappeared, Max muttered, "Like usual."

Only a few seconds later, Drummond returned. "We've got a problem."

"Yeah?"

"Gil Dun is down there. I'm assuming it's him. There's a skeleton dressed in the clothes of a man from the 1800s. I checked the lid, too. Nothing to suggest it had been pried open."

Max smacked the side of his head. "We're stupid."

"Speak for yourself."

"Of course, that's Gil Dun. The corpse that's been used for over a century had to provide a boost to magic energy for the Dun family. Well, Granny Witch has made it abundantly clear that the Dun witches never had much power. They required that boost to stay strong. Why would they get that from another Dun. And a man, at that. What they needed was the energy from a powerful witch."

Drummond clapped his hands once. "Like a Westra. Like

Rosie Mae. I'll bet that we'll find her remains behind that door in the house."

"Oh, crap. Sandra and the Westras think they're a diversion, but we can't stop anything from here."

Grabbing the shovel, Max hurried out of the woods. When he hit the tree line, he halted, his heart hammering as he saw the clouds blacken. "Oh crap, crap, crap."

"It's Callie," Drummond said, pointing to the house.

Gazing out a window, Callie raised her middle finger. Max didn't bother returning the gesture. No time. The gathering storm rushed a heavy rain as lightning streaked across the sky.

No. Not across the sky. Only above the house.

"Max, hold onto something." The shocked fright in Drummond's voice pulled Max's eyes toward the side they had walked up to reach the forest.

A clear, early-evening sky with a half-moon could be seen on the other side of the property line. But on the Vellmer side, a storm raged. Thunder cracked. The wind picked up.

And it started to spin.

"Is that?"

Max couldn't get anything else out. A noise loud as a runaway freight train rumbled from the ground as the spinning air pulled dirt and stone, tree limbs and leaves. The rain pelted his face, hitting from the side. All that spinning debris formed a funnel from the roiling clouds to the shaking ground.

A tornado.

Chapter 26

GROWING UP IN MICHIGAN, Max had experienced several hurricanes, two blizzards, hailstorms, and torrential rains. He heard about tornadoes touching ground in nearby towns, but nothing bad ever happened. No damage. No deaths. Just a grazing of the earth. He had seen the devastation twisters had wrought in other states, too, but he had never seen one himself. Never experienced one. And since this one had been created through witchcraft, he wondered if it was unique in its horror or if all tornadoes terrified the living as greatly.

Max stood rooted to the forest floor. He watched the storm widen as it moved over the yard. It slowed, holding between the forest and the house. An unnaturally summoned bit of nature turned into a blockade.

The sheer volume of noise would quell most brave people. The wind howled, shrieked, roared, and screamed all at once as if a hundred animals fought in a giant war of the forest. Trees splintered and cracked. Metal whined as it bent in directions it did not wish to go. And dancing between all these thunderous sounds, Max heard the gentle tinkling of glass shards by the thousands. A soft song spinning ever higher into the air.

But more than the racket of destruction, the wind itself petrified the heart. Max had known fear. Plenty of it. In his line of work, fear was a prerequisite. But this — the same wind that cooled a body, that scented the air, that played with a balloon, or flickered a campfire now whipped against the world with a giant's strength and a child's mindless tantrum.

"Max!" Drummond floated into view. "Get out of here!"

But Max had nowhere to go. If he ran deeper into the forest, he knew the tornado would follow him. If he aimed to the sides, off the property, the windy beast would snatch him from the ground and pummel him back to where he stood. If he tried to reach the house, to reach Sandra, it would slam him against the grassy ground, smash his head into the dirt and rock and mud, break his bones, and hold him there until he died. This storm had witchcraft behind it — Callie's witchcraft — and that meant it had an agenda.

A ferocious gust shoved Max several feet as if to make its point. But that also made Drummond's point. He couldn't simply stand at the forest edge and watch a tornado conjured to destroy him.

Time. That's what he needed. Not for him, though. For Sandra.

Max wrapped his arms around the nearest tree that wasn't too big but also looked sturdy, looked well-rooted. This storm couldn't last forever — well, technically it could last as long as Callie lived, but it required her attention, her focus, her energy. The longer the tornado raged, the more chances Sandra and the Westras had to alter their tactic from a diversion to an offensive. They didn't need to figure out that Rosie Mae's bones were behind that door. They only needed to break the spell locks and grab those bones.

"Hold on," Drummond yelled. "I'll find something to help."

The spiraling winds shot around, blasting Max with dust like needles into his arms. He tucked his face low, but that offered limited protection. Squinting, he tried to reposition so that he faced the house, but his fingers slipped, the racing air took hold, and he flipped to the ground, pushed by fierce winds, spun like a tire, until he bashed sideways against another tree. Little stones ripped everywhere along his skin, stinging like hundreds of papercuts.

"Max?" Drummond called out. "Where are you?"

Max tried to respond, but the moment he opened his mouth, he inhaled particles of debris. Coughing and spitting, he cried out a long moan — the best his brutalized body could manage.

Pale dots like moonlight pushed through the breakneck winds. Drummond appeared, instinctually ducking his head against the storm though none of it could touch him. Hovering low beside Max, the ghost said, "I checked in the house. The spell for this tornado is huge. Takes up most of the bedroom floor. Callie must have had it ready to go."

"Of course," Max shouted. "She knew all about this."

"She's got that spell going and another one to fight off Sandra and Granny Witch. They're at a stalemate right now. I couldn't see a ghost ward on Callie, and I didn't feel one. That's good. If I can figure out how to get to her, I can break this spell."

"What's the problem?" Max spit out more dirt that flew into his mouth.

"Wyatt can see me. He's busy fighting, he's already knocked out Luke. Just him and Billy now. I'm guessing whatever pendant he has giving him strength, he has another giving him a lot of stamina. Even as he's fighting, he still had the presence of mind to warn Callie when he saw me."

"So, what then? I get to hang out here and hope I don't die?"

"I'll go back and do everything I can to stop the spell. But I can't guarantee I'm going to succeed. You do whatever you can to survive. So, yeah, hang tight and don't die."

Despite the attempt at humor, Drummond's brow pulled down in grim acceptance. They held a look as if to say goodbye without uttering the words. Max marveled at the ability for human beings to pack a lifetime into one short nod.

With that, Drummond disappeared. Max closed his eyes and counted to ten. He focused on the numbers, trying to clear his mind of all the panicked thoughts threatening to overwhelm him. To survive a dire situation, he knew he had to pour his attention into the next step and the next and the next. Don't worry about tomorrow. Don't worry about consequences. Don't worry about anything but the next moment in front of him.

He opened his eyes. First thing he saw — his shovel. The winds had blown the blade into a thick oak tree where it got stuck.

Uttering a groan, Max crawled against the storm until he reached the big tree. The winds pushed him against the bark, attempting to force him through the trunk. Fighting for each motion, he reached down, gripped the shovel, wrenched it free, and dropped forward, flattening against the ground.

He wanted to take three deep breaths but didn't dare open his mouth that wide. So, three shallow ones. Stay focused. On the third, he vaulted to his feet, darting out of the forest and across the grass. As he felt the spiraling whirlwinds attempt to pluck him from the ground, he thrust the shovel into the dirt and held on with a white-knuckled grip. If the tornado wanted to chuck him high, it would have little trouble freeing him from the shovel, but if it simply blew him forward, he could maintain his position.

He didn't expect the tornado to do both.

Dragging him away from the shovel as if it held onto his ankle, the storm howled. It yanked him loose. Not only did the shovel fail to anchor him, but now he worried the flying tool might become a threat. The storm raised him into the air — only a few feet — and dropped him, his body rolling across the grass.

Max tried to get up several times, but the winds kept knocking him down and over. He felt like a mugger had taken him by surprise and wouldn't let him stand. Blood coated his tongue.

The fourth time, however, the blasting wind hit softer. The storm's hold on him had dwindled, and he pushed up to his knees. To the side, he saw the neighboring property — calm, serene, untouched. Did the storm's strength weaken the closer to the edge of the property? Lunging towards the property line, he felt the tornado snake around him. He pushed harder, but the tornado — however reduced — still had more strength than a single man ever could. It jerked him in one direction, in another, and then into its vortex. Max curled into a ball, afraid to let his limbs flail about — breaking bones would not be helpful to anybody.

The tempest tossed him to the ground, bowling him like a toy for its amusement. When he came to a stop, he understood how apt that word fit — *amusement*. This storm did not behave like he imagined the tornado that had ripped through Olin and destroyed Gil Dun. This storm did not behave like any natural occurrence diverted by magic and finding its way through its otherwise normal course. No, this storm had been created to play with Max, to hurt him but not kill him, to keep him occupied and confused and unable to aid those inside. Callie might as well have conjured a forty-foot golem that could juggle him from one hand to the other.

As if his thoughts had cast a spell of their own, the wailing cries sputtered into silence. The debris that pelted his body now pelted the ground. Max lifted his head from beneath his arms and watched as the whipping winds dissipated into a quiet, cloudless, moonlit night. The heat returned with a vengeance, and sweat beaded upon his body in response. A thousand new stings assaulted him as his salt mixed with his open cuts.

One breath later, Drummond hurled out of the back wall of the house as if punched by the giant golem Max had envisioned. He soared through the air, arcing overhead, roaring in pain, until he disappeared amongst the forest trees. Sitting up, dazed, Max watched the tree line. By the time he found the energy to stand, Drummond had returned, moving slow and with effort.

"That hurt," the ghost said.

"I take it you were the one to stop her spell?"

"Bit of advice — the bigger the spell, the worse it hurts you when you break it."

Max let out one short chuckle. Then he looked at the house. "What's the situation in there?"

"Not good. The downside of breaking that spell — besides it blasting me into the woods — is that Callie no longer has to focus on it. It's still two witches against one, and I always will bet on Sandra, but I don't know how much longer this standoff can go."

"And Wyatt?"

"He knocked out Billy, too. But he's not about to get in between three angry witches. At least, not unless our side starts to win."

Walking towards the house with a slight limp, Max said, "Let's go see what we can do to help."

Drummond tipped his hat. "My thinking exactly."

Though the ghost could have swept ahead, he kept close to Max, and Max appreciated it. He wasn't entirely confident he could make it back to the house on his own. Not that Drummond could do much, but at the least, he could inform Sandra where his body fell in the end.

However, Max did not die. He managed to place one foot down, then the other, and in short order, he found he could walk. Each step forward brought with it a speck of energy, a tiny thrust of adrenaline, and a miniscule acknowledgement that he would be okay.

"Man, I hate this job somedays."

Drummond said, "Yeah, but think of all the benefits."

"What benefits?"

"I don't know, but I'm sure there are some."

By the time they reached the backdoor that led into the kitchen, Drummond's jokes and Max's recuperating body managed to bring Max to the point of functioning. He wouldn't be running a marathon anytime soon, but he could talk, he could move, and he could think. That would have to be enough.

They entered the house.

Chapter 27

From the kitchen archway, Max watched as reality smothered those flickers of hope that had sparked inside him. Callie blasted arcs of red energy across the house — reaching from where she stood at the head of the hallway, through the living room, into the entranceway at the front door, and careening into Granny Witch. The old woman had been standing inside a small casting circle, the lines of which glowed a soft blue. But Callie's attack threw Granny Witch aside, smacking her into a coat rack, and thrusting her to the knees. The casting circle dimmed into chalk lines and nothing more.

Drummond rushed through the walls to help. But the moment he appeared in the living room, Wyatt blocked the way. Drummond ignored the man. Until Wyatt threw a haymaker that landed on Drummond's flank. The ghost shouted — both in surprise and pain — as his spectral body flung to the side.

"The pendants," Max said. "They must make it so he can touch you."

"Ya think?"

Drummond lifted toward the ceiling, but Wyatt pointed at him and said, "If you interfere, I'll bash in your partner's head."

In response, Drummond lowered. Until he floated right in front of Wyatt. Then the ghost pulled the brim of his hat down. "I don't like you," he said.

Before Wyatt said another word, Drummond threw an uppercut, catching the man on the chin. Wyatt fell to the floor, rolling as the world spun around him. Drummond hissed and shook his hand. It didn't take long for Wyatt to regain his senses and return to his feet.

Drummond raised his fists. "It's been a long time since I've gotten to pummel a dirtbag human. This'll be fun."

At first Max had no idea why Drummond would engage in a fistfight in the corporeal world. But as the ghost's cold body rushed by into the kitchen and Wyatt's heat-soaked fists followed, Max understood. As long as Drummond kept Wyatt engaged, Max had full access to the witches.

Not that he had any magic or wards or witchballs or anything that would help. In fact, Max realized he would have to rely on the one skill he always had with him — his mouth. Having just stepped out of one magic storm, he had no desire to enter another. But Sandra needed him.

He could see the stress on her brow. Now that Granny Witch no longer played a part, Sandra strained from the intensity. Though she tried to hide it, her fatigue showed enough — Callie had to have noticed, too.

Max entered the living room.

Like a traffic cop he raised both hands indicating to Callie and Sandra that they should stop. Neither of them did, but he did not expect it. Rather, he simply got some morsel of their attention.

"It's over, Callie. You have my word that if you cease casting your spells, my wife will stop hers as well. You won't be harmed."

Callie never let her focus drift from Sandra. "This only ends when you give up. You turn around and leave. And when the day comes, you accept my rule over all magic here."

From the kitchen, pots clattered to the floor. Wyatt barked in pain. Good. At least Drummond could hold his own.

Max lowered his hands and faced Callie. "You are a strong witch. We can all see that. You would be better as an ally than an enemy. We've already fought against the bigger threats that face us. Put this day to rest. Let us talk like we did in the beginning when we were friendly. You can pour a tall glass of sweet tea, and we can be adults about this."

"I don't think Granny Witch or her grandsons would like what you're saying."

"This feud has been too destructive for too long. Now that there is a real witch war going on, a real feud worthy of our attention, the Westras and the Duns are wasting time and energy on some foolish love story from centuries ago."

"It's the Westras that caused it all. They could've been happy for Rosie Mae. They could've welcomed Gil as their new son. But they are so wedded to their mountain ways that they no longer think with reason or compassion for anybody else."

Behind him, Sandra said, "We have plenty of compassion."

He heard the dark rumble in her voice and knew he had given her all the time she needed. He had become the diversion, and relying upon the connection between a couple married for years, he knew his wife understood what he had attempted.

Max dropped to the floor.

Two pillars of light careened into each other, sending sparks off in all directions. Covering his head, Max crawled beneath the fierce battle of magic. Once free from under the spells, he scrambled to one wall, pressed his back against it, and watched Sandra and Callie. The houselights dimmed as all power in the area pulled into these two women. Callie ground her teeth and snarled. Sandra widened her gaze and shouted.

It happened in seconds. Like gunfighters, the buildup to action lasted far longer than the event itself. Two stark white waves of smoking energy torched each witch. Both Sandra and Callie were thrown back and crumpled against the first walls they hit.

Max rushed to Sandra's side. He caught a glimpse of Wyatt, bruised and bleeding, as he hustled toward Callie. Drummond drifted over, moving slower, breathing hard, and grimacing as pain cycled through him.

Cradling his wife, Max looked for any visible injury, but he found nothing. She lay unconscious, so he couldn't ask her if she had internal pain.

"She better be okay," Drummond said, "or the Duns are going to find out how terrible an angry ghost can get."

From the mouth of the hallway, Wyatt held his wife and stroked her hair. "Come on, sweetie. Let me see that bright as day smile."

Her head lolled to the side, but Max caught her eyes flutter. He looked down at Sandra. "Hon, wake up." Kissing her brow, he snatched another peek at Callie. That witch let out a groggy groan. To Sandra: "We need you."

A few feet away, Billy stirred, but his attention turned straight to his granny and then Luke. Max gave Sandra a shake.

Drummond said, "Don't hurt her."

"If she doesn't get up, what are we supposed to do?"

"If you keep shaking her, she won't ever get up."

Max withdrew from holding Sandra and eased her onto the floor. Standing, he checked across the room. Wyatt had Callie sitting up, though she still appeared disoriented. With a head motion, Max suggested Drummond lend a helping, frosty hand.

Drummond frowned. "I don't know if I can take another hit of the physical world tonight."

"You're doing it for Sandra."

The ghost gazed down at her. "Of course."

He floated through the living room, rubbing his hand as if anticipating the torment that would come when he plunged it into Callie's head and froze her into unconsciousness. But when he neared, Wyatt vaulted to his feet, glowering as he raised his fists.

"Back off, ghost. I only fought you to let my wife cast her spells. You come any closer, and you'll fight a man protecting his wife, defending her. That's a whole different matter."

"Aw, my love," Callie said, using Wyatt as a crutch until she could stand. "That might be the most charming thing I ever heard you say." Her hand glowed softly — a fast spell she had prepared hours ago.

Drifting back, Drummond's lip lifted in a sneer. To Max: "You better get Sandra awake."

But as Max dropped to his wife's side, Callie stepped closer. She rolled back her shoulders and crackled her neck from side to side. Clearly unsteady but full of anger, her severe line of a mouth rose into a morose grin.

"You have all failed. The Dun family is the winner today, and we will be the winners tomorrow, too. You will bow to our future rule, and you might as well start now. Billy Westra, you can be first. You are going to lower your head and say that this feud is over, that the Westras submit to the Duns, and that you will obey me as the leader of all magic." When Billy did not move, she added: "Or I can kill your dear granny in a most unpleasant manner."

Max nudged Sandra, put his ear close to hear breathing, touched her neck to check her pulse. She lived but showed no indication of waking soon. As Callie moved in, Billy bowed his head — not in obedience or subservience, but rather in acceptance. Max saw a man who refused to be ruled by another and accepted death as the result.

"A waste and a shame," Callie said. "But I do praise you for the loyalty to your family. Not enough of that these days."

In all the commotion, Max never heard the truck arrive — nobody did — but when the front door opened and Brenda Byrd entered, Max knew the situation had changed. Not because of Brenda herself, but because Brenda would only have shown up if she had succeeded in her assigned mission. Max knew who would follow in her wake.

Long thin legs and jeans stepped into the house. A salty beard covered an angular face, and stern eyes locked onto the scene with clarity and concern. "Callie Anne Dun Vellmer, what the heck do you think you're up to?"

Her eyes drifted to the man. She dropped her hand to her side. Her mouth forming a small hole as her brow quivered.

"Uncle Monty?"

Chapter 28

As Montgomery Dun entered the living room, Callie inched back. He wore a ratty denim jacket, and when he removed it, he revealed dozens of pendants and wards wrapped around his forearms from wrist to elbow like ancient bracers. Eight necklaces surrounded his neck.

"I suggest we sit down and have a proper talk," Monty said, the cigarette scrape in his voice deep and rich.

Wyatt growled as he stomped forward. "You get out of my house."

He threw a pendant-enhanced punch, but it never landed. Wyatt's fist smashed into a barrier around Monty.

Scowling, Monty said, "Look at me, you fool. I'm prepared for anything."

Cupping his hand, Wyatt slunk back toward his wife. It looked to Max like the man sought another attack, but Callie put out her hands and flashed a cheerful smile. "Why Uncle Monty, it's so wonderful for you to visit. Have a seat. Would you like some sweet tea on this hot night?"

"That would be kind of you."

"Anything for family."

As Monty lowered to the couch and waited for Callie to return from the kitchen, Brenda found a spot on the floor next to Max, pressed her hands on Sandra's shoulder, and closed her eyes. "I'm still a beginner, but considering our line of work, your wife figured I should know some witchcraft first aid."

"She's smart like that." Max edged out of the way to let Brenda do whatever healing she could accomplish.

"You're not too dumb yourself. It took hardly any convincing to get Mr. Montgomery out here. All I had to do was mention that name you gave me, and he couldn't move fast enough."

Max rested his head against the wall. He watched Callie serve the sweet tea much like she had when he first visited her. She patted the empty chair for Wyatt to join and waited for him to get the message. Once he sat, she perked straight up, crossed her legs, and continued to flash her fake smile — fighting off great discomfort with a grin.

"I'd introduce you to our other guests," Callie said, gesturing to the half-unconscious crew sprawled in the entranceway and along the edge of the living room, "but I imagine you already know them all."

"I do." Monty scratched his beard as he thought. "I'd say I know a whole lot more than you do about what's what around here."

"Is that a fact?"

"Callie Anne, Wyatt — let me be plain spoken."

"It's the only way you should ever be."

Monty grimaced like he swallowed milk gone bad. "You keep smiling at me like that, your cheeks are going to break."

As if slapped, Callie's cheeks reddened. She stopped smiling. "I'm trying to be polite."

"I appreciate that. I do. But what you're doing here, what you've already done, goes beyond all that. There's no more room for being cordial. What you need now is a hard dose of the truth."

Her right hand started to glow. "I don't like the way you're talking."

Monty jangled one ward covered arm. "Are you as stupid as your husband? I came in here completely prepared for you. My mother made all these, and she had me put them away in a safe spot, never to be used, until this day came."

"You saying she could see the future?"

"Not by witchcraft. But she knew things. She listened to the world well, and she heard what the winds had to say. She knew somebody would want to get into this house, would want to break through that door in the hallway. So, she made me its guardian."

Wyatt said, "Except this house ain't yours anymore."

Under Brenda's watchful administrations, Sandra stirred awake. Max kissed his wife, and she patted his chest. He mouthed *Thank you* to Brenda before turning back to the Dun family reunion.

Monty chuckled without any humor. "That was one of the sneakiest, lowest things ever done to me. Stealing my house right from under. If you hadn't been family, I might have seen it coming. But it never occurred to me that another Dun would try to hurt me."

"Oh, you know it wasn't like that," Callie said. "I love you. But there was no way you were going to give me access to that door. You're a bit old school when it comes to our power. I don't mean that to be offensive — merely honest. You see, Wyatt and I have been trying to move the Duns forward. Our family has the greatest opportunity right now to take hold of magic, force all witches to work through us."

"That door doesn't exist to feed your ambitions."

"No. I know better. That door was made to protect the family, give us the power to fight off the Westras. That's why I need it. When I take the reins of power, it will not only enrich our family for generations, but it will put an end to this feud. I'll be able to destroy the Westras, hurt them hard enough that they won't ever touch a Dun again."

He shook his head — not with anger or disappointment or disagreement but with pity. "I've always believed that we should never blame the younger folks for behaving young. More, we should never criticize them for having ideas different from our own. Each generation is responsible for moving the world forward. But more than that, being angry at the next generation is plain ignorance. After all, we're the ones who raised them."

Callie hesitated. "If you're trying to scold us, I'm not understanding what you're saying."

"Not scolding you at all. I'm saying that you young folks may have a point."

Max stood. This was not his plan when he thought to bring Monty into the picture.

Drummond floated next to him. "I don't care how many

wards he's wearing. If he tries to join up against us, I'll bash him to pieces."

"But don't get too full of yourselves," Monty went on. "I know more about this house than you do — and not just because I lived here for longer."

"Does that mean you know how to open the door?" Callie clenched the bottom of her shirt.

"Of course, I know. You would too, if you hadn't stolen the house from me. If you'd waited your turn to own it, I would've shown you every little thing you need to know."

"Then show us now. We're family."

"We are. I would never deny that. And when it comes to family, the love of a family, I can tell you that there are two kinds of love that you end up dealing with. There's the love that comes in the shape of unconditional support. That's the love I'm showing you right now while making sure you and Wyatt don't end up in jail for seriously hurting these people. I won't say you were right to hurt them at all, but I'm always going to have your back."

Wyatt said, "What's the other kind?"

"That's the harder one. That's the tough love sort of thing. It's the same kind of love you show a horse when you're forced to put her down because she broke a leg. Not something you ever want to face, but when you do, it's because of love that you do it."

Max took one step forward. "He's going to betray us."

Staying close, Drummond said, "Not sure how he can do that when he never was with us in the first place."

"Because I found out that —"

Wyatt snapped his attention toward them. "Don't take another step."

But Monty waggled his arms to shake all the wards and pendants, sounding like a demented wind chime. "Oh, don't worry about anybody else here. Their witches are out of commission, and I'm fully armed against everything any of you can throw. Nothing they can do."

Drummond faced Max, frustration forming pale wrinkles.

"He probably isn't wrong."

As Wyatt sat back, keeping a watchful glower upon Max and Drummond, Callie said, "Uncle Monty, you started this saying you would speak plain, but now you're babbling on about family love, and I don't see how that matters here."

"I'm no babbler and I am speaking plain. You just aren't listening. Let me say this — you want that door opened, and I can open it. That plain enough for you?"

"I feel there is a *but* coming along here."

"Not exactly. More a question. If you push away your desire to be the leader, to rule, if you let that all go and think clearly about that door, about how it came to be and still is, the question then becomes — do you really want me to open it?"

"I absolutely want you to open it. What do you think this is all about?"

Shooting to the edge of the couch, Monty said, "You're not hearing me. You're not thinking. You still see the prize behind the door and want it so bad that you won't slow down and use the gray between your ears. Don't look at your husband or your enemies or anybody else in this room. They can't help you, most won't, and they don't know what's going on either." Monty sent a piercing sneer at Max. "Not even you."

Drummond said, "What's that mean? What do you know?"

Glancing back at Brenda, Max said, "That maybe I shouldn't have had her bring Monty here. I might've really screwed up."

"I am paying you my fullest attention." Callie uncrossed her legs, dropping all pretenses, and looked at her uncle with contrition.

Monty said, "Better. You got to understand that despite what you've done, you're still my little niece. I love you. I want you to be happy in your life."

"Opening that door, finally ending all of this Westra nonsense — that's what'll make me happy."

"I need to be sure, that's all. I need to know that you can handle what happens, that you're ready for the sacrifices that come with power."

"I'm as prepared as a witch can be." That old smile returned, but Callie dropped the act the second she realized she had started. "I've been dreaming about this my whole life. Since I was seven, at least, and I knew from back then that the only way to end a war is to destroy the enemy. Mercilessly. If you allow some other form of loss, some way to for them to lose with dignity, they'll come back one day and ruin you."

"Then this is about the Westras and not about ruling magic."

"It's always about the Westras. The other part is how I'm going to end the feud. Becoming the ruler is merely a benefit."

Monty stroked his beard, concentrated on Callie, then Max. "Since this is going to change all of us, I think everyone in this room should follow me to the hallway. Luke, too, if you can wake him. It's time we opened that door."

He stood with grim resolve, but Max couldn't tell if it was that of the criminal headed to the gallows or that of the executioner.

Chapter 29

THE PROCESSION DOWN THE SHORT HALL moved with solemn respect. All but Luke attended this event, and Luke had been propped against the kitchen archway so that he could watch — though Max imagined the man would only see everyone's backs and whatever light filtered between them. Still, the befuddled young man wanted to experience whatever small amount he could, and Max understood that much. After all, nobody stopped Monty from leading the group to the door.

Then again, nobody was in a position to do anything significant. Callie and Wyatt had no desire to interfere. Sandra, though awake and aware, required Brenda as a crutch. Billy carried Granny Witch, setting her against the section of wall opposite the bathroom door. Though Billy might have been able to find the strength for a final round of fighting, Granny Witch whispered in his ear, and that halted any further action. He stood in the bathroom, poking his head into the hall to observe. Max guessed Granny Witch recognized the futility of an assault from such a weakened point and did not want to waste the lives of her grandsons. As for Max, he knew too well when to act and when to wait. Charging in now, without any backup, would be suicide. Even Drummond couldn't help thanks to Monty's wards.

When they stopped, Monty nudged the casting circle drawn at the foot of the door. "This wasn't ever going to work."

"I had to try," Callie said.

His chest slumped — only a slight movement but enough for Max to pick up on the man's disappointment.

Callie raised her chin to stare right into Monty's eyes. "What's so bad with having ambition? You talk about it like it's such a terrible thing, but think of all the good that could be done. Our family deserves as much as we can aspire to, and I was taught to aspire high."

He placed his hands on her shoulders with affection and warmth. "Ambition is only as good as the person wielding it. Same with the power that it can lead to. My mama taught me plenty growing up. I got a better education from her than in any school. Philosophy, religion, sciences, and even witchcraft. She wanted me to know things so that I would be ready when this moment came, when I had to choose whether or not to open this door."

"You already said you'd open it. Are you changing your mind?"

Wyatt stiffened. "That ain't right."

"What I'm doing," Monty said, keeping his attention on his niece, "is offering you a chance to change *your* mind. I don't have to open the door. You could say that you've had enough. We could let all these people go home to their loved ones and forget all about what's happened this evening. You'll still grow in power from what the house can offer."

"But not the fullest extent of power it can truly provide."

"Not the fullest."

Callie playfully slapped Monty's chest. "You're a teaser. Why would I want to do any of that? I've come all this way, done all I could to get this thing opened, and you want me to change my mind? That doesn't sound like me, does it?"

He smiled with glistening eyes. "No. It certainly does not."

"Well, then, that's all settled. Open the door, and let's make this a new world."

Monty kissed Callie's forehead before motioning her back a few steps. The rest in the hall pressed forward. With Granny Witch in front of him, Max had a clear view over her head, and he could feel Sandra resting on the side of his shoulder.

He never thought defeat would be so calm. It didn't have to be. He could shout at Monty, rush forward, flail about. Drummond would help him and the witches — well, Sandra, at least — would cast whatever they had left available. But all of that would start from a weak position and it would only get weaker as they fought against wards and spells and pendants.

None of this held back Max from watching each face closely, searching for any opportunity to stop Callie. But he found nothing.

Raising his hands wide, Monty spoke with booming command. "Open sesame." He looked over his shoulder and winked. "Just kidding."

Only Callie reacted — a childish giggle — and Max realized that she had been the intended recipient of the joke. Nothing could have worried him more. When he had sent Brenda after Monty, he assumed Monty would be angry at Callie for stealing his home. Perhaps he still harbored some resentment over the act, but clearly the familial bond proved stronger. Instead of weakening Callie's position in all of this, Max had accidentally emboldened her.

He had to find some way to disrupt the proceedings. Halt it to buy time for … well, that was another problem. The back up plan had been Monty. They never had a chance to form a Plan C. Didn't matter, though. Even if such a plan existed, Max knew he had no chance of getting through the hall to reach Monty. Not only would he have to overcome Wyatt and Callie, but he would have to wrestle through Billy and Granny Witch first.

Max appraised each one to confirm his suspicions. They all wanted to see that door opened. Even Sandra gripped his arm in anticipation. The only help he could count on would come from Drummond, but that wouldn't be enough.

We are so screwed.

Monty gently lowered to his knees and placed both his hands on the door. He dropped his chin to his chest. A resonant moan like a monk in deep meditation grew from within him and rumbled upon the door.

"This could take a while," Sandra whispered.

Max shifted his gaze down at her. She was aware enough and strong enough to make a comment. That told him not only that she would be okay, but that she could still be counted on in the present. Maybe not at her best, but she hadn't been knocked out of commission. Max put his arm around her and squeezed.

Nothing more happened for a few trailing minutes. Max knew

firsthand how difficult it was for a man to cast a spell. He never understood it completely, though Sandra had explained it several times, but for whatever reasons, women tended to be more attuned to the natural world. Witchcraft manipulated that world, played with its energies, and so, witches tended to be women.

In a weird way, it made sense that Monty had been the one to hold the key to opening the door. The whole point of the door was to act as a safe, to be difficult to gain access. By entrusting the unlocking spell to a man, it meant that nobody could open the door with ease. Of course, a witch could have tortured him or used magic to get the spell from him, but only if he could explain it properly — another problem entirely. Max's experiences casting spells usually meant that he had to say things and do things he didn't understand. He doubted he could explain a spell to another, even a witch, and not botch it up.

The men in the hallway shuffled their feet. The witches watched riveted as if pulled into a great drama. Max peeked at Drummond. Though male, he was a ghost, and a ghost by nature could feel the world's energies more like a witch. Max wouldn't want to rely on Drummond casting a spell any more than himself, but he did see that Drummond's intense focus matched Sandra's. He saw something — or felt it — more than Max, Billy, Luke, or Wyatt.

The hall light sputtered. A burnt plastic odor drifted over them. While unable to feel subtle energies like a witch, Max certainly could feel major changes like this. All eyes shifted to Monty and the door.

Blue light glowed from beneath his palms. A soft hum like a whirring window fan rolled through the hall, but it did not come from Monty. He still maintained his monkish drone. No, this hum came from the door, and as the blue light spread out, the door hum grew louder.

In three rapid pulses, this light spiderwebbed in all directions across the door. In its wake, the spell revealed numerous witch symbols — some in vertical columns, some along the edge of a casting circle that dominated the center of the door. All this writing glowed in concert with the steady beat beneath Monty's shaking hands.

Each witch leaned closer. Sandra's lips moved as she read what appeared on the door. Callie's face reflected the light like a night prowler tracking her next meal under a full moon. Granny Witch closed her eyes and bowed her head — not out of reverence, Max thought, but more from defeat.

Monty set one foot forward as if preparing to propose. The same glow that pulsed under his hands spread up his wrists and then further. Jangling flashes of light in different directions, the various spells and wards wrapped around his forearms came to life. They flowed in concert with the steady rhythm, and a haphazard pattern of light brightened as several clumps of pendants began to emit their own radiance. More and more of the pendants and wards dazzled the hallway until both of Monty's forearms became too bright to look at.

A single, loud click like a shorted breaker, and all the lights went out.

They stood in the dark hall. Waiting. Listening. Only shocked and excited breaths broke the quiet.

When the hallway light flickered back on, Monty stood, his face red from the exertion, his hairline rimmed with sweat. He placed one trembling hand on the door knob.

And he opened the door.

Chapter 30

AT FIRST GLANCE, the door opened into a walk-in closet that traded clothes for books on either side and a small, tabled area in the back. But the longer Max looked, the darker the room turned. More sinister. Many of the books had the ancient tome bindings he had become familiar with over the years — most covered in animal skins; some covered in human skin. One row of books contained nothing but copies of *The Long-Lost Friend*. Long-abandoned spiderwebs dusted the ceiling corners as well as some of the space between books and shelving. Upon closer inspection, the table in the back served as an altar. Covered in melted candlewax while dried blood stained the wood in thin rivulets, it appeared diminished but not useless. Above the table, where a window had originally let in the sun's warmth, bricks blocked out the light. But more than this, all eyes drew toward the body on the floor.

Desiccated, gray skin stretched thin over the back of a woman curled upon a casting circle. Dust covered her blouse and skirt from decades gone, and her skull peeked through her sparse hair. The decayed skin on her sides hung in tatters, revealing her ribs, part of her pelvis, and the empty gap where her organs once functioned. The rest of her — the legs, the arms, the feet — all of it was nothing but bones. In a few spots, even the bones had gone, leaving behind piles of ash-like dirt.

Callie walked forward, but Monty pushed her back with one arm. "Not yet," he said. "You should know what you are looking at before you go in there."

She tried to peek beyond him, her deep hunger causing her to bounce on her feet. "Stop playing games with me."

"Be quiet and listen."

She shoved aside the arm and entered the room. Stepping

around the corpse, she ran a finger along the dusty titles on the shelves. If her triumphant smile could have grown, her skin would have torn. Breathing in the stale air as if inhaling a bright meadow, her chest puffed forward, and she arched her head back.

"It's far stronger in here than I had ever thought it could be." She sucked in more air. "Oh, Wyatt, we are going to be so much more than we thought."

"Get out of there." Monty spoke harsh enough to stun her into silence.

But then Max saw that it wasn't Monty's tone causing the sudden obedience. It was the corpse. It rose.

Staying within the casting circle, the heap of brittle bones and decomposing skin, of degrading clothes and soulless form, moved with the creaking pain of the elderly and infirm. The woman's head turned, and she wore only half the face she should have — even that was gray and hollow with death. Lacking many muscles, she finally stood hunched and twisted. The spell that animated her could do no more.

Callie's eyes grew larger as she whispered, "Rosie Mae."

But Max looked closely at Granny Witch, saw her eyes close to clamp back a tear, and he knew his research had been right. "No," he said. "That's Mary."

The corpse's one eye reacted to the name. Even the skeletal hole in the other socket seemed to know.

Callie turned back and demanded, "Who's Mary?"

Max waited for one of the others to answer. Didn't seem like it was his place. But neither of the families spoke up.

"She's your great aunt," Max finally said, drawing more than a few angry glares. "Ask Monty. That's his mother."

"How is it that your Porter Agency has succeeded all these years? Anybody can see that is Rosie Mae." Callie turned to Monty. "Right?"

In a soft, caring tone that slapped Callie hard, Monty said, "After Gil died, his brother built this house. The tornado had done more than level the old house, though. Gil had buried Rosie Mae in the back, but it had been a shallow grave. The tornado ripped her out. So, Dale buried her beneath the house. His wife was a witch, and she knew what kind of power that could create."

Mary lifted a shaking, bony hand. She lacked her ring finger and thumb. When she lowered her head and moved her jawbone in a quiet murmur, Max garnered a dark suspicion.

Sandra confirmed it. "I think she's casting a spell."

"Can you tell what it is?"

"Too much dust on the floor. And she's standing on part of it."

Monty noticed, too. "Stop, Mother. She needs to know."

Callie skirted around the circle to face Mary. "Tell me. Ignore him and tell me."

Pressing closer to Max, Brenda came up behind. "What's the old lady doing?"

Max and Sandra turned their attention towards Granny Witch. She, too, had lowered her head and murmured to herself. Crap.

Max asked his wife, "Can you do anything to stop this?"

She shook her head. He checked on Billy and Luke. Neither appeared capable nor willing to interfere. If anything, Billy held his stomach as if he might throw up. Good thing he stood near the bathroom.

"I am here to continue the Dun legacy," Callie said to the rotting corpse before her. "I'm sorry that I believed our power came from Rosie Mae. Clearly, it comes from you. You deserve our praise."

"Callie, stop it." Monty reached towards her but refused to cross into the closet. "You don't know who she is."

"Max Porter just told me. Or did he lie? Is she not my great aunt?"

"She is."

"Then what's the matter?"

"She's not a Dun."

"Of course she is. Your father was a Dun, and that makes her one, too."

"They never married. They couldn't."

"What do you mean by that? They didn't want to?"

Granny Witch took one step into the middle of the hallway, lifting her hand out towards the dead witch.

Drummond said, "I'm thinking we should get out of here."

Max said to Sandra, "I'm thinking he's right."

"They loved each other," Monty said, his voice breaking. "Spent all their time together. They wanted to be husband and wife. Build a real family with me. But they weren't allowed."

Callie's face wrinkled. "Were they siblings?"

"No. Not anything like that. You're not thinking clear."

"Then tell me."

Granny Witch lifted her head. "Westras are not allowed to marry Duns. Her name is Mary Westra, and she is my sister."

Mary's head snapped up, her face blazing with rage as her jaw dropped wide. A horrid screech emanated from deep within her. Bypassing her throat and echoing out of the room, the shrieking slammed down the hall like a subway train braking hard but moving too fast to stop.

All but Granny Witch dropped to the floor. They clasped their ears as the attack splashed over them.

When no further attack came, Max pushed up and helped Brenda and Sandra. To Callie, he said, "Do you understand now? All the power the Duns have used all these years, it comes from the Westras. And Mary and Rosie Mae aren't the only Westras to have fallen in love with a Dun. It's happened plenty of times. Your two families act like they hate each other, but they keep falling in love."

Sinking back against the altar, Callie clutched her chest. "No, no."

"Westra blood and Dun blood have been mixing for generations."

"That can't be."

Wyatt said, "If that's true, then why are we having this feud for all this time?"

With a snap of her wrist, Granny Witch sent a powerful eruption through the hall. When it crossed the threshold of the door, a gale sent Mary teetering on the edge of the casting circle.

Her index finger on her outstretched hand broke off. It smashed into the back wall, disintegrating into dust.

"It's because you Duns won't accept the truth," Granny Witch said. "The real witch power comes from the Westra line. Every few generations, you crawl back to the mountains and seduce one of us. Replenish the strength in your line. Then you go on mating with others until things get too diluted again. My sister Mary was only the most recent."

Seeing doubt still crossing Callie's face, Max called out, "It's all the truth. I researched your genealogies, traced them back straight to Gil. Rosie Mae and Mary Westra were just two of the Westra witches that have been brought into the Dun lineage. There are two definite others that I could find, a few more that were not recorded properly to be sure, and possibly more that were not recorded at all." When he had Brenda go find Montgomery Dun, when he had understood how this all connected, Max could not know if the information would change any attitudes, would stop this fighting, but he had to try. "Wyatt is right in asking why you're fighting. The Westras and Duns don't need to keep this feud going."

"Shut your mouth, boy," Granny Witch said.

"Callie, look at me, please. Rosie Mae and Gil and your Great Aunt Mary — all of them wanted to join these families."

"I'm warning you," Granny Witch said.

"They didn't do it for power. That's why the other Westras fight you. That's why so many Duns play these games. They're all about the power. But that's not the inheritance these women wanted left behind. They didn't care about power games like that. They were in love. Your great aunt knew that. She understood it because she was in love, too."

Granny Witch whirled around. "Liar!"

A hurricane conjured solely for him threw him down the hall. He crashed into the end, half his body breaking through the drywall. As white dust rained over Max's head, Drummond shot fourth. He punched his fist into Granny Witch's body. His screams from touching her were drowned by the old woman's horrid cries.

"Sister," Mary cried out — though with only partial lips and half a tongue, the word could barely be understood. Her actions were clear enough, though.

Another shrieking subway train of energy raced down the hall. It ripped Drummond away from Granny Witch, carrying him straight at Max. When he reached the end of the hall, Drummond kept going through the wall, possibly out of the house.

"Enough of this." Callie screamed the words until the hallway settled and everybody focused on her. "Whatever the reasons, I don't care. This power has belonged to the Dun family for generations. If it came from the Westras, clearly most of that family doesn't approve. If it was born from love, so be it. Wyatt and I love each other. To appease my ancestors, we'll wield this power through our love."

With a sweeping motion of her hand, Callie moved Mary out of the casting circle. The moment the corpse's legs staggered over the circle's line, Mary dropped to the floor, disintegrating into a heap of bones and dust and the shredded remnants of clothes.

"Sister!" Granny Witch let a short, girlish gasp escape her lips.

"I can already feel her power coming into me," Callie said. "I have all the books and all the energy that has been stored in this room for decades. Porters, Westras, and whoever you are in the back —"

"I'm Brenda, bitch."

"— you would all be smart to leave now. Stay and you'll be my first examples to the witch world that I run things now."

Max struggled to extract himself from the wall. When the drywall beneath him crumbled under his weight, he folded forward into a ball on the floor. Covered in chalky dust, he dared to peek over his shoulder — fearful that he might see Drummond hurt; fearful that he might discover Rosie Mae's decomposed corpse in the open wall. Instead, he saw wood framing and some plumbing. When he returned his view to the hallway, however, the real fear began.

The energy of that tiny room at the far end pulsed with

sinister calm. Each time Callie inhaled, the room, the hallway, even the house closed in towards her. The walls creaked. The paint cracked. The carpet swelled off the floor. Each time she exhaled, it returned to normal, relieved as if a heavy burden had been lifted.

Sandra moved alongside Granny Witch, and they held hands. Without any prompting Max could see, the two women chanted in unison using one of those languages forgotten by all but the witches. Its eerie tones and unsettling utterances pushed Max's hair on the back of his neck as he walked up the hallway once more.

With a laugh fit for a movie villain, Callie said, "I'm sure you can feel the power I'm taking in. Do you really think the two of you can do anything against me now?" To Sandra: "Take your husband and your ghost and leave. I promise you will not be harmed. I will end this witch war by the morning, and when I rebuild the witch community, I see a prominent place for you by my side. But if you stay, you'll be another body we'll have to bury."

"Stop it," Monty said, all his previous strength sapped leaving behind the tones of a broken man. "Please. This is not what I wanted."

Another breath that pulled in the house. "You're the one who opened the door for me. Now you get cold feet?"

"I opened the door because I had to. My mother demanded it."

Blinding energy emitted from Sandra and Granny Witch. Like a bowling ball rumbling along waxed wood, it sped down the hall and invaded the tiny room. Callie dropped back one step, always remaining within the casting circle.

Keeping her eyes firmly on the witches, she lowered her head. She growled, and the sound echoed through the walls as if a thousand ghosts had been awoken. Her casting circle glowed a soft green.

She's preparing another spell. With the power she had shown, Max guessed she would be able to cast much faster than a normal witch.

He rushed up and grabbed Brenda's hand. "We need to get out of the way."

"But Sandra."

"She can hold her own, and we'll do more damage if we break her concentration. Come on."

Too late. As they turned for the living room, a charge of energy sounding like static electricity sizzled through the air. Max smelled burnt hair when he felt the sledgehammer blow into his back. A spike of pain and he crashed onto his belly, the cries of Billy, Luke, and Brenda growing around him.

Rolling over, he saw that the attack had not harmed Wyatt or Monty. Callie had cast a spell so fast yet had been able to select her targets within a crowded, cramped hallway. Only Sandra and Granny Witch remained standing and only because they had formed a protective bubble around themselves.

Sitting up, Max tried to gauge Sandra's stamina. A thin line of sweat stained her clothes along the spine, her free hand shivered at her thigh, and one leg trembled. They had never come across power like this. It was too much.

Monty dropped to one knee and clasped his hands. "Please, Callie Anne, please. I'm begging you."

Max opened his mouth, prepared to berate Monty for begging when clearly his niece had lost her senses to a lust for power, but his researching intuition leapt into action and stopped him cold. It began with a simple question — the same question Callie had asked. Why had Monty opened the door if he had not intended for her to take all this power?

Using the wall as a brace, Max rose to his feet once again. He thought about Mary and Rosie Mae. He thought about the feud and the way the Westras tried to contain the power buried here. He thought about the first grimoire and the brutal magic that had been used throughout the day as well as in the past. And he thought. He didn't understand so much as pictured what needed to be done — or, in this case, said.

Planting his feet in a wide stance, Max summoned the will to speak as forcefully as he could manage. "Monty, get up and be a man."

The Dun family members stiffened as they looked beyond the witches in the hall to the crazy little man behind them.

"Your mother made it clear to you," Max said, not knowing what exactly he referred to but believing he spoke truth. "She tasked you with a job today, and you are spitting upon her memory by pleading with your niece."

"What's he talking about?" Callie asked.

Monty squinted at Max. The two men shared a voiceless conversation. A strange moment to be sure, all the stranger since Max could not be certain of his end of the silent exchange. They nodded at each other.

Wyatt must have caught the subtle looks because he yelled, "They're up to something. Stop them."

"I'm finished with this," Callie said. "You've all had your chances. It's over."

She stepped forward as if to strut down the hallway, but her knee slammed into a barrier. Placing her hands around her like a mime trapped in a cylinder, she discovered the barrier followed the outer-line of her casting circle.

Her face opened in panic. To Monty: "What have you done?"

With both arms cactusing outwards, several of his pendants glowed anew. "I tried to get you to stop. You'd been given your opportunity, but you chose this. You wanted all this power, and it is yours now. Perhaps someday you'll be able to share a trickle of it to some young witch."

With several more pendants coming to life, Monty reached towards the door to close it.

"No." Callie raised her arms, her eyes glowing fiery red, and spewed out a fast litany of words both guttural and disturbing.

Chapter 31

GUNFIRE CRACKS WHIPPED ALONG THE WALLS as wooden framing splintered inside. Wood shrapnel shot out through the drywall in puffs of white. Two long shards stabbed Max's leg. Billy's enormous torso took seven hits. Brenda and Luke crouched and covered but still had their backs peppered.

The previous storms that had been created paled against the typhoon winds that swallowed the hallway. Monty tried to close the door, but the winds drove him back. Wyatt slipped around the doorjamb, settling in next to his wife, standing at attention, ready to strike anybody who dared assault her. But Sandra and Granny Witch did not have to approach to fight back.

Thunder rolled through the howling winds as one electric ball after another cut through Callie's storm. Granny Witch pulled another witchball from her pocket, and with Sandra's aid, they grew it into a new electric ball of energy. Each one zipped towards the door. But each one deflected before crossing the threshold.

Max tried to walk forward, his leg limping — same leg that had just healed from their recent encounter with Madame Ti and her new coven — but the storm kept him from making progress. He leaned forward, dug his chin into his chest and shoulders against the wind as if trying to dislodge a massive object.

"Billy, I need your help." Max looked over at the large man. Blood cried out of numerous wounds on his chest and stomach. "We've got to close that door."

Billy turned his head toward Callie, and he nodded. Stepping into the storm gusts, he maneuvered one thumping footfall after another. Bellowing, mouth fully open, he blocked Max, taking the brunt of the torrential winds. Together they pressed on. Once they passed in front of Sandra and Granny Witch, the two women would no longer be able to safely attack Callie. Max crossed his fingers that their witches would take that into consideration.

Step after step, they inched along the hallway. When they maneuvered beside Sandra, Max glanced over. If she saw him, she gave no sign. Another thunderous crackle sent two more balls of electricity forward. One slammed off into the upper corner. The other broke through the doorway and dissipated against the same barrier that housed Callie.

Wyatt clearly itched to put his body in front of his wife, but when he motioned to do so, she snapped at him. "Stay still. It's better if I see my targets."

Max and Billy managed another foot. While Sandra and Granny Witch had not sent another electric ball, he did not know if that was out of safety or simply taking time to recharge. "Keep going."

"I'm trying," Billy said.

Peeking around the big man, Max saw Callie rise into the air. Damn. Nothing ever good came from a witch lifting off the ground.

From the shattered wall to the right, a band of wound electric wires tore free. Like a hose gushing water, it sent sparks as it flapped about without control. It slapped the floor, the walls, and the ceiling, nipping out like an enraged snake, until it sunk its sharp copper ends into its victim — the largest target to find. Billy.

His massive body grew rigid. The lights in the house dimmed and flashed as Billy jittered. Smoke rose above him, and Max felt the fleeting gratefulness that Callie's storm blew that smoke far away. He did not want to have to smell Billy's burning flesh.

It lasted mere seconds, but to Max the death of this giant required infinite time. Billy dropped to his knees, his body jolting nonstop, and his head arched back. His mouth foamed. A nightmare inducing gurgle crept between the bubbles that formed on his lips. When he finally flopped forward, there was no time to mourn. No time to watch in shock. That electric wire snake reared its head looking for a new victim.

It found one quick.

Max hunched over like a wrestler searching for a move. But he felt no courage to launch at the snake-wire. Though the harsh winds slapped at him, he strained to hold still as if the snake could see him, would react to him, rather than being a puppet of the witch behind it.

"Easy there," he said, wondering why he spoke at all. Wires couldn't hear. Even if they could, talking to a real snake would never have helped him. Talking to an animated wire bundle had no hope of helping.

He needed to think. Yet as his mind rifled through all the information it held, he could not find anything suitable to his current predicament. Never had he experienced anything under the heading *Attacked by a magically controlled snake wire.*

With sparks of electricity arcing between its open heads, the wire weaved and curved in the air. It moved like a real snake, like a cobra trying to mesmerize its victim. When it finally hissed a sizzle of sparks, preparing to strike, Max found no answers. His mind was empty. He stared at this thing, petrified, unable even to move his legs.

It shot forth, aiming straight for his chest.

"Never." Sandra's hands appeared in front of Max slicing away from him. The wires yanked to follow, ripping out of the wall, and breaking at the far end. The long mass of twisting electricity sagged to the floor as dead as Billy.

While many of these events had slowed in Max's eye, the next few seconds doubled in speed. To destroy the snake, Sandra had to break the spells she had cast with Granny Witch — the electrical witchball spell as well as the protective spells. They were vulnerable now.

Callie seized her opportunity and struck. But for her to do so, she had to stop her storming spell. And in that short break, Max had a chance.

As all three witches raised their hands at each other, as they raced to cast anything against the other, Max sprinted forward. Shouting as he pumped his legs, fire raging up from his bleeding wounds, he came alongside Monty and threw his shoulder into the door. The two of them pushed hard, managing to close the door halfway. Wyatt dug in on the other side, bracing himself with one foot against the doorjamb.

Unable to see her victims, Callie resorted to returning her gale force winds.

Pressing his back against the door and digging in with his legs, Max's injuries screamed in agony. Down the hall, he saw Granny Witch drop to one knee — panting, teetering. Brenda and Sandra went to help her.

Flipping back, Max put both hands against the wood. Monty groaned as he called upon a reserve of energy. They pushed and pushed, gaining small bits of ground, but not enough to seal the door.

Wyatt's fingers peeked over the edge. If he could get a better grip, they might not be able to beat him. They were hurting. They were drained. Until now, Wyatt had spent the hallway fight standing by his wife's side. He was as fresh and ready as if the night had only begun.

"Coming through," Drummond yelled from the far end of the hall.

Max didn't dare look back for fear of losing his grip. He didn't need to, anyway. A mass of ghostly cold swished next to him and bashed against the door. As Drummond cried out, the door slammed against the jamb, catching Wyatt's fingers. He shrieked and fell back into the tiny room. Together, Max and Monty gave one final heave, smashing the door closed.

"Hold it tight." Monty whirled around Max to stand in front. He raised both hands, and every pendant he wore blazed alight. The writing reemerged, and warmth radiated from the dark-stained wood. The carved wolf's head peered down, its wooden eyes shining with the spell.

"Don't do this." Callie cried, but Monty did not even flinch.

Still, as he sealed the door, reengaged the spell locks, cast a spell to soundproof and close off the room, tears trickled down his face.

A moment later, he lowered his arms and then his body to the floor. Sitting with his head hung, panting, he said, "It's done."

Chapter 32

AN HOUR LATER — after Monty double- and triple- checked each of the safeguards surrounding the door and room, after Drummond tested the spells by attempting to enter through the outside walls, and after Sandra bolstered security by casting a few spells of her own — everybody met in the living room. Granny Witch had been stretched on the couch while Luke attended to her. Both despaired over the loss of Billy and spent much of their time consoling each other. Monty, too, spent much of the time with his head hung and his face contorted in efforts to hold back further tears.

"I am so sorry for your loss," Monty said for the third time since closing the door. This time, however, he added, "We are entering a new era. A time of healing between our families. At least, I hope as much. In that spirit, perhaps you would like to bury Billy in the back. He could rest with Gil, and the two could serve as markers of the beginning and the end of this feud."

Granny Witch did not answer, and all in the room took that as a good sign. She did not say *No* outright. She, at the least, considered the proposal.

As Sandra returned from casting a final spell on the door, she used her hip to scoot Max over a little, making room to share a folding chair. Brenda tended to Max's injured leg with a First Aid kit she had found in the bathroom. But Max hardly noticed any of this. His mind had been trying to piece together the events into a clear image.

"From my research, I had figured out that you and others were mixing these families together, but was this always the plan? Were you trying to end the feud?"

Without changing position, Monty said, "Never occurred to me this could happen. What you're really wanting to know is if

Granny Witch Westra and her sister, my mother, had put this together? Was all this some grand scheme? Well, Granny Witch — Auntie — was it?"

The old witch shook her head. "I never knew any of it. When Mary left to be with that Dun boy, my heart broke. She's only two years younger, but I acted like it was ten, like I was the big sister who knew the world so much better. I begged her to stay away from the Duns. I told her Ma and Pa wouldn't understand, wouldn't care about her feelings of love and such, but she refused to listen."

"That sounds like my mama. Stubborn as a tired mule on a hot, summer day."

Granny Witch cracked a grin for an instant. "Once, when we were very little, she was by the creek hunting frogs and whatnot, but it was Sunday, and we were dressed for church. I kept trying to get her to stop, to come back to the house before Pa found out and gave her a whooping, but she refused to listen. I kept saying that she had to be careful of her dress. At least, do that much. But she plunked down in the muddy bank and sunk her hands into the water. She was so stubborn that even when Ma started calling for us, she refused to go. She wanted to catch her frog — I remember she started calling it *her frog* and she hadn't even caught nothing yet."

Monty snickered. "She get a whooping then?"

"Oh yes. And so did I. Big sisters are supposed to look out for their littler ones. More than anything else, that's why I hated when she came down here. I couldn't stop her, but I was supposed to."

Max sat up. "You knew she was in that closet all this time. Sending my mother here with a witchball — that wasn't about holding back the Duns from having power. You were trying to control your sister."

"I was protecting her." Granny Witch tried to rise, but Luke eased her back. "I didn't want anybody, least of all a Dun, to find her and use her. How horrible would it have been if Callie had succeeded? How horrible for Mary? She would exist within Callie, knowing she aided that psychopath to harm other witches, and eventually Callie would turn her anger upon the Westra family and me. Mary would have had to watch as her power was used to destroy her own sister, her own parents, everyone she loved. Maybe even Monty."

Max glanced over at the man. "Is that why your mother did it? She did build that room, right? Cast those spells?"

"Some of it." Monty stroked his beard and sighed. "My mother was an idealist. She always thought of things as how they should be not how they were. That went double when it came to matters of love and matters of witchcraft. She didn't like all the hatred associated with both. You see? Being a Westra and loving a Dun, all she encountered was the stupidity of this feud. And when it came to witches, the hatred attacked from all sides — especially when she declared that she would be different. She would be a good witch."

From the back of the room, Drummond said, "Doll, don't take it to mean anything."

Sandra said, "And was she? A good witch?"

"I think so," Monty said. "I never saw her harm anybody, and she didn't go around making witch deals that hurt anybody. She could have, too. We moved into this house, and she had access to all that power. It radiated off the walls, she said, and sometimes it pounded so hard, she suffered migraines and body aches and all kinds of afflictions. Then one morning, she called me to the kitchen, and she told me that she'd had a vision."

"A vision of the future?"

"Maybe. I don't know, for certain. She saw things, but never like a clairvoyant or anything. I only know that this one time, she told me about this one vision. She said that she saw how the power in this house would go on and on, forever destroying the families around it. The Duns and the Westras would never be free from their hatred, and as a good witch, a witch that had the ability to fix this, she had decided she would make a sacrifice. I was seventeen. She had me cut off the end of that hallway with a door. She had me hunt down copies of *The Long-Lost Friend*. She had me collect all sorts of things for her spells. Then she had me crawl under the house and dig up Rosie Mae."

"How awful."

"I didn't mind. I was helping my mother and helping my family. Once everything was ready, she went casting. Took her three days. When she finished, she had made all these pendants and wards, and she instructed me on how to cast the door spells. By locking her away and containing herself in that casting circle, she hoped to contain the full power of the magic that had grown in this house. There'd still be enough to satisfy most Dun witches that came to live here in the future, but nothing like what she had been enduring, fighting against. Because that's why she had those migraines and aches and such — she fought against the allure of it all; the corruption. Without that power available, my mother thought there would be healing between the families."

Max said, "So when you opened the door for Callie, it was some kind of test?"

"I suppose. Maybe I knew all along she would fail — which makes it a trap. I think I hoped for the former but expected the latter. That healing my mother wanted, it hadn't come yet. The kind of talk Callie was making, I just couldn't let her do half of what she claimed she would do. My mother sacrificed her life, allowed herself to be locked away until she died and then beyond that. For what? If I allowed Callie to become the evilest witch alive, I'd be allowing my mother's work to be ruined."

"But you had to give Callie a chance."

"We're family. What else could I do? All she had to do was let it go. All she had to do was understand what my mother wanted and respect that. If she had turned away, closed that door, we could have reached out to the Westras. We could have explained everything. We could have changed things."

"And Wyatt?"

"A victim of his love for Callie. He's stuck in there with her. Nothing to be done for it."

"What then? He starves to death?"

"I suppose there's a spell or two she could cast to have him join her, but I think she truly loves him. She'll show him mercy and put him down."

A brief moment of stillness. Then Luke spoke, his voice

creaking. "Now what happens?"

Granny Witch pushed away his fussing as she sat up. She waved for her cane. "Now," she said, firm and cold, "we bury Billy."

Chapter 33

THE DIVISION OF LABOR went along traditional lines — the men trekked out back to dig the grave while the women prepared the body. Nobody demanded these roles. Instinct drew each person to their task.

Monty grabbed three shovels from the garage, and Max led them to the grave of Gil Dun, using his phone's flashlight to navigate. Since the deceased was Luke's brother, Max and Monty gave deference to Luke's desires. The man stared at Gil's tombstone, and the others waited.

"I don't think Billy would want this," he said, dragging his shovel at his side as he poked through the overgrowth in the nearby area. "We always said we were mountain folk. We would never marry a girl from down here and definitely not a Dun."

Monty said, "That's all over now."

"Not for Billy. He don't know."

"Sure he does," Max said. "He gave his life to save me, to save Granny Witch, to save all of us. Being buried out here isn't what you imagined for him, but don't you think he'd want to do it, if that meant ending the feud? The next Callie that comes along and moves into this house will find a Westra buried in the back alongside a Dun. She'll know that the stories she heard about this day, about the end of the feud, and about what happens to those who let their power corrupt them — she'll know it's all true. Billy's grave confirms it. That might save more than all of us here. It might save everybody in the world."

Max worried he had spread it on too thick, but Luke did not call him out for being melodramatic. He simply stood there, glowering at the grave, and he thought.

At length, he plunged his shovel into the dirt beside Gil Dun's resting place. By the time he dug out his third shovelful, Max and

Monty had joined him. The North Carolina clay always fought back against digging, but with three tackling the job instead of one, it moved rather quickly. Luke concentrated on each shovelful and clearly wanted to be left alone.

Max had some questions for Monty, though. "I'm curious, if you don't mind — when we met at the Wallburg Baptist Church, you spoke with a lot of anger about the feud. About Granny Witch, too. But you and your mother were trying to stop the feud. Why would you say those things?"

Monty dug into the deepening grave three more times before he answered. "Granny Witch is my mother's sister. When the Westras turned their backs on my mother, Granny Witch should have been there to support her. She had promised her love to my mother many times growing up — at least, that's what my mother said — yet when needed the most, that old witch betrayed her." He ticked his chin at Luke. "Sorry. Don't mean to be disrespectful to you. She is your granny."

"Guess that makes you my cousin." Luke threw more dirt to the side. "Our blood ain't as close, but I like you. Granny — well, Billy and I worked for her because we had to. Good jobs in the mountains are hard to find right now, and she is our granny. Scared of her, too. But I'll say this — all the stories we ever heard about our Aunt Mary were good ones. Granny Witch never badmouthed your mama."

Max had other questions, but he decided to let it go. Family was complicated and convoluted. Whatever mental gymnastics Monty had to twist through to make sense of it probably only followed his own, personal logic. Somehow, he found a path to balance out his resentment toward Granny and the Westras with his mother's desire for peace.

A half-hour later, they carried Billy's body out and placed it in the hole. Sandra and Granny Witch had cast several spells upon Billy in the hopes of keeping him at rest. A man dying the way he did had a strong chance of haunting this haunted area. Or worse.

"I don't see him anywhere," Drummond said, taking his hat off in respect of the funeral. Sandra confirmed it with a nod. The ghost added, "Guess he's moved on. Good thing, too. If ever there was a death that promised to loop a ghost, that was it. Thank you, doll, for whatever spells you cast. I'd hate to have seen him locked in a fight to reach that hallway door that would never end."

Standing over the open grave, Granny Witch gazed down, sniffling and dashing at her eyes. "Billy and Luke's parents died years back, and I took them in. I finished their raising, and like a mother, I watched over them, made sure they learned right from wrong. Being a witch means learning to see the darkness in people. That's often the kind that come to us for help. But Billy never judged. He saw the healing we do, and he wanted to spend his life finding ways to heal others, too. Now, in death, he can continue this fine work. Buried here, he will forever help to mend these families and protect us all from our less-than-noble desires. Good luck, Billy. Watch over this home. Watch over our family."

Luke stepped up next to his granny. "My brother. My friend. Just as you sacrificed yourself to save another, I wish I could have sacrificed my life to save yours. You were the better of us, and I'll live the rest of my life trying to be as good as you."

He might have intended to say more, but a wave of tears left him leaning on Granny Witch's shoulder. Max and Sandra held hands a few feet away. Along with Brenda and Drummond, they watched and listened — observers, not participants.

When Monty came to the edge of the grave and peered down, Max tensed. He didn't want to jump between fighting and grieving people — especially with one being a witch. Thankfully, they all behaved. Perhaps there was hope to be found. Perhaps they could truly leave this feud behind.

"Billy was my cousin," Monty said. Luke's head popped up as if ready to argue the point, but Granny Witch patted his arm which provided enough of a signal to stop him. Monty went on, "From all I have seen and heard about him, he was a cousin I wish I had known. But his death will never have been pointless. Not as long as I live. Today, the Westras and Duns begin to heal our old rifts, and I vow upon this grave that I will use all within my ability to see success where others have failed. Granny, Luke — I hope you will join me in my pledge to Billy. I promise the days of the feud are over. We will convince the families. Because there is no sane way forward otherwise."

Granny Witch walked around the grave, leaning hard on her cane, and when she reached Monty, she hugged him. "You are my nephew."

He smiled and squeezed her gently. "You are my aunt."

Luke paused, processed, and finally smiled. He clapped his hands — sounding a lot like Drummond — and said, "Well, let's clean this up and get some food. I'm starving."

"Sure," Monty said.

"You better like Lexington barbecue."

"Greatest food in the world."

Chapter 34

JORGE OSORIO GRUNTED as he backed through the kitchen carrying one end of a heavy dresser. Huffing and drenched at the other end, Max slowed. They would have to figure out how to navigate the corner to get the dresser into J's bedroom. No, not J's bedroom anymore. The room now belonged to Max's mother. He had to wrap his head around that more than once.

Over the weeks after the events in Olin, the reality of Mrs. Porter's situation became undeniable. Her eyesight had returned, but it lacked the clarity of before. The doctors said she shouldn't expect further improvement. She shuffled around her apartment with overly-cautious steps, afraid of every shadowed corner. Max knew that part of her refused to adjust to her new, poorly visible world. Another part, however, feared what she could not see. Though he promised the matter of Granny Witch Westra had ended, that the witch deal had been cancelled, and that the large man who had terrified her was dead and buried, Mrs. Porter still acted as if an attack could be launched against her at any moment.

J spent a lot of his time with her. After school, weekends, and on a few mornings, he made sure to visit her, clean for her, cook for her, and do all the things Max should have done but often was too busy with his caseload. At least, that was the excuse Max gave himself. More truthfully, after spending time at his mother's place, he would feel unnerved and depressed. Talk of ending her life had vanished — perhaps it had been Granny Witch's doing all along — but his mother had lost her spark and showed no urgency to find it.

J noticed this, too, and had been the first to suggest the move. "I can sleep on the living room couch for a few months. After that, I graduate and then college. I won't need the room anymore."

That first time J mentioned it, Max gave a non-committal, "We'll think about it."

A few days later, J pushed on the idea again. "If she lived with us, she would feel safer, and you wouldn't have to drive out of your way to see her."

That time, Max said, "It makes sense. We'll see."

J's final attempt hit hard. "She's declining. You don't want her to die and wish you had done things different."

Max simply said, "I know."

For Sandra's part, she never put pressure on Max. He appreciated that. When he finally broached the subject of having his mother move in with them, she had already started preparing.

"You knew?" he asked.

"I've known for years that she would be joining us. It was simply a matter of when."

Osorio groaned under the heavy dresser before setting it down, half in the kitchen, half in the hallway. He surveyed the doorway, the ceiling height, and shook his head. When he finally looked up the short hall toward the living room and the front door, Max knew what the man would say.

"We're going to have to take this back outside and enter from the front of the house."

Max wiped his sleeve across his face. "What if we angled it up on end? We could get it around the corner, into the hall, and then back into the bedroom."

"Sure. That'll work. Except the two of us are panting like old dogs. I don't see us lifting this heavy SOB onto its end."

Max had hoped to avoid taking all his mother's prized furniture through the front door — longer trip that way — but Osorio was right. Heck, Max had hoped to avoid taking any of the furniture to begin with. However, between the crying and the screaming, his mother made it clear that certain pieces — this heavy dresser, for one — had to come with her. He supposed he should be thankful she parted with most of her furniture at all. Besides, as difficult and annoying as moving the furniture had become, it was easy compared to when he suggested the move in the first place.

"Why would I want to move in with you?" Her nose had wrinkled at the idea.

They sat on her long couch that stretched the length of one wall — another piece of furniture she had insisted would come, but he had managed to talk her out of that one. She had made a pitcher of iced tea — non-sweet, Northern tea — but she shattered a glass and cut her foot in the process.

Max thought about pointing out her bandaged foot but chose to speak in broader terms. "You can barely see. You need help. Nothing wrong with that, but we have our jobs and J has school. It would be better if you were at our house. We could help you easier that way."

"But Sandra —"

"We've been through this before. You've known that one day you would have to move in with us. That day has finally come. I know you want your independence, but you're not able to watch yourself as well anymore."

"Nonsense."

He hated to do it, to say it aloud, but he knew the card to play that guaranteed a win. "It's up to you, but you can't be on your own. If you don't want to live with us, that's fine. But we'll have to make arrangements with an assisted living facility —"

"Fine, fine, I'll move in with you."

Giving up most of the things she had collected over a lifetime had been hard, but they had limited space in their small house. The majority of her furniture, pictures, statuettes, and other knick-knacks would have to fit in her bedroom — J's old room that he had cleared out for her. That meant making hard choices.

One morning while J was in school and Sandra worked in the office, Max helped his mother sift through several dusty boxes stashed in her bathroom closet. She insisted they all come with her, but when Max opened the first box, he found towels from the 1970s — paisley, scratchy, and smelling of mold. The second box contained unopened sleeves of crackers that probably also dated back nearly half-a-century. He was about to comment on her witch-like hording behavior when he opened the third box and found a photo album.

Sitting on the cool tile of the bathroom floor, Max turned through the stiff pages of the album, the smell of forgotten moments and forgotten people rising with each photograph. They were all black-and-white, many had waved edges, and quite a few had browned with age. Images of people at birthday parties, vacations, or simply enjoying summer fun. People at a public swimming pool, having a cookout, costumed up for a Halloween party, or dressed to the nines for a fancy evening. The only strange part of it all — Max did not recognize a single person. Nowhere did he see his mother or father or anybody he knew.

"What is this?" he asked, bringing the photo album into his mother's bedroom while she separated items to go to the house from those going to donation.

Even with her poor eyesight, she could tell before he came too close. "That's your father's family."

"But I didn't see a picture of him anywhere."

She scooted to make room for Max next to her and taking the album, started turning pages. She stopped at a photo of a hefty couple smiling at a wedding reception. "That's your Great-Grandmother and Great-Grandfather Porter. Most of the pictures are from their life. Here's some of their son, your grandfather, and then there are a bunch of him growing. But if we turn to the end —" She did so. "— here it is. This is Grandma and Grandpa Porter. Standing in front is your father, he must have been about four."

Max looked at the old photo, bent in the bottom corner, and pointed to the baby in his grandmother's arms. "Who is that?"

"That is your Aunt Janie."

"Dad had a sister?"

"That's right. Jane was a wild one, always causing trouble when she was little. When I met your father, she had run away two or three times already, always shacking up with some man that she said was the one and that she loved and planned to marry. Never lasted, though."

Max stared at the pictures, his mind pounding as he tried to fit this new person into the family. "How come I never heard of her before?"

"Your father and her had a falling out. He cut her out of his life, and she did the same to him."

"What happened?"

"I don't know. When Grandma Porter died, we went to the funeral — you probably don't remember since you were only five at the time — and that was the last we ever saw of Jane. Something happened, but your father never wanted to talk about it, and I learned long ago not to press about things that don't matter."

"Don't matter? She's part of our family."

"Not really. She's blood, but that doesn't mean much."

"Well, is she alive?"

"I imagine so." Mrs. Porter closed the album. "This is all ancient history. None of it matters anymore."

Not too long ago, Max would have accepted that as the end of it. He knew his mother kept a lot of their family's past in darkness. He often thought that's why he liked to research other people's lives so much. But having recently seen the dangers of allowing a wound to fester between families, he couldn't simply let this go. He had an aunt, and something broke between her and his father. Just because his father had passed away didn't mean the pain between them was gone. Not if Aunt Jane still lived.

As Max and Osorio finished cluttering J's old bedroom with the apartment furniture, Max thought about that photo album again. He couldn't help but wonder how many more secrets his mother held, and if he should be concerned that she now revealed them. The more he put his mind to these questions, the more he noticed other problems. Like the fact that she so easily agreed to move in. A year ago, she would not only have fought against the suggestion, she would have locked her apartment door and refused to come out. They would have had to get the police, the fire department, and a mental health professional involved, and even then, they would probably have had to break down her door and remove her forcibly. Yet here he stood, panting along with Osorio, looking at the room in his house that she would now call her own. Did she think this would be the last room of her life? It probably was. And what better time to unload the family secrets than at her end?

"You okay?" Sandra said, handing both men a cold beer.

He nodded but knew she saw through him.

"J called," she went on. "I told him you were done. He took your mom to a movie and then they had an early dinner. She hasn't mentioned what's going on, but she's fully aware. Her eyesight may be fading but she's still sharp."

Max tipped back the bottle. He didn't like beer, never understood the fascination, but he liked the cold of it now.

Osorio finished his, ripped a loud belch, and looked properly apologetic. "I should get going. I'll take the rental truck back in the morning. You don't need to worry about it. I know how it can go, bringing in an elderly family member. The next few days are going to be a lot of adjustment. So, let me make one little thing easier."

"Thank you," Sandra said, and walked the detective out.

Maybe the photo album doesn't matter. Maybe the lost aunt or his father's brush with the supernatural doesn't matter. Max knew better, though.

His entire career centered around uncovering and understanding the past. For crying out loud, one of his business partners was a ghost from the past. Drummond was a piece of history. And if The Porter Agency had learned anything over the years of fighting witches, breaking curses, releasing ghosts, and navigating ancient politics, they learned that nothing stays buried forever.

The Duns and Westras kept coming across that lesson and refused to learn it for generations. Hopefully, that would change. Max figured the Porters needed to change, too. Whatever stood between his father and his aunt no longer mattered, and if he could find her, then perhaps they could heal this hidden wound, make the family stronger. It helped that finding lost things was part of research, and that was something he knew well.

The temperature dropped, announcing Drummond's arrival,

and Max took a final swig of his beer. "It's going to be a tight fit around here," Max said, "until J heads to college."

"Be thankful you have a house to cram together in." Drummond floated behind in the hall. "I lived through the Great Depression. I can remember when my office was the only home I had."

Max had lost track of time, but he must have been standing there for a short while — he could hear car doors slamming as J helped Max's mother toward the kitchen side door.

"It'll work out," Drummond said. "Trust me. You'll all be fine."

"Sure, we will. And if we aren't, then Sandra will end up killing her, and you can deal with her ghost."

Drummond tipped back his hat. "Don't even joke about that."

Before I get into the good stuff — the part you're really reading this for — I've got to say thank you to all of you for reading Max Porter over and over. This is the 18th (!) book and I'm constantly amazed when people come up to me to gush on how much they love Max, Sandra, Drummond, and the series. Please know that your love never gets old, never gets taken for granted, and is part of the fuel that keeps this series going.

Now, to the good stuff:

To start with, Olin is a real town in North Carolina, and it was hit by a tornado during the infamous Enigma Tornado Outbreak in 1884. As far as I know, that particular tornado, amongst the many that touched ground that day, was not conjured by a witch but rather a natural occurrence.

The quote from an 1884 newspaper is entirely fictitious. Of course, there were many real reports about the tornadoes in numerous papers across all the states involved, but this particular quote is from my imagination.

The Long-Lost Friend is, in fact, a real book and considered the first grimoire published in America. As of this writing, you can get a copy on Amazon. It deals mostly with folk remedies and advice for crops and animals. But there are quite a few strange entries including the one that I refer to.

The 1928 murder of Nelson Rehmeyer that involved *The Long-Lost Friend* is true. All the details of the case required no embellishment from me. The impact of that murder contributed to the demise of the grimoire's popularity and gave the vocal minority that wanted to end all things they did not approve plenty of ammunition.

Finally, the town of Wallburg is real as is the speed trap I refer to. The police don't always have somebody there, but I have seen it in use, and I've seen people caught by it. So, if you're ever in that neighborhood, perhaps tracing Max Porter's steps, you've been warned.

Acknowledgements

After eighteen books, you would think I might run out of people to thank, but that doesn't ever happen. Each book requires unique knowledge that I lack, and so, I must rely on others to help me. This time around, the duty of educating me on Appalachian witchcraft began with fellow author, Michael G. Williams, and continued with his suggestion of H. Byron Ballard's *Roots, Branches, & Spirits: The Folkways & Witchery of Appalachia*. Once again, I relied upon my friend, Jordan Harris, for her firsthand knowledge of dealing with multiple sclerosis. She's an amazing person, and Mrs. Porter's difficult journey would be sorely lacking without Jordan's input. Special thanks goes to Randy Miller, who saved me from a huge boneheaded error that I should have caught myself (hence, the bonehead). Of course, no book is complete without my thanks to my wife and son.

And, in the end, I always reserve my final thanks to you, my readers. Without your loyalty, Max and the gang would never have lasted eighteen books, and I'd have a different career.

Thank you.

About the Author

Stuart Jaffe is the madman behind the Nathan K thrillers, The Max Porter Paranormal Mysteries, the Ridnight Mysteries, the Parallel Society novels, The Malja Chronicles, The Bluesman, Founders, Real Magic, and much more. He trained in martial arts for over a decade until a knee injury ended that practice. Now, he plays lead guitar in a local blues band, The Bootleggers, and enjoys life on a small farm in rural North Carolina. For those who continue to keep count, the animal list is as follows: one dog, one cat, one aquatic turtle, and three chickens. As best as he's been able to manage, Stuart has made sure that the chickens do not live in the house

www.ingramcontent.com/pod-product-compliance
Lightning Source LLC
Chambersburg PA
CBHW051123300726
48981CB00022B/520/J

9781963517170